I0818116

TWISTED PAGES
BOOK ONE

OF THORNS AND BEAUTY

ELLE MADISON ⚜ ROBIN D. MAHLE

Of Thorns And Beauty: Twisted Pages Book One

First Edition

Cover by *Covers By Combs*

Map by *Enchanted Quill Press*

Copy Editing by *Jamie Holmes*

Proofreading by *Kate Anderson*

For Sarah and Gideon.
We will never think of Frosted Flakes
the same way again.

"You are not hopeless,
though you have been broken,
your innocence stolen..."

—Lauren Daigle

KENSLEY SPRINGS
JOKITH
CASTLE ALFHILD
COLBY
CORENTIN
PALAIS DE ETIENNE
BONDÉ
LÉ BOIS D'ENCHANTE

INGDOM OF MAYIM
MIRRORE
DESSERT
EASTERN
LANDS
VILLA
PARADIS
ISLA
DELPHINE

"You think you know the tale as old as time, but you've already got it wrong.

There never was a beauty and a beast,
only a girl who was both.

And that girl was me."

CHAPTER 1

I will never be free.

I have been chained for so long, I'm not sure I would know what to do with freedom. And now, I will never find out.

We're nearly there now, my new prison.

Jokith.

Even the name sounds cold and brutal.

Just like its endless frozen landscape. Just like the rumors of its beastly king, the man I will soon belong to.

Tales of the seclusive warrior people run wild.

Whispers abound of how they drink blood from the skulls of their enemies, of the beasts they become on the battlefield and the bodies they leave torn in their wake.

I shiver at the thought. It will be interesting to navigate the facts from falsehoods.

It's not like I had time to do any real research. Six hours. That's how much notice I had before I left on a journey that would change my entire life.

Six hours to hear the barest details about this kingdom and its king, my soon-to-be *husband*. Six hours to sit perfectly still while my wedding markings were inked onto my arms and wrists, remnants of a culture I can hardly remember.

Then, eight solid days to dwell on all the goodbyes I didn't get to say.

I want to scream.

None of this even makes sense. Arranged marriages haven't been done in centuries, even in the Eastern Lands.

It's not surprising that a king would marry a woman a third his age, but why one he's never even met? For that matter, a man in his position should have his choice of brides. What prompted him to purchase a lady of middling importance from a neighboring kingdom?

Madame is persuasive, but surely even she has no influence over the Jokithan King...unless he truly is a barbarian, and all he wants is a bride he could use up and dispose of. Someone no one else would miss.

Icy tendrils edge slowly in through the window, and I can feel them winding their way throughout my body, down to my core. The handle on the carriage door mocks me with empty promises of escape.

Damian notices my glance from the seat across from me and gives me a cruel smirk. But it's not Madame's watchdog who keeps me from fleeing.

It's not even the day-long trek back to the inn at Colby in my silken slippers and thin wedding ensemble. Truthfully, facing a blizzard with no clothes at all would be preferable to the future I'm hurtling toward.

The reasons I don't flee are my sisters.

The few lady's maids who were sent with me stare ahead with dead eyes and lifeless expressions. Even when they shiver and struggle to keep their seats in the jostling carriage, their faces remain neutral.

The only time they show any emotion at all is when they cringe after capturing Damian's wandering eye.

He brushes his knee against mine, watching my face for any sign of the reaction I refuse to give him, though my skin crawls at each point of contact.

"This plan has been a long time in the making," he says in the eerily calm tone he always uses. "Try not to ruin it."

"Perhaps I would be more likely to succeed if Madame had seen fit to give me more than half a day's notice," I shoot back.

His features turn feral.

"Mother, you mean."

I swallow a gag. She is not my mother. She's not even my aunt, as the castle has been led to believe. She's just the woman who took everything from me.

But for all that she bribes and tortures the rest of the world into submission, Damian follows her out of sheer devotion. In turn, she lets him off his leash to be a sadistic monster. Already, I fear for the ladies in the carriage when I leave.

But that's one more thing I have no power to control.

"Yes, of course. *Mother*." At least, I can try not to provoke him. "I'm sure it will be fine."

"Good." He smiles, but there is no warmth to it. "We all know what happens when you aren't at your best."

And there it is. The reason I am here at all.

My sisters would pay for my disobedience. *Hadn't they before?*

I take a deep breath, willing the emotion from my face.

The carriage rattles and shakes as we draw nearer the ancient gray stone walls ahead. With each bump and jolt, my stomach sends waves of nausea through me. I focus on what lies beyond the frosted window — anything to distract myself.

The top of the castle and the outer walls surrounding it come into view at last. The enormous façade is outlined by a lifeless, overcast sky and the black, choppy waters of the canal that encompass it.

The slow groan of an iron gate rattles the world around us, a foreboding greeting playing out in each clink of metal as it lifts high enough for our carriage to pass through.

Ahead of us stands Castle Alfhild, a massive edifice of dark, imposing turrets.

Morbid curiosity takes over as I scan each menacing brick and snow-covered tower. The castle has exactly one splash of color. Almost as if it was an afterthought, a single stained-glass window sits high above in one of the spires, mocking me with its depiction of a black-stemmed, blood-red rose.

Rose.

The word is like a curse that follows me everywhere I go.

I sit up straighter, pushing the thought and its painful associations out of my head. I smooth out the skirts of my beaded red bridal outfit, more to occupy myself than because I actually care.

Because I need to think about anything other than my frantically beating heart and the ceremony ahead that will surely break what's left of it.

"You look lovely, *Lady* Zaina." Damian twirls a lock of my midnight hair around his finger, his words dripping with a vulgar sort of lust.

His other hand reaches up my thigh, and I sit perfectly still, forcing a playful smirk to my lips. Slapping him away would only invoke his wrath, and I wouldn't be around long enough to subdue it.

"Thank you," I say with a wave of my finger. "But no touching. We're nearly there now, and I wouldn't want to give my new husband the wrong idea about our relationship."

He laughs, and it only encourages my nausea.

"Don't kid yourself, Zaina. It's not like anyone could mistake you for a virtuous bride, even with this." His fingers play along the chain that runs from my golden nose ring to my matching ear cuff.

"And as far as our *relationship*." He says the word like it's something dirty, and I fight the urge to shudder. "I know Mother has had her reasons for keeping me out of your bed, but there will be time enough for that down the line."

I swallow down the bile building in my throat, my smile freezing on my face. I don't need anyone to remind me that I'm tainted goods. Damian knows better than anyone that choice was never mine.

A few more moments pass by in silence until we finally come to a rocky halt. Damian steps out of the carriage to be met by a shadowed figure that towers over him. A man, I realize.

They converse in low tones until I hear the clipped edges of the sadist's words, enough to realize that he's upset.

I can't hear what the newcomer is saying, but the whispers that linger at the end of each syllable send tremors down my spine. Their conversation is a brief back-and-forth until Damian rips open the door. His dark eyes are furious, but his voice is calm when he speaks.

"Looks like I won't be allowed to so much as walk you in."

I bite back a satisfied smile at his frustration. I'm not sure why he expected anything different when we had known I would face this alone.

I give the servants one last glance. I wish I could help them, but I can't even help myself at this point.

Reluctantly, I take Damian's hand to step out of the carriage. The man who had been speaking to him is now visible, and it takes everything I have to face him bravely.

This is it. There's no turning back now.

I force my chin a little higher, refusing to play the part of a startled animal facing the den of a hungry beast. This king cannot be worse than anything I have faced in my life already.

A beast he may be.

But I am a far cry from being anyone's prey.

Chapter 2

"Lady Zaina." The man's voice is more unnerving than the imposing castle in front of us. "Welcome to Castle Alfhild."

He is covered from head-to-toe in black and grey, and his hands are gloved under his dark, hooded cloak. But what stands out most is the mask he wears with dark rounded lenses over the spaces for his eyes, punctuated in the middle by a long, sharp beak. A silver wolf's head is stitched into the side.

Do all of the servants here wear masks, or is this a personal quirk?

I give a small dip of my head.

"I apologize again for this necessity," the man says.

Somewhere through the formal tone and the hissing syllables in his voice, I can detect sincerity, but that could mean nothing. I've heard Damian apologize in that same tone right before he takes a man's life.

It does pique my curiosity, though. Why would it be a necessity for a bride to have not a single friend at her own wedding?

Another group of servants joins us. Those with more feminine forms under their black and gray clothing wear veils, too thick for me to make out their features. The men all wear the beaked masks.

A northern wedding custom? Or something else?

Damian hands off my trunks to them with more force than necessary.

"I'll miss you." He winks.

His words creep up my spine as surely as the mountain air does.

Then he returns to the carriage, and I am almost relieved before I remember what faces me on the other side of the imposing doors.

"It is a pleasure to meet you, at last. My name is Leif, and I am at your service." The man offers his arm, and I hesitantly reach up my hand to wrap around it.

At nearly five-and-a-half feet, I am considered tall for my people, but these servants make me look like a child. Leif is no exception. His proffered elbow nearly reaches my shoulder.

Taking a deep breath, I put one frozen foot in front of the other.

The doors open with a groan, and Leif leads the way. The other servants aren't far behind, but they veer off to take my trunks to another part of the castle.

Earlier, I had thought of this place as a prison, and it's an apt description for the dark stone walls we wind our way through. I try to focus on the rooms we pass, making mental notes of the places I see and every possible exit, anything to differentiate these castle walls from the dungeons I grew so familiar with at the château.

Endless nights in a darkness so thick, it was more like a physical blindfold. The shadows would close in around me, suffocating me, shutting me off from reality.

Why are there no windows here?

The hallways are lit by sconces on the wall, and it's too similar to the walkways down to the dungeons. I half expect to hear the clinking of my own chains, the scurrying of creatures staying just out of sight.

How many times had Madame dragged me down there on a whim? To teach me a lesson. To make me stronger.

She always had a reason.

During the wan light of day, I would stare at the sea water trickling in through the cracks and wonder if it would keep coming in, faster and faster until it covered over me and I surrendered myself to an inevitable watery grave.

That's what happened to most of her enemies. Why not me?

"Are you all right, Mistress?" Leif's voice startles me from my thoughts. He's studying me through his mask, like a creature from my nightmares.

"Yes, very well. Thank you," I say quickly.

His head turns to the side for a moment, as if he's carefully interpreting each word, before he nods and continues leading us forward.

My damp slippers slap against black stone floors as I follow him to the enormous entry room. For all its size, the space is unnaturally still and airless. A massive fireplace sits on the far wall, but it is devoid of flames.

If the castle is reflective of the king, it becomes clearer why he has had to import his bride. Even the halls are ominously empty, the only sound the weight of Leif's left foot gently scraping along the floor as he walks.

"Nearly there now," he says over his shoulder. "We're just taking a quick shortcut."

He leads me through a large door to the outside once more, and I brace myself for the biting cold. I don't complain, though, because at least there is light here...and air.

Still, I bundle my cloak tighter around my bare midriff and wonder if perhaps I was wrong before about drowning.

If instead, this kingdom will be my frozen tomb.

Leif opens another door at the end of the walkway leading back indoors, and I force myself to follow him to the dark interior.

"Nearly where?" I ask when he makes no move either to the right or the left.

A naïve part of me is hoping he will say we're nearly to my rooms, but that doesn't seem likely.

Instead, he gestures to the door directly across the hall and it feels as if my heart has stopped beating. I hear the music drifting from behind the wall before he can answer.

"The ceremony, of course." His expressionless mask tilts to the side as if he's confused by my question.

Of course.

When I had been told to wear my bridal gown, I had expected the marriage to happen today, but not before I had a moment to use the privy or collect my thoughts, or, even more ludicrous, to meet my groom.

Nothing for it now. I plaster a bland smile on my face and head for the door. Leif reaches out to stop me.

"Your cloak, My Lady." He holds out a gloved hand.

I suppress a sigh. I'm not in a hurry to be any colder, but I can't very well walk down the aisle with my cloak on.

Handing it over, I give myself ten more seconds to breathe, straightening the ruby dangling on my forehead and smoothing out my silk headscarf. Once I'm finished, Leif nods his beaked head and opens the door to the ceremony.

The candlelit aisle is lined with rows of pews, at least twenty on each side, but only a handful of those are occupied. Though the guests are dressed in rich velvets and furs, they, too, conceal their faces with coverings similar to those of the servants. The only differences are that the haunting masks of the men are overlaid with fine silks, and the ladies' veils are embellished with thick layers of intricate lace.

The abundance of short swords and axes, even among the women, makes me grateful for the knives I have hidden on my person. At least I'm not going into this completely defenseless, even if it feels that way.

Finally, I force my eyes to follow the path of the aisle to the man who has kept his entire kingdom away from the rest of the world.

I suck in a breath.

With everything I have seen in what feels like an obscenely long twenty-two years, I had begun to believe that astonishment — just like hope — is an emotion I am no longer capable of.

But when I see what awaits me at the end of the dimly lit room, I realize that's only one of the many, many things I've been wrong about.

Chapter 3

Standing at the end of the aisle is the king of Jokith, a mountain of a man clad in gray and white furs with an enormous axe strapped to his back and a short sword at his side.

By all appearances, he looks more prepared for battle than matrimony.

Or, are they the same in his mind?

But that's not what surprises me. I wonder, for a moment, if he is the king at all or if this is all part of an elaborate hoax. King Einar is a solid sixty-five years old, but the man in front of me appears to be no more than thirty.

My heart sinks. Is this how Madame arranged for me to come here? Had she given him one of her potions? It's true that Jokithans live several times as long as the rest of the world, but it never occurred to me that they wouldn't age in the meantime. Besides, no one looks this perfect without the use of alchemy.

I shake the thought away. That wouldn't make sense. Her role as an alchemist is wholly separate from the one she plays as a noblewoman.

His long white-blond hair is braided close to his scalp on the sides of his head, far enough for his silver crown to rest on before falling down in a straight line.

A slightly darker beard covers the lower half of his face; a small braid is woven into this, too, ending a few inches below his chin. A silver chain glints around his collar, dipping down to fall under his shirt.

When his glacial blue eyes meet mine, I'm taken aback by the fury burning within them. His gaze barely roves over my figure before he stiffens, his knuckles going white around his clenched fists.

Whispers sound throughout the small room as veils and beaked masks lean closer to one another, likely to discuss the king's reaction to the strange new addition to their castle. Or the fact that I'm still standing here, frozen as the world around us.

Still, I don't move. My legs have turned to marble, cold and heavy and utterly unyielding. Mentally, I chastise myself. *I know better than to make a scene.*

Einar scowls in my direction, a timely reminder that he has all the power here.

Taking Leif's proffered hand, I place one foot forward. Then another, and another afterward. My heart beats a furious rhythm within my chest, punctuating each halting step the masked man and I take toward the end of the aisle.

When we stand directly before the king, Leif bows to us both before moving to stand behind him at a place of honor.

Interesting.

Einar stretches out a massive hand for me to hold, and I force myself not to cringe while placing mine in it. I can't help but notice that his warm fingers are calloused, one more thing to set him apart from the noblemen I've known.

The officiant opens the ceremony in the aggressive, clipped tones of the Jokithan language, and our wedding is now underway. Einar repeats his vows in his own language, promising things he has no business swearing to a girl he's only just met.

When it comes time for my vows, the officiant surprises me by giving them to me in the desert language. The tongue of my people. His accent is thick, but the words are there, clear as the noon sun.

My body goes rigid, and it takes everything in me not to scream and run from this place as fast as I can. It is one thing to vow my life and future to a man who is as foreign to me as the language he speaks.

It is something else entirely to be forced to make promises in my heart language that I never wanted to make in the first place. Somehow, it makes me feel...exposed. Like one more piece of me has been offered up for the taking without my consent.

I close my eyes, trying to will calm into my breaths, but the only thing I manage to do is morph my vulnerability into a wave of white-hot anger. It's an emotion that will get me nowhere, though, so I shove it back down and repeat the words I will never be able to give to anyone else.

When I am finished, the officiant holds a hand out to Leif, who passes him something from the pocket of his cloak.

Rings, I register as he hands one to both Einar and myself. The King takes my left hand in his and slides the delicate band over my finger. I reciprocate the gesture with a quick, impersonal motion.

"King Einar and his consort, Lady Zaina of Jokith." The officiant announces our union along with my new title and I fight to keep my features neutral.

Consort? No one has used that title in half a century except for the Emperor of the Eastern Lands, and even he only uses it in reference to his concubines. Surely even Madame didn't agree to this, not with her aims.

Then again, she does love to see me humiliated.

I push back the heat trying to creep its way into my cheeks. These people and their king will not see how this title affects me.

The officiant makes an announcement with the word *koss,* pulling me back to the moment. The king steps closer, his lips curling in distaste as he pulls me roughly against him.

Before I can even brace myself, he has crushed his mouth against mine. His scruffy beard is even more abrasive than the kiss itself, scratching at the soft skin of my face.

I focus on that momentary discomfort instead of the gesture that is as empty as our marriage will surely be.

CHAPTER 4

Applause rings out, and congratulations assail us both from every direction.

I know I should at least be feigning the role of a blushing bride, but I don't have it in me to pretend. Not yet. I'll have enough of that to do tonight.

My jaw clenches at the thought, and I fight to at least keep the half-smile I have on my face now.

The king nods in thanks but says nothing as we leave through the open doors back into the hall. A guard closes it behind us with a loud bang that echoes down the silent halls.

He doesn't speak again or even glance in my direction as he practically drags me along next to him, unaware or unconcerned by his much longer strides. Just when I wonder if he is intentionally fraying the edges of my sanity with this endless walk, he finally drops my arm, halting before a solid oak door guarded by two more hulking, and unsurprisingly masked figures.

I move forward as soon as one of them opens the door, ready to get this cursed ordeal over with. When I take a step, the king does as well, practically barreling over me with his giant form.

The servant coughs on what I assume is a laugh as Einar pointedly clears his throat. The brute is obviously unfamiliar with chivalry. We stand locked in place, both waiting for the other to budge, for what feels like an eternity.

My lips part, and I am about to speak when Einar heaves a sigh before he roughly grabs my wrist, pulling me into the room. As soon as the door closes behind us, I carefully extract myself from his grasp.

My other hand itches for the knife sewn into the skirts at my side, though I know I can't use it. This is what I'm here for, but all the notice in the world would not have prepared me for this moment.

"Blazing sands!" The words escape my trembling lips as I squeeze my eyes shut and take a deep breath.

My stomach is leaden, and my heart races, but when I open my eyes again, the king is watching me with an impassive expression.

"What is the matter with you?" Einar's voice is dripping with condescension, but he makes no move toward me.

If anything, he seems to be putting an intentional space between us, and I'm reminded of his extremely reluctant wedding kiss. Looking around, I see he hasn't brought me to a bed after all. Only a dimly lit chandelier, an ornate porcelain basin, and a black chaise lounge fill the small space we're in.

"Did you bring me to a fainting room?" I ask my own question instead of answering his, my brows furrowing in confusion.

"Where did you think I was taking you?" He huffs.

Heat floods my cheeks, partly from embarrassment, but largely from the fury that is slowly ebbing in, crowding out the fear that has been driving it.

"The way you yanked me down the hall, what was I supposed to think?"

He looks nonplussed.

"You should have said something if you couldn't keep up."

My last, fragile thread of patience splits apart with that comment.

"I'm beginning to see why you had to import your bride with

manners like these," I snap. "Have you actually encountered a woman before, or is this an entirely new experience for you?"

His eyes narrow, and he opens his mouth to respond, venom dripping from every word.

"I can assure you, I've encountered many a woman." His eyebrow raises, a cocky smirk playing on his lips.

"Just none that would stick around, then? I wonder why." I feign contemplation.

His expression goes flat, sharpening the angular lines of his face and only emphasizing his barbarism. He looks me over from head to toe, but there's nothing flattering in his gaze.

It's predatory. Scrutinizing. The way he looks at me makes me feel as though I'm wearing clothes far more revealing than my bridal outfit. With another man, I might be afraid, but I know the signs of a body thrumming with violent intent.

The king is not going to hurt me. At least, not physically. Not yet. When he finally speaks, his voice is deeper and colder than it had been when we said our vows or even a moment ago.

"You should clean up, *wife*." Einar points to the basin. "There's a feast in our honor."

"Clean up what, exactly?" I counter, stopping myself before I can ask why I'm allowed such a privilege now when it wasn't even offered *before* my wedding.

He gestures to my hands.

"I didn't figure you'd want to eat with dirt on your hands, but of course, that's entirely up to you. All that is required is your presence, not your cleanliness."

Red flashes through my vision. I may have only vague memories of my early childhood, but I remember dreaming about my wedding day, about the privilege of having such exquisite markings on my skin to let the world know I belonged to someone.

I never imagined my life winding up here. With him. Insulting me and my culture.

"Certainly. While I busy myself scrubbing at the very intentionally and carefully applied bridal paint," I use a description I think the oaf might actually understand, "perhaps you could spare a moment to remove the revolting animal from your face." I gesture to the braided beard with unconcealed disgust. "I wouldn't want it consuming your meal before you get the chance."

Einar's jaw might have dropped, though I can hardly tell behind the mass of hair. He visibly collects himself before letting out an audible sigh.

"As much as I'm enjoying spending time in your delightful presence, we should go, Zaina. My people are waiting."

"Sadly, my feminine sensibilities are far too overwhelmed with the emotion of this joyous union to leave just now." I sink down on the chaise pointedly. "It was certainly an astute move on your part to bring me here. Truly, your understanding of my weak constitution is most appreciated," I add, noticing the way his jaw tightens at my words.

For all of my bravado, I can feel myself spiraling. I'm desperate for a moment to collect my thoughts alone.

He stares at me for a long moment with an expression I can't quite decipher.

"Very well then," he finally says. "I certainly hope you don't starve." He flashes his teeth in what is more a snarl than a grin, like that thought is appealing to him.

What's more is that he clearly thinks his comment will sway me, like I'm some spoiled heiress who has never spent the night hungry. If only he knew the consequences of gaining an unsightly pound in my household.

But I refuse to think about the dungeon when I've finally banished its images from my head.

"I'm sure I'll survive," I reply with a smile that doesn't quite reach my eyes.

"Yes, of course," he says, his body taut with tension. "The fates would never be kind enough to grant me anything less."

The fates haven't been kind enough to grant it for me, either.

I don't say the words out loud. I don't say anything at all while he sweeps out of the room, slamming the door shut behind him.

CHAPTER 5

Despite my brave words, I already feel the gnawing of hunger in my stomach. Part of me wonders what it is they'll be serving for the feast, and another tells myself that I shouldn't care.

Before I can deliberate further, an eager knock sounds at the door.

I'm fairly certain it isn't the king. I doubt the man knows how to knock, much less would bother with it.

The door opens, and in bustles a tall, round figure sporting a black veil. With the wedding over, I'm beginning to wonder if this is a custom all the time here.

"*Æ, dúllan mín*!"

I'm a bit taken back by her familiar greeting, so I respond uncertainly.

"Hello."

"You have even more beauty up close." Her accent is thick, and there's something like wistfulness in her chirpy voice.

"Can you see through that, then?" I finally ask what I've been wondering since my arrival.

She halts, but whether she's affronted by the abruptness of my question or the veil itself, I can't tell.

"Yes. I could not help His Majesty while not see."

I'm gleaning nothing from her carefully neutral inflection, so I decide to push a little further. I need more information to navigate the murky waters of this strange place.

"Surely, it would be easier to work without it, though."

She lets out a surprisingly wry laugh for such a high-pitched voice, shaking her head.

"I now understand His Majesty's temper," she says instead of answering. "He is angry like wolf."

I bite back a sigh.

"So, you've been sent to coax me to dinner, then?"

She bristles.

"I am not sent anywhere, Mistress, though why a bride needs to be coax to come to her own wedding feast is very much confuse to me."

"I see." My tone is clipped, my fury rising to the forefront again. "Is it also confusing for you to understand why a bride might want a moment or two to collect herself, to use the facilities, or, odder still, be introduced to her groom before their wedding?"

I don't even mention whether it's beyond the whole twisted lot of them to see why I might have wanted a single familiar face here. Though, at this rate, I wonder if the only face I'll ever be familiar with again is the king's, considering everyone else hides theirs.

My eyes sting unexpectedly, and I look down. I don't cry. Ever. It must be something else. The damnably frigid air, perhaps.

When the woman's posture slackens ever so slightly, I want to disappear in between the freezing floor stones.

"It is not done, Mistress. A bride and groom are not see each other on the day of marry. If you had --"

"No," I interrupt her. "It is not done *here*." I don't need to say the rest. That not a single consideration was given to my needs, to my traditions.

A beat of uncomfortable silence stretches on until I finally break it.

"I apologize --" I drop off, not sure what to call her.

"You call me Sigrid," she supplies. Or orders?

"I apologize, Sigrid," I tell her sincerely, lifting my fingers to massage my throbbing temples. "I know none of this is your fault."

She huffs and waves her hand.

"Do not have worry. I am sure you had long journey, Consort Zaina."

Another stilted moment passes as I cringe at the title my husband has bestowed upon me before she reluctantly speaks up again.

"I suppose you do not want hear this, either, but is no good to stay shut up in this room. In Jokith, the union is not being final until the partake."

"Partaking?" I parrot back to her.

"Yes." She pauses and scratches her cheek through the veil. "The two of you have witness when you partake what the other offers."

I freeze in my pacing, mouth agape. Either the language barrier is stronger than I thought, or she's suggesting our wedding night will be performed in front of others.

I run through my knowledge of the ice kingdom and come up short. No one engages in public consummations anymore. Not even Jokith can be that archaic.

"But, what about the feast?" I ask hesitantly.

Her head cocks to the side, the black fabric swaying below her neck.

"That is where it is happen." She sounds confused, like it's obvious.

"You have got to be kidding me," I say under my breath as I clench my fists.

"This is usually considered not a hardship, Mistress."

I say nothing, because I can't imagine the type of women they breed here if that truly is the case.

"Come, Mistress. It is over before you know." Her tone is softer this time.

I finally find my voice.

"And just where is this..." I search for her words, "partaking to occur?"

She stops and turns back toward me, her head tilting to the side the way I've seen birds do when they are listening to something.

"In dining hall, of course." Again, she sounds bewildered by my confusion.

And again, I am stunned into silence.

The dining hall? I wonder if there are furs on the ground or if he plans to take me right atop the cold stone tables.

I grit my teeth and curse the woman who forced me to come here.

But of course, it scarcely matters how I feel, I remind myself. Not to Madame, nor the king, nor anyone else in this sands-blasted castle.

There is little use in delaying the inevitable. I muster all the dignity I possess, but the words still come out baked with resentment when I finally respond.

"Lead the way."

Chapter 6

"The king is good man." Sigrid's incessant praises of the king have not stopped since we stepped out of the fainting room. I'm beginning to wonder if he has a kinder twin brother I know nothing about, or if the woman is truly insane.

If it was not for the signs of age in her voice and stature, I would ask why she hadn't married the king herself.

Perhaps she isn't as keen on public dining table sex as she pretends to be.

"Indeed."

I should at least try to be charming, to ingratiate myself to the people here rather than making them like me even less, but somewhere between my frostbitten toes and my impending "partaking," I can't quite dredge up the energy for courtesy.

The steady hum of conversation reaches me as we near the dining hall, but once I round the corner, it cuts off entirely.

The sound of chairs scraping against the stone floor echoes off of the cavernous walls as everyone stands to greet me. Even Einar follows after a moment.

So, he is capable of chivalry. He just doesn't bother when his people aren't there to bear witness.

A second examination of the room stops me dead in my tracks.

Three long, empty, wooden tables with ten occupants on each side are aligned parallel across the room. One smaller table sits perpendicular at the end of the room, with only the king and an empty chair beside him.

There is no food anywhere, even though I am decidedly late. No servants stand by with covered tureens. Not so much as a single stein of ale or glass of mead clutters the long, rectangular tables of veiled and masked courtiers.

Just when I had begun to hope Sigrid simply possessed a truly horrendous sense of humor, I can see she was neither mistaken nor joking about what was to take place here.

I feel the blood drain from my face, and the ambience in the room turns even more tense than it had been. I am acutely aware of how very *other* I am here, in my red skirts with my bared stomach, dripping with ornate jewelry yet covered in the markings I now know they all believe to be dirt.

But I refuse to cower, or even to fidget under the weight of their stares. I make my way to the king, where he holds out a chair for me.

His face holds no sign of what's to come, so I have little choice but to take my proffered seat. Once I am settled, the rest of the room follows suit. A lutist, likely the same one from the wedding, starts up a subdued tune, and gradually, a halting, stilted conversation overtakes the room. Though, none of it seems to be directed toward me.

No, I have the immense honor of being at a separate table with Einar as my only conversant, not that he has bothered to glance in my direction since I sat down.

And here, I thought this ritual couldn't get any more awkward.

A servant places a chalice at my right, and I examine the contents for hints of poison. It was impossible to grow up in Madame's household without a basic knowledge of alchemy. Having watched her do everything from turning a prince into a frog to outright murdering people, I had long since learned to be cautious.

Fortunately, though, all I can discern here are dark and frothy scents of barley and malt with a sweet, chocolatey undertone.

"It's just ale," the king grunts without looking at me, but I don't miss the way his lips curl in disgust.

I resist the urge to glare at him.

"Obviously, you're well-enough acquainted with it," I mutter, noting the sour note of the drink on his breath.

He sucks in air through his nose but doesn't respond. I take a tiny sip of the brew, letting it linger on my tongue for a long moment before swallowing. It's surprisingly smooth, if a bit sweet. It's that last part that gives me pause.

I hold my breath for a moment, but there is no burning, no unexpected effects of any kind. Of course, it's not doing much to keep out the cold, either. What I wouldn't give for a cup of chai masala right about now, but I doubt the anyone here even knows what that is.

A fireplace roars in the opposite corner of the spacious room, but it offers no more warmth over here than my thin bridalwear does. I will myself not to shiver, not to show any weakness, but the idea of shedding even more clothing in this room is nearly as unappealing as the ritual itself.

Several tense minutes later, a servant arrives with a covered silver tureen. Einar slams his metal stein down on the table several times, causing the ale inside to slosh out. The sound is loud enough to get the attention of the room, and my insides seize.

"What is on that tray? Why is it just for us?"

Einar gives me a puzzling glance before speaking to the room in Jokithan. They all pound their fists on the table in agreement with his words, and that's when my husband deigns to look in my direction.

"Are you ready?"

Is it my imagination, or does he look hopeful that I will decline? That's all the incentive I need to lift my chin and answer in a strong, clear voice.

"Of course."

The tray is placed in front of us, the lid removed to reveal...food. Just a bit of roasted fish and potatoes. He cuts a small bit of potato, then spears it with his knife before holding it out to me. I lean forward, taking the bite into my mouth and deftly removing it from the knife with my teeth before he can stab me.

His impassive gaze burns just a bit brighter while he watches me but remains otherwise unchanged. He stares for another moment, finally clearing his throat to remind me that it's now my turn.

Well, then.

I reach for a knife as well, though it's more like a dagger, and the handle was clearly designed for a hand much larger than my own.

"Can you use that?" The king raises his eyebrows, and I blink back a glare.

"You mean with my delicate constitution? I'm sure I'll manage, as long as I don't faint first." I stab the end into a large chunk of potato with perhaps a bit more force than is strictly necessary, then lift it up to Einar's lips. Well, his mouth, anyway.

Who can say where his actual lips are in all that mess.

He rolls his eyes, but dutifully plucks his bite off of my knife, baring his teeth in the process.

The room gives a polite smattering of applause, and the feeling of expectation begins to ebb away, but I don't let my guard down just yet.

"So," I ask cautiously, "is that it? There's nothing else?"

"Not meeting your lofty expectations?" The king scrutinizes me for a moment, his brow lifting as he takes a gulp of ale.

I narrow my eyes but don't rise to his bait.

"I was led to believe that we would be *partaking* of... each other..." I lower my voice so only he can hear.

Einar's eyes meet mine for a half second, and then he does the last thing I would have expected him to do.

He laughs.

Eyes crinkling and deep, baritone chuckles, all while I sit at his side, likely the butt of his joke.

Does this mean there is more?

"What did you call it?" he finally manages to ask.

"The partaking," I say, then add somewhat defensively. "You know, that whole wedding ritual you didn't bother cluing me in on."

"That's what you thought we were doing, and you still came to the dining hall?" He doesn't wait for me to answer. "Quite the exhibitionist I've married." This throws him into another fit of laughter at my expense while I glare at him.

It's easy enough for him to laugh, the man with unlimited power in a room of people who do his bidding, as though I would have had a single sands-damned choice if that had been our purpose here.

While he's laughing, a man with a single silver star on the beak of his mask rises from his seat at one of the other tables. The king's laughter cuts off abruptly, the mirth in his features replaced by the stony face from our wedding.

Interesting.

The man slides toward us, his footsteps too muted to be entirely casual. I suppress an arched eyebrow, guessing at his purpose before he even reaches my side.

"Consort Zaina." He stresses the title, like he suspects how it rankles me. "We have not yet had the chance to become acquainted. I am Lord Odger. I wish to offer my congratulations." The obsequious tone coming clearly through his mask tells me I've taken his measure correctly.

Sure enough, he takes my hand with both of his in what can only be described as a proprietary gesture. His fingers stroke the inside of my wrist, making my skin crawl, but like earlier with Damian, I don't pull away.

I feel the king's gaze on me, though I refuse to turn in his direction. Like it or not, I am a consort, not a queen. Einar may as well have called me his plaything for all the power he's bestowed upon me, here in this place where he has made sure I am without friends or allies.

Besides, Odger is hardly the first to touch me without my consent, and I doubt seriously he'll be the last, not in my lifetime or even on this day. My wedding night still awaits.

"I confess, that was not my only reason for approaching," the man says, righting himself. "You looked to be freezing." His western accent is particularly prominent on that last word, rolling the R and turning the Z sound into an S.

"It is warmer where I come from," I respond noncommittally.

Where is he going with this?

He answers my unspoken thought by reaching for his cloak pin. His heavy fur is off his shoulders and around my own with a speed that is unnatural, even to me.

The king is nearly as fast.

He is at his feet with his sword drawn in a movement I can barely track. The tip of his blade presses into Odger's bare neck just enough to draw the tiniest drop of blood.

The casual violence from a man who was laughing less than a minute ago is jarring. But then, I should have expected no less. I knew who he was before I came here.

A man who would draw a sword on someone for daring to offer me warmth in this frigid mausoleum he calls a castle. A *beast*, as they say.

My opinion is solidified by the reticence of the room. The king's authority is absolute here.

Odger slowly holds his hands out in a gesture of surrender.

"Forgive me, My King." He sounds not the least bit sorry. "Knowing your lofty position precludes you from seeing to such minor details, I only thought to make your bride more comfortable in her new home."

Judging by Einar's murderous expression, he hears the thinly veiled scorn as plainly as I do. With his free hand, he rips Odger's cloak from my shoulders, not so much as glancing down at me.

I scarcely have time to fight down a shiver before the king replaces the cloak with his own.

"I have seen to it. You will have no further need to approach Lady Zaina. For anything." Threat laces his words, but he is more like a child refusing to share a toy than a man protecting his wife.

This isn't about my comfort. It's about his property.

Odger returns to his seat, and Einar sits back down like nothing happened, except for the thrumming of fury I can still feel waving off him. The rest of the room takes their cue, but the conversation in the air feels markedly more forced now.

I wait until their talking creates a steady hum again before I murmur my next words through a smile as false as our wedding kiss had been.

"Perhaps I should just stand still while you drop your trousers right here to mark your territory on the ground around me." At his confused look, I add in an overly pleasant tone, "That way, you wouldn't have to suffer without your cloak."

"If I'm suffering through this meal, it has nothing to do with my cloak," he mutters, sizing me up in a glance. "But I could never deny a lady her wishes."

He gestures gallantly for me to stand, and I shoot daggers at him.

"I'm only saying that somewhere between our never-ending vows and shoving potatoes down my throat, I would think you had sufficiently staked your claim." My cheeks redden in anger, but I force my smile to stay plastered on my features. "That you feel the need to continue doing so makes me wonder what you might be compensating for."

I want to take the words back as soon as they are out. I can't remember the last time I spoke without thinking, let alone allowed my emotions to cloud my judgment this way. I need sleep, and warmth. And my sisters.

But his next words duly remind me that it will be a long time before I have any of those things.

"I guess you'll find out." He gives me a crooked grin, his eyes glinting. "Or have you forgotten it's nearly time for our wedding night?"

Chapter 7

For the second time in an evening, I find myself off-kilter. I swallow, fighting to keep my expression pleasant for the courtiers.

"Shouldn't we finish the feast?" My attempt at nonchalance falls flat.

"Of course. I wouldn't dream of interfering with your enjoyment of the meal." He shoots me a phony smile, waving a hand toward the food I scarcely touched, like he knows I can't stomach another bite.

All traces of my earlier hunger disappeared when the king pulled his blade on a man for an offense as innocuous as showing him up. For daring to care for what was his, whatever the motives.

"I was only thinking of our guests," I try again, though I'm not sure why I bother postponing the inevitable.

"They'll eat after we leave." He says it like it's obvious.

Perhaps it is, given the masks and his overdeveloped sense of authority.

"Well then, Husband, I see no sense in making them wait," I say with a boldness I don't feel, then stand from the table.

Even if I was hungry, I couldn't sit here in good conscience and stuff my face while they watched with empty bellies.

Einar stares up at me for a moment before I see the smallest hint of a smirk playing at the corner of his mouth. Either he knows I'm bluffing, or he's pleased with himself and where he imagines this night going. Regardless, he follows suit and stands next to me.

A thud sounds, followed by another and another until every beaked figure at the tables before us is slamming their fists down on the table. Cheers erupt, and they stand and beat their chests with the same fists, while the veiled figures applaud.

I raise my glass back to them and chug the contents in one go. If I'm going to endure this, I might as well have a drink first...or several.

Neither of us speaks after that. An endless walk up a large staircase and down three hallways with nothing adorning their walls finally leads us to a large set of doors.

The engravings on the dark wood offer some of the only adornments I've seen in the entire castle. I wonder if the carver had meant for it to sit in a palace far more lovely than this bleak prison.

Two large guards open the massive doors for us. If I thought that Einar dwarfed me, he seems average compared to the men who are protecting the room. That shouldn't surprise me, given their reputation of being a warrior people, but I'm still getting used to being the shortest person in the castle.

"I'll be back in a moment," he says in his deep, growling voice.

"Do hurry..." I respond through gritted teeth.

The words are right, even if the tone is all wrong. His glacial stare meets mine as he leans in to place a mocking kiss on my hand.

"I wouldn't dream of making you wait," he adds before turning to leave.

I wait until the door clicks all the way shut before I collapse in front of the blazing fire in the center of the room. I can hardly breathe for the weight of the day, and the worst part isn't even over.

At least I can finally kick off my damp shoes and burrow my feet into the plush white fur rug. Pain seeps in as they begin to thaw, but there is warmth as well.

My trunks are here and opened, the colorful fabrics in such sharp contrast to the monotony of the room that I suddenly find it unbearable. I'd rather not be reminded of home right now. Of anything personal.

My eyes flit to the rustic table nearby. A decanter and two glasses sit upon it. I lean over and grab the decanter, pouring a few drops of the amber liquid into a glass. Swirling it around, I take a sniff before dipping my pinkie finger into it and bringing the drop to my lips.

It burns, but no more than ordinary alcohol. Between my rapidly fraying nerves and the chill I can't seem to dispel, I am desperate enough to actually want some. I take a small sip, then wait a few minutes. Nothing.

Another sip and I finally feel the heady warmth of the alcohol beginning to work its way through me, numbing me, just like I need it to. With some relief, I pour myself a heavy dose of the amber liquid and drink it down before I can even feel the whiskey burning at the back of my throat.

Liquid courage is all I can count on to get me through this night, so I go ahead and fill it up a second time.

The crackling of the fire draws my attention back toward the hearth, and I watch as the flames lick the air around it. For a moment, I imagine I am one of the embers that dances away from the blaze, flying through the air to freedom.

Minutes pass by — or hours, I'm not sure which — while I imagine and dream of a different world, one where I have a say in my future.

The sound of the door latching shut pulls me from my pointless thoughts, and I stiffen. I am not ready for what comes next, no more than I was when he left.

But then, is anyone ever truly ready to hand over their body to a stranger?

CHAPTER 8

I feel the king's presence behind me, the warmth of his body overpowering that of the fire in front of me.

Slowly, I turn to face him.

With most men, I can immediately tell what they want from me, but I'm finding it difficult to read Einar. The rise and fall of his chest tells me that he's breathing quickly, but his sharp features reveal nothing. He stands immobile as a mountain range, looking down on me like he's expecting something.

He's too smart to expect me to run. And surely by now he knows I'm not the type of woman who simpers. So, what is it that he is so clearly anticipating?

The way he shakes his head is so subtle, I nearly miss it. He moves toward the sitting chair next to the bed and slowly, methodically unties the laces on his boots. He places them on the floor next to him and stares up at me.

I swallow hard, walking toward the one feature of the room I've been doing my best to ignore. I gulp down the remaining contents of my glass just before it slips from my hand, landing soundlessly on the rug beneath our feet.

"Are you drunk?" Einar asks as I sit down on the massive bed that looks as if it was carved from one of the enormous trees we passed on our way here.

The grooves in the wood resemble bark, and the branches at each corner stretch upward toward the ceiling. I run my fingers along the post, marveling at the craftsmanship.

Einar repeats his question.

I turn back too quickly, and the room begins to spin.

"I am *never* intoxicated." My eyebrows raise in offense, even as I teeter sideways. "I simply thought it would be less of a burden on both of us if we were more...relaxed. I left you some in the decanter. Help yourself." I wave a hand toward the table.

He moves to examine the nearly empty container and crosses his arms. Then, he stares down at me like I am nothing more than a fascinating marionette, playing a part he's not quite sure of while he towers over it all.

We both know what happens next. There is no use in delaying it any longer. I preempt any attempt he might make in removing my clothes and decide to do it myself. I wouldn't want him to wonder at the carefully concealed weapons stitched into the fabric.

Pushing aside all the reservations that have no place in this moment, I stumble to my feet. First, I remove my long silken scarf, carefully disentangling it from my hair and letting it fall softly to the ground. I capture his icy blue gaze with my own, noting that it doesn't waver from where it's focused on my face. Only my face.

Next, I pull down my heavy beaded skirts, neatly stepping out of them. Again, his eyes don't falter.

But when I place my hands on the short blouse that covers the only remaining part of me, I swear I hear a sharp intake of breath, though his expression is as resolute as ever.

I slip the top up over my head, shaking my hair out from the ornate beading before I reopen my eyes.

This time, he has let the smallest molecule of that stone façade slip. His gaze is heated, his lips parted, and his eyes find their way slowly down my body.

Content with whatever power I have managed to wrangle from this situation, I shoot him an arrogant smirk. He has his strengths, and I have mine.

What I don't expect is the way he stalks toward me, closing the space between us until he has all but erased it.

Until I am close to being plastered against the freezing leather of his belt and the warm, rich furs of his tunic.

Until I forget, for the tiniest increment of a moment, that I'm not supposed to want to be here. To want any of this.

I lean toward him, in spite of myself and the way I have done nothing but dread this moment for days. Tilting my head up ever so slightly, my gaze travels from the chain at his neck and up to his lips, which are slowly parting.

"Stop." The words are not mine, but his.

I pause briefly, any warmth I felt moments ago being once again stolen by this wintry castle and the people in it.

"What?" I ask in a voice that is unfamiliar, even to me.

Did he want to be the one who undressed me? Or is he unhappy with what he sees? I look down to be sure nothing is amiss, and nearly lose my balance.

Einar catches me with steady hands, careful to only touch my arms and nothing else.

"Is something not to your liking?" The whiskey has made me bold and reckless.

"Just put your clothes back on." He clenches his jaw.

I narrow my eyes at him. *Surely, he doesn't mean it.* That would be too much to hope for. And it makes no sense.

His frame towers over mine, and I can feel the heat emanating from him once again. *Is that why he keeps the fires so low? Because he is his own source of furious, unyielding heat?*

I fight down a shiver as my gaze moves from his piercing blue irises to his full, parted lips.

We stand there for a moment, and not even my rapid breaths dare to make a sound. He leans in, and it's all I can do to stop myself from leaning right back into him, stealing some of his warmth for my own.

But he doesn't tilt his head downward. Instead, he grabs one of the heavy gray furs piled atop the bed and dangles it next to me.

"If you were freezing earlier, you must be ice by now." Not unlike his tone.

I stand there, puzzled, abruptly aware of how very exposed I am. Holding the fur in front of me, I back up to brace myself against the tall, plush mattress.

Is he turning me down?

I war with feelings of relief and something else I can't quite figure out as I voice the question aloud.

"Isn't this why you chose me?" If Madame's alchemy hadn't come into this, my beauty is the only reason anyone would have picked me from a sea of eligible ladies.

I had been called beautiful my entire life. My light brown skin and my wide, almond-shaped, honey-colored eyes were rare in these parts of the world.

Exotic.

I didn't take any pleasure in it. That's why Madame had taken me to be part of her macabre family. It's why I was so *useful* to her.

And I suspect that's why the king chose me as well.

Of course, that would mean his features are all his, genetically. I try not to stare at his perfectly chiseled jaw and the unnaturally straight line of his aquiline nose.

He sizes me up with a glance that is almost cursory, crossing his colossal, muscled arms before giving me his answer.

"I didn't choose you. My ambassador did." He could be reading a shipping ledger for all the inflection in his voice.

No malice. No anger. Only a calm, collected, factual tone that has me steadily losing my grip on what's real and what isn't. Trying to gather my thoughts and utterly unsure why I'm staring this gift horse so directly in the mouth, I speak up again.

"Regardless of what either of us wants," I begin, my voice going even colder than this stone floor. "Surely, we have to...consummate, at some point?"

I stop just short of saying "produce heirs," though that's really what I mean. It's the main reason I was sent here.

His eye twitches infinitesimally, the first outward sign of emotion I've seen from him. I tuck it away for future me to think on, though I'm observing it through my swimming, inebriated vision.

"Tempting as it is to spend this evening — or any — in your delightful company, I'm certain I could find a more appealing prospect elsewhere."

I squeeze my eyes shut, trying to decide how to respond, but when I open them, he has vanished. There hadn't been a creak or a clink of the door latch shutting. He was simply gone.

I'm left to collapse naked on my bed, confused and unsure, and worst of all, completely unable to escape the dawning horror that this is my life now, chasing after a man who clearly hates me for reasons I don't begin to comprehend.

And *not* chasing him isn't an option I have. Things stand to get much, much worse if I fail to produce an heir.

Especially when Madame finds out.

Chapter 9

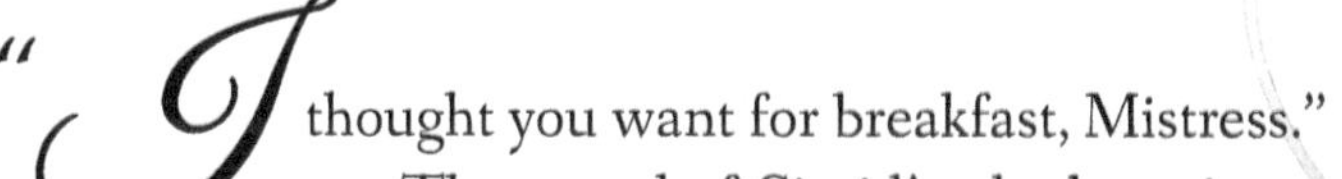

"I thought you want for breakfast, Mistress."

The sound of Sigrid's plucky voice and bright rays of golden sun pouring through the windows pull me from my fitful sleep. I want nothing more than to throw the covers back over my splitting head and die.

"Here," she says, resting a tray beside me on the bed.

One sniff of the savory meats has bile rising in my throat. I sit up too quickly and barely make it to the other side of the bed, grabbing the nearest container I can find and vomiting every ounce of liquid in my stomach.

I use my free hand to hold both my hair and the golden chain linked from my nose to my ear safe from the trajectory. It isn't until I'm finished that I realize it is one of Einar's boots that is the lucky recipient of my stomach's contents.

Well, it couldn't have happened to a more deserving piece of footwear, at least.

Sigrid comes to my side without hesitation.

"Oh, no. It must be the mountain sickness."

"The what?" *As in, the mountain of alcohol I consumed last night?*

"The mountain sickness, Mistress. It takes everyone when they are first arrive." Sigrid chuckles and helps me move my hair away from the mess I've made.

Ah, that explanation makes much more sense, and in no way involves the several — or more than several — glasses of the amber liquid I treated myself to. That, at least, is a relief.

My temples begin to throb again, and all I want is for the mountain sickness or whatever it is to finish me off.

"I see the wedding night was success..." I don't miss the amusement in her voice as she picks up the pieces of my wedding garb and folds them neatly across her arm.

"Yes. It would seem that way," I croak out, throwing the furs back over my naked form.

I remember last night in bits and pieces, mostly drinking nearly an entire decanter of whiskey and then being rejected by my *husband*.

Which begs the question, *Is our marriage even secured yet?* Does he no longer wish for it to be?

If his ambassador chose me, what did he gain from any of this? Einar clearly didn't want *me*, and I was beginning to wonder if he wished to be married at all, based on his behavior at our wedding.

My spinning thoughts are interrupted when a panel of the wall to my left slides forward with only a quiet shuffling sound to announce its entrant. I am unsurprised by the motion, having surmised there were passageways coming and going from this room.

It's the king. *Of course.* After his vanishing act last night, it makes sense that he used a secret door.

I force myself into a sitting position, glancing at him with more anticipation in my expression than I had intended. It is warranted, though. At this point, he's the only person who can answer any of my questions.

If he can manage to string together more than two hateful words today.

His expression isn't hateful, though. It's so neutral, it borders on lifeless until his gaze snags on his defiled boot. Even then, he only lifts a single silver eyebrow the barest fraction of an inch before turning his attention to Sigrid.

"*Gooan morgin*, Sigrid."

"*Gooan aptan, Úlfur.*" She says the words insistently, her tone a gentle chiding, and I can't help but marvel.

Her head would not have been long attached to her body at Villa Paradís, the château I had grown up in. Madame scarcely let the servants speak at all, let alone refer to any of us with a nickname, but the king doesn't so much as blink at the exchange.

So, he's not opposed to showing kindness. He's only opposed to me.

Einar walks to the tray while Sigrid pours a steaming cup of milk. My stomach flips again, and I press a hand to it, taking a slow breath through my mouth.

Though he hasn't directly looked at me once, the king shoots me a sideways glance.

"The privy is through there." He points to a small door. "If you would like to empty the contents of your stomach into something other than my boot."

Sigrid turns to face him, her veil fluttering with the quick movement, but I'm too focused on keeping my food down to do the same.

"I just tell her about the mountain sickness."

He looks me over with a deliberate slowness.

"Ah, yes. That must be what ails her." His voice is condescending, and I think seriously about throwing one of the plush velvet cushions at his pompous face.

I just glare at him instead, but at least I don't vomit. I'd rather be caught dead than have him watch me run naked to the privy.

Yes, things are going splendidly.

Sigrid makes a quiet exit, leaving me in a stilted silence with my...husband.

"Do they always wear the masks and veils?"

"Yes." His clipped tone leaves no room for further questions.

Swallowing back another round of bile, I gesture to the passageway and try an attempt at humor to change the subject. Anything to make the man act like less of an ass.

"So, is that how you go to visit your more agreeable wives?" I lift my lips in what I hope is an apologetic smile.

"Are there agreeable wives out there somewhere?" He doesn't smile back, but he doesn't quite frown either, so I take it as a victory. "Sadly, it leads only to my own chambers."

He sits on the foot of the bed near the tray, dumping nearly the entire bowl of honey onto one of the bowls of porridge. Adding a scoop of deep purple-colored berries, he proceeds to drown the whole thing in milk before finally mixing the horrid concoction together.

I grab my own bowl, carefully keeping the sheet close to my chest, and begin to eat it plain. He looks on in clear revulsion.

I sigh.

"Is there a reason you came into *my* rooms to pass judgment on the way I eat *my* breakfast?" I quip.

His eyes narrow.

"And by your rooms, you mean the rooms in *my* castle?"

So much for him acting like less of an ass. His words are a slap in the face, a cruel reminder that I have nothing here, not even a small pocket of space to let my guard down long enough to eat a sands-damned bowl of porridge the way I like it.

I feel my face turn to stone while I attempt to collect whatever vestige of dignity I can muster while naked in a bed that doesn't remotely belong to me.

"My mistake," I say quietly. "In that case, do help yourself to any pocket of sanctuary I eke out in this lifeless tomb of a castle. It's not as though I could stop you," I add.

He closes his eyes for a prolonged blink, and when he opens them, they are completely devoid of emotion.

"I don't suppose you'd like to see the rest of this...lifeless tomb, then?"

Like is a strong word, but I need to know my way around this place sooner than later.

"That would be helpful," I answer honestly. "I can dress and meet my guide within the hour." The quicker I get out of this oppressive room, the better.

"The staff is busy," he all but snaps. "I will be your guide."

Wonderful.

"All right, then," I say, but even I hear the grim resignation in my tone.

We finish our breakfast in silence before he leaves me to dress.

Chapter 10

I meet Einar just outside my room. My sapphire gown is a stark contrast to the monotones around me, which must be why his eyes are fixated on me from the moment I step out the door, since he hasn't shown interest in me before this.

His gaze lingers on the criss-crossed straps that wrap from my collarbone to tie around my neck, then over the sheer sleeves that gather at my wrists with golden cuffs, and down to the flowing, gauzy skirts.

My slippers are as impractical as the gown is, but it was by far the most suitable thing I found in the trunks I hadn't been permitted to pack myself. Each outfit had been more stunning than the last, the clothing from my home culture blended seamlessly into Delphine's far more revealing styles.

Most have low necklines, bare midriffs, and no sleeves at all. By comparison, at least this one covers my cleavage and offers some modicum of protection from the elements, though I'm already fighting down a shiver.

Sigrid had returned to fix my hair. There was little time to converse while her lightning-fast fingers whipped my hair into a half-updo, taking yesterday's curls and making them look artful, even after a night of sleep.

When the moment stretches into awkwardness, I finally clear my throat to speak.

"Well then... lead the way," I say with a begrudging smile.

It's only been a day since I got here. Surely, we can still turn this around.

Einar stares down at me, and I swear I see his steely gaze soften a fraction. He opens the large wooden door and gestures for me to walk through it.

My head throbs as I take in each hallway and corridor. He only names the important places like the barracks, the throne room, the great hall, and the kitchens. The list goes on, and I make mental notes in the map I'm drawing in my head.

All of the spaces are spartanly decorated. Shields are the only decor on the walls, along with other weapons that are obviously well-used.

It's almost as if they keep their arsenal close by in case they are attacked at any moment. I can't help but wonder if it is a habit that has been ingrained in them from the days of constant war between Corentin, Jokith, and the other mountain kingdoms, or if it's merely a matter of pride among their people.

For a moment I imagine the giant beside me running toward an opposing army, swinging his battle axe in full regalia. A shiver runs down my spine, and I begin to understand why such barbaric rumors have spread about these people.

Most of the castle is as dull and lifeless as I had expected it to be, but there is one room that catches my eye. He calls it a study.

It's a long, rectangular room with an enormous fireplace on one wall, and floor-to-ceiling windows on another. There are shelves of books, a smattering of musical instruments, and several places to sit and converse. It looks like a room where someone might actually enjoy themselves, and I have to wonder what it's doing in this castle.

I have to pull myself away from it rather reluctantly to return to my meandering tour.

We trudge up and down several sets of stairs, and I'm certain that I will vomit again all over them. I feel sicker than I should, even accounting for my rare indulgence last night.

"We can take a shortcut back, through the courtyard." The king gestures ahead of us to an area at the bottom of the staircase.

It's the small square of freezing outdoor air Leif had walked me through only yesterday. I glance down at my sheer clothing and thin slippers.

If it was anyone else, I would assume they were joking, but I'm beginning to believe he is just genuinely oblivious to the needs or feelings of any person apart from himself.

"The long way is fine," I say shortly, swallowing back the burning feeling in my throat.

The nausea doesn't concern me, but I can barely seem to keep my feet beneath me. Maybe there is something to this mountain sickness.

My foot slips ever so slightly on the final step, sending me teetering backward. But Einar's reflexes are quick, far more so than I would expect of someone his size. Before I have time to right myself, one of his hands is on the small of my exposed back, while the other is gripping my upper arm.

My eyes lock onto his for a moment while I take his measure. I can feel the heat emanating off of him just as it did last night. Shaking my head, I step out of his hold and smooth out the layers of my gown.

"Thank you," I say softly.

Einar simply nods and continues to move forward on the tour. I am about to reach out to him, to link my arm in his for support when I catch sight of one of the veiled servants hunched over on the floors, scrubbing what looks like a trail of green slime from the stones.

She wipes at her brow, fidgeting with the veil that is so clearly hindering her, when the king calls out to her loudly.

The words he uses are in his native tongue, but his meaning is clear enough.

She needs to keep her face covered.

My blood runs hot as I stare from him to the woman on the floor.

I deliberate over my response. True, I'm trying to appeal to whatever slightly better nature he possesses, but where does that end? Do I sit back and watch him mistreat others just to avoid upsetting him?

I flash back to Damian in the carriage, and a hundred memories before that. *Hasn't that been enough of my life?*

"What's happened?" I decide to interject.

I search for the kinder tone I'd used earlier, but my fading energy makes the words come out more forcefully than I mean for them to.

Ice creeps back into Einar's irises and his jaw clenches.

"Nothing you need worry about," he grits through his teeth.

The servant has ceased moving, cowering so much that she appears to be disappearing into the very cracks in the floor.

I try again to assess her stance with his fury before deciding to speak.

"Surely, she would be able to work more quickly without the hindrance of the veil." I offer him a sincere expression, placing a hand on his colossal forearm.

He hesitates for a moment, his entire body stiffening and his gaze going predatorial.

"What did you say?" His voice is a growl, offering a glimpse of the beast I saw in him yesterday.

"I was only thinking that the servants --"

"Don't. It isn't your place to think where my staff is concerned."

There's that word again. *My.*

I nod. It's all I can manage, weighed down by my mounting resentment. I know one thing, though. I was wrong before, when I thought there was still time to turn it around. But at least there is consistency in this.

At least I don't have to worry about my emotions getting in the way of what I came here to do.

Chapter 11

Einar insists on walking me back to my room, though I would much prefer to be alone and could find my way back blindfolded at this point. I nearly take him up on his suggestion of going through the courtyard just to shorten the tense walk.

Considering what a failure today has been, though, I don't bother to argue or to make suggestions.

Sigrid waits at my door, practically bouncing on her toes.

"It is here at final," she says to Einar.

He sighs, and his clear unhappiness piques my interest.

What's here?

Sigrid clucks her tongue at one or both of us before opening the door with a sigh of her own. I'm beginning to realize the woman misses nothing.

"I will leave two of you now." True to her word, she's gone before I can question her enthusiasm or the way she continues to address the king with such informality.

I reach a confident hand to the door, refusing to show any outward hesitation, and Einar doesn't stop me. If I had hoped to be less confused on entering, though, I am sorely disappointed.

I hate surprises under the best of circumstances, let alone with my head swimming and my temples throbbing. So of course, that's what awaits me.

The space has been cleaned, the bed made, and my trunks are no longer in the center of the room. I wonder where she took my clothes, and if she found the weapons carefully hidden within them.

Would it even matter now that I know the Jokithans keep their weapons so readily available?

The middle of the room now hosts a nondescript wooden crate with shapes seemingly carved out at random on each side. I move toward the box, vaguely registering Einar coming in behind me and shutting the door.

A shuffling noise from inside stops me short.

Have I misjudged Sigrid's nature entirely? Is it a snake?

I glance back at Einar, but his face is as inscrutable as ever.

Fine.

I flip the lid off one-handed and take a half step back, my heart thundering. When nothing jumps out at me, I inch closer, but what I see leaves me more confused than ever.

It's... a tiny cat, of a sort, covered in bright, shimmering, silver-colored fur with deep sapphire stripes, the exact color of my dress. It's staring unflinchingly at me with eyes the color of the waters around Villa Paradís, the bluer side of turquoise.

When it opens its mouth to yawn, two metallic canines stand out amongst its sharp teeth.

I was raised in a place far grander than most palaces, surrounded by the most extravagant things in the world, but I think this cub might top them all. I only wonder what strings the king will attach to this gift.

Though it's hard to imagine that this is a gift, in the light of all his caveman-style territorialism. He has made it clear nothing is mine. Why should this be any different?

Tall, pointed ears — too large for its small body — twitch, but the thing makes no move to attack. Again, I wonder at its purpose. I am both in awe and terrified of the fuzzy creature as it curls into a ball and falls asleep, completely undeterred by our presence.

The king's features give nothing away. Most men, I can read like a dossier, each part of their component crystal clear. But not him.

I am at a rare loss for words, something he must notice, because he finally speaks up.

"The chalyx was supposed to be here yesterday," he explains without inflection. "I procured it when I was more hopeful about the whole arrangement."

I try not to let his last muttered statement sting, but it does. There are only a handful of reasons that come to mind why he despises me so much after so short a time.

Does he know about Madame's subterfuge? She told him she was my beloved aunt, that she had taken me in when my parents were killed. She had falsified my lineage and hers, all to make this happen.

And I, of course, had gone along with it. Surely, if he knew that, it would mean more than cruel comments and dirty looks. It would mean my life.

Which leaves another explanation.

"Did you know I was from the Eastern Lands?" I ask him quietly, studying his face for a reaction.

His brow furrows before he answers.

"Yes. My people vetted you before you came here," he says flatly. "Why?"

So my story had checked out, and it wasn't an objection to my people. Just me.

"I just wondered if that was why you chose this animal. Tigers are common there, though I haven't been back in some time." I keep my features perfectly neutral, turning my gaze back to the chalyx.

"Clearly, the gesture was ill-conceived." His tone is even sharper than before, and I'm already tired of trying to cater to his moods.

"Clearly," I echo in a hollow voice. "Pets are frivolous." I nearly cringe as I hear Madame's voice echoing in my head.

I inspect my fingernails rather than meet his eyes and let him see the uncertainty swirling in mine.

"But thank you for the thought," I add in a tone about as genuine as his gesture was.

I finally glance up to see the smallest twitch in his eye, the only sign of any emotion from him.

"I am tired and in need of a bath. Would you please fetch someone to help with that?" I say with all the imperiousness he has already ascribed to me.

I hear the breath he takes before he turns to leave the room without a word. As soon as he's gone, my shoulders slump and I rub my temples.

Without him around to scrutinize me, I take a solid look at the kitten. It's not really a tiger, but it still brings me back to another life, one I barely remember. Vague, scattered recollections of tiny cubs running rampant while careless children laugh and play with them.

"Were you taken from your siblings, too?" I whisper, pulling the creature out of the box and cradling it against my chest. "Do you have sisters who miss you? Parents who don't know you're still alive?" And though I know it's not reasonable to sympathize so much with an animal, I trace the thing's nose with a finger, whispering reassurances it's still young enough to believe, and wishing I still could.

I can't seem to make this go any better with Einar. I tried during our tour. I practically threw myself at him last night. But nothing. He is as impassive and impervious as a brick wall. Sands, if only he was one. I would probably get further with him then.

At least walls can be scaled.

CHAPTER 12

The only sounds in the room are the crackling of the flames in the hearth and the gentle snores of the cat, or whatever the creature is. It's nearly enough to lull me to sleep. I take comfort in the melody of the two until the door opens and Einar's heavy footsteps remind me of my purpose here.

I hastily plop the chalyx back into its box before he opens the door. Taking a deep breath, I turn and see that Sigrid has followed him, pushing him toward me like he's a child being rebuked.

"Good afternoon, Mistress. I will start bath." She immediately sets to work in the small room off to the side of this one.

I had glanced briefly at the fixtures this morning before I got dressed, relieved to see pipes and faucets. Plumbing is something we had gotten only a few years ago in the château, but it looked like theirs had been installed for a while.

For being so closed off from the rest of the world, they seemed to be advancing well enough on their own.

The king lowers himself onto a small sofa, one that looks like children's furniture once his massive frame covers it.

Still, I ignore his presence and that of the gift he gave me, the latter of which is scratching at some cedar shavings in the box she slept in. Sigrid shuffles around in the privy, and I wonder if she is taking longer than she needs to on purpose, to force us to communicate.

If so, it's a wasted effort. There is nothing I especially want to say to him right now.

Actually, there is one thing.

"Why is it so quiet here?"

He shoots me a pointed glance over the book he has brought with him, indicating that I have clearly interrupted his reading.

"Is it? I hadn't noticed." If he is trying to irritate me with his answer, he has succeeded.

The image of him doing something so...normal is so at odds with his appearance. His hair is still braided to the sides of his head, but, this morning, the long mass is pulled up into a knot. The sleeves of his tunic hug his biceps as he turns another page of the book that looks terribly small in his hands.

I add it to the list of contradictions about him.

"Is hiding their faces not enough for you? You'd prefer no one in the castle speaks, either?" I am genuinely curious about this, but I am also happy to return his ire in spades.

"Did I imagine Sigrid's greeting just now, then?" he growls over the book but doesn't look up at me.

I'm sure he is only pretending to misunderstand what I am implying. I feel my temper rising again.

"Fine. I suppose it's hardly my business if everyone in this castle is miserable."

He shuts his book, placing it forcefully on the table before he matches my furious gaze with one of his own.

"Have you considered that the only miserable person in this castle is you, and if its inhabitants seem so in your eyes, then perhaps it is only because you manage to siphon the joy out of every room you walk into?"

My jaw drops open at his audacity.

"If I siphon the joy out of any room, it's only because you're following me into it with your revolving carousel of moods. You would think sixty-five years would have given you time to sort out your emotions, but please, tell me, how are you feeling now, Einar?" I hold up my fingers as I count off his various unpleasant dispositions. "Is it to be hostile Einar? Self-centered bastard Einar? Or my personal favorite, downright unlikable beast?"

I am practically shouting on the last word, and the feeling is so foreign to me that it stills my tongue.

Einar opens his mouth, but his response is cut off when Sigrid practically comes running into the room, confirming my assumption that she was less preparing than she was giving us space...space she clearly no longer thinks we will benefit from.

"Sorry I not have this ready early, Mistress," Sigrid says in a forcefully cheerful tone. She gestures for me to come over. "I was want for you have surprise kitten."

I try to let myself be soothed by her matronly mannerisms and the cheerful way she speaks the common tongue. "That's all right, Sigrid. I --"

My words are cut short by the sight of a large bath that is filled almost to the top. I am already frazzled, and the still water mocks me. The deep tub was clearly built to accommodate the average Jokithan.

But for me...

I place a hand to my throat, swallowing hard, fighting back the images that come unbidden.

Disobedient soldiers, spies, and anyone who was disloyal... I see their wild eyes and hear their pleas as they are locked in a cage and lowered into the raging seas.

Shipwrecked trespassers who have nowhere else to turn are forced to swim to the continent.

None of them make it. Even if they can swim, their bodies are dragged down to a watery grave by Sharks, or, even worse, the Mayima, the cursed sirens off the coast of Delphine.

A bubble rises from the drain breaking at the surface of the bath, but all I hear is the gurgling, final breaths of each of them, the sounds of death and drowning. My mind spins as each of these gruesome scenes play on repeat for me until I can't take it anymore.

"Remove half of this at once," I croak out, not caring for a moment how rude I sound.

Sigrid freezes, her head tilting to the side.

"Pardon, Mistress?"

I try to collect myself, to come up with a reason that makes sense, but it's all I can do to speak in a halfway reasonable tone.

"Remove at least half of the bath water," I repeat. "Please," I tack on belatedly.

Sigrid tsks and mumbles under her breath in Jokithan but does what I ask before leaving the small room. She's probably gone to complain to Einar about my manners.

Not that he would have room to judge.

I rub my temple again, close the door behind me, and lean into the dark spruce frame.

I've never been so far from my sisters, and I can't help but wish they were here to help me figure this whole mess out.

I undress and climb into the tub of steaming water, bracing myself. Most people find baths relaxing, but they are nothing short of torture for me.

Sigrid comes back in as I'm methodically washing each inch of my skin. She doesn't even hesitate before kneeling down on creaky joints to start in on my hair.

"Thank you," I say after a moment.

She nods, and the veil moves with her forced breath. But whatever words she is about to speak are cut off when I get to my stomach.

I immediately regret not sending her away. The water has washed away the balm that concealed the carefully hidden row of scars along my abdomen. Madame could have made them disappear with one of her concoctions, but she insisted they were a healthy reminder for me.

I forget about them most of the time. It's easy enough when I refuse to look at them, but here they are now — white, stark slashes against my tawny skin.

I squeeze my eyes shut against the hideous sight of them and the visceral memories of the man who gave them to me. They are a harrowing remembrance of the night my innocence was stolen. With one quick glimpse of them, I can practically smell the peppermint leaves on his breath all over again, and I want to be sick.

Shivering, I swallow hard, and belatedly attempt to cover them with the small washcloth in my hands.

The servants in Villa Paradís were accustomed to seeing much worse than a handful of healed wounds here and there, but that isn't how I want to be seen here.

Sigrid's hands still, but she says nothing. When she eventually starts applying the oils to my hair again, her touch is softer. Maternal.

And I'm not sure how to interpret it.

When she finally finds her voice, it's not to ask about the scars, as I expected. She says something else entirely.

"You are so beautiful. But you have too many...thorns." She pauses, and I wonder for a moment if she's referring to the obvious physical flaws she has just borne witness to, until she speaks again. "You prick at his Majesty...use sharp where soft would work. You do with everyone, I believe."

I know I've been rude, harsh even, but her mild scolding is an unwelcome reminder of how differently things have gone than I wanted them to. Even if the overgrown toddler that serves as Jokith's king is largely to blame. Still...

"Sometimes thorns are useful," I add after a moment. "Sometimes they're even a protection."

"This is true." Sigrid sighs. "And it is difficult to be in new home, be with new people so far from ones who belong you." Her voice trails off, and I hear the sadness etched into each word. The empathy. "But you will never have happy here if not you try."

Truer words...

She pats my shoulder and goes back to rinsing my hair without waiting for a response. The rest of our time passes in a silence that leaves too much room for the thoughts and memories that haunt me.

CHAPTER 13

Once I'm out of the bath and dried off, Sigrid wraps me in a thick, warm robe and sends me back out to the bedroom.

Einar pointedly ignores my presence as I sit across from him at the fire, pretending to focus on the book he's reading. He looks even angrier than he had when I left, and I'm not sure I have the energy to try anymore today.

Hadn't he just accused me of sucking the life out of a room, of making the servants miserable with my mere presence?

It hadn't been fair when he'd said it, but it felt uncomfortably true now.

When Sigrid emerges from tidying the privy, though, she places a gentle hand on my shoulder. She clears her throat and faces him, her expression concealed by the veil, but something in his countenance softens.

He sighs and arches an eyebrow, then goes back to his book.

Sigrid huffs, then scolds him in Jokithan, and I can't help but wonder how she gets away with it. I've yet to meet a lord or lady who tolerates such a thing.

Einar's eyes narrow as he closes his book. He doesn't respond to her rebuke. Instead, he stands and moves toward the door.

"You'll have to excuse me. I have matters to attend to," he says, reaching for the knob.

"What matters?" Sigrid boldly asks, placing a hand on her hip.

Einar's hand freezes, and he glares back at her.

"I am King still, am I not?" he asks calmly.

"Of course, *Majesty*." She uses his title condescendingly. "But Leif has already everything in control. Remember? You have nothing but to know your new wife today."

"I don't mind. I would hate to take him away from something so important. I'm not feeling very well anyway," I interject.

Even though he hasn't outwardly reacted, half a lifetime of watching servants be punished for less has left me unreasonably afraid of what her obstinance will result in. And besides, it's not untrue; my head and stomach are still vying for my attention while they do somersaults.

Sigrid only tsks again and walks over to the king's side. Whispering another rebuke, she pushes him bodily back to his chair.

"I get tonic brought up for sickness, Mistress. You are feel better after."

At this point, I'm not sure if the words are encouragement or a command. With that, she walks out of the room. Judging by the slight spring in her step, I would say she is quite pleased with herself.

As soon as the door clicks shut, a squeak sounds from the crate at the center of the room. The chalyx is back securely inside of it, but I'm hesitant to make any moves to let it out just yet, especially under Einar's watchful gaze.

Einar's knee bounces repetitiously as he stares too long at the same page in his book, and I continue to watch the flames dance in the hearth.

Another meow has him glancing from me to the cub and back again. He shakes his head, presumably because I've shown little interest in the thing he purchased for that very purpose.

The silence stretches on until I have no real choice but to break it or spend the rest of my evening in the suffocating tension that has permeated every inch of this room.

"So," I begin. "Leif is taking care of your duties? Your...ruling duties?"

The king's eyes meet mine, and he grunts what might be an affirmation. I'm missing something here. The man wouldn't grant his own wife a shred of power, so surely not a subordinate, one he forces to wear a mask for reasons he refuses to even hint at.

Though Sigrid would point to a different dynamic entirely, I assumed she was a unique case.

"I thought he was just a servant?" I seek to clarify, and he slams his book closed.

"He isn't *just* anything."

His gaze doesn't waver from mine for several heartbeats.

"My mistake," I offer, not breaking eye contact. "I am only trying to understand --"

He stands abruptly, cutting me off before I can dance around all of the things I had just been thinking.

"You understand nothing." He looks at me for a final, stilted heartbeat before stalking off to the passageway.

Well, then.

I sit in stunned silence while I try and fail to make sense of him and my purpose here. He doesn't seem to want to be married, or have any interest in me at all, for that matter.

Every woman I'd seen on our journey since crossing the border was tall and broad-shouldered, strong-looking, with fair hair and eyes. Their skin was either dark as coal or white as snow, and I am simply a middle-ground of sorts between the two.

While I am of average height back home, I feel like a child here. Even Sigrid towers over me.

My skin is much darker than Einar's, as is my hair. And my topaz-colored eyes are far different from the various shades of blue I've seen on every person in Jokith.

Am I so different from what he is familiar with that he finds me disgusting?

From the way his pupils went wide when he saw me bare before him, I would say no. There are some things you can't lie about; your traitorous body always gives you away.

I shake my head at the whole situation, mulling it over again and again and always coming up short.

I've been direct with him. I've tried subtleties. But nothing has worked.

The man is impossible.

The tonic Sigrid had sent up does seem to be helping ease my body aches and nausea. I was even able to eat some of the roasted venison and carrots from the dinner she had delivered, though there was no plate for Einar.

He still hasn't returned, and I'm unsure of what to make of that.

A squeaky growl reminds me that I am not the sole occupant of the room. Leaning over the side of the bed, I peer down at the cub, who is desperately trying to gain my attention.

It raises its little paws up, seemingly reaching for me.

"You're spoiled already, I see," I coo, but I pick her up anyway.

The servant who brought up our meal also saw that the cub was fed and taken outside to relieve itself, as well as inform me that my new pet is a girl, in case I wanted to name her.

"What is it that you want?" I ask the cat. "To annoy me? To make me crazier than these walls are already?"

Metallic teeth flash as she opens her mouth to yawn, rubbing her small head against my palm. Her fur is softer than the finest silks I've ever touched. Softer than gosling feathers or a butterfly's wing.

I'm still marveling at her when she presses her sharp teeth against my flesh.

"*Khijhana!*" I gasp a word from home in surprise, one that roughly translates to *little nuisance.*

I pull my fingers away to examine them, but she didn't seem to draw blood, or even break the skin. It was just a warning nibble that there is something she is wanting from our exchange as well.

She nestles in closer, her turquoise eyes opening and closing slower than before.

I narrow my eyes at her.

"If I let you sleep with me, you're not allowed to bite me again. Understand?"

The cat purrs, vibrating through my chest.

"Fine," I sigh.

I plop her down on the bed and lie down next to her. She goes straight to my pillow, kneading the fabric with shimmering claws until she's satisfied.

"*Khijhana,*" I say again, more amused this time. "It would seem that we have found your name, at least."

She stretches and purrs before closing her eyes to sleep.

I wish I could follow suit.

Over-thinking is getting me nowhere, but neither will closing my eyes and wishing this all away. I force my eyes to stay open, trying desperately to turn the gears in my weary mind.

I need to find a way to make this better, and I need to do it soon, before this convoluted mess of a situation gets any worse.

CHAPTER 14

This is an awful idea, but I can't seem to stop myself.

No sooner do I hear the king's voice echoing down the hallway outside my bedroom than I find myself slipping through the panel in my wall. The one he said leads to his room.

I don't stop to think. I don't even spare a second for shoes, instead slipping along the freezing stone floor on the naked soles of my feet.

Madame always did say desperation makes a fool.

I can hardly deny that now, not when I'm shivering and he could return at any moment. But I need to know something, *anything* about the man if I have the furthest chance of making this work.

I leave the panel cracked for a trickle of light but don't dare take my bedside lantern. It hardly matters. I am no stranger to the shadows.

In fact, as I make my way down the hallway, I realize how much I have missed the darkness, the ease of hiding in the shadows, of seeing without being seen rather than being on constant display in the full force of an unforgiving light.

Here, no one can see my scars.

Perhaps my cat, for all her seemingly nocturnal preferences, was an apt gift after all, if only I could believe it was meant that way.

Speak of the siren.

The tiny, exquisite terror is making her way behind me with footsteps even more muted than my own, but her shadow plays like a giant on the wall, giving her away.

A smile tugs at my lips, in spite of myself and this wretched situation. Without time to backtrack, I have little choice but to scoop the vixen up and bring her along for this little reconnaissance outing.

Ill-fated though it may be, my gamble has paid off already. Before I even make it to Einar's room, I discover something new about him. Something altogether less surprising than I wish it was.

This passage leads far beyond my room in both directions and has at least half a dozen hallways breaking off toward the eastern and northern wings. Unless the man has chambers the size of Villa Paradís, the king is a liar. And a rather gifted one at that.

A soft glow to my left seeps from under what I assume is his door. Pressing my ear to the wood, I listen to be certain no one is on the other side. I feel around for a knob or lever until my fingers graze the cold metal of the handle. One slow twist and the door is creeping open.

I steel myself for what my excuse will be for coming into his space unannounced. But we are married, after all... I'm certain no one else would take issue with my visit, even if my husband undoubtedly would.

Closing the door, I allow my eyes to adjust to the hazy light coming from the lanterns in the room. I'm not sure what I expected from such a calloused man, but it certainly wasn't this.

Plants cover half the surfaces in the room, potted on tables or the floor, hanging in the windows. Some of their leaves and stems are cut and rest on his desk. A closer examination shows drawings of the plants and hand-written explanations of their health benefits.

Books, unsurprisingly, line every shelf, some stacked on top of one another, some spread open on his bed and the table next to it.

Some are new, but most are worn, the bindings frayed and torn as if they have been read many times by many different people.

The cub mews, and I put her down so she can do some of her own exploring. I make a mental note to keep track of any mess she might make.

I'm careful when I move the pages to place everything back just the way it was. Each of the leather-bound notebooks has extensive information on various herbs and the oils that can be derived from them.

The clinking of glass alerts me, and I barely have time to catch two glass vials as Khijhana's tail knocks them from their home on the shelf.

I curse at her under my breath, and her ears lay flat, as if she understands me.

I place the glass bottles back on the shelf and take a moment to study it all. The number of vials and tomes on the dark oak shelf are puzzling. Each of the journals seem to be filled with the same subjects: flowers and shrubs, weeds and grasses, herbs and even some trees.

But nothing like the rose on the tower window I saw on my way into the castle.

Who knew he had such a passion for botany?

I snap my fingers gently to get Khijha's attention before she gets too close to the fireplace. She reluctantly comes back and rubs against my legs as if she isn't the annoying creature that her name implies. Fortunately, she follows me as I take in the rest of the room.

A few pictures line the walls. Judging by the azure gazes and the silver hair, it's easy to tell these are paintings of his family.

His father's skin is dark as midnight, while his mother's pale complexion looks like a reflection of the pearlescent moon next to him. There is no in-between, no various shades of brown or peach or tan. Only these two magnificently contrasting colors.

No wonder I stand out so much here.

The traits that tie them together, though, are the piercing blue eyes and heads of silver-white hair that they all share. I study each of the faces in the paintings and try to imagine what it would've been like to grow up with a family related to me by blood.

There were six of them. And he is the only one left.

I don't know what happened, exactly. Just that it was an accident, and they all died at once. It was sad to learn about, in a distant sort of way, but it's a harder pill to swallow when you see their faces and stand in their home.

The mid-sized of the fair-skinned children, I decide, must be Einar. There is something in his countenance that makes me certain it's the case, despite the lack of scowling and the notable absence of that wild animal he calls a beard.

In each painting, it's clear to see the kindness, love, and adoration the family had for one another. The artists couldn't have added that on their own; this is too genuine.

If only Einar possessed a fraction of those feelings now --

I cut the thought off with another. I know full well what losing family can do to you. How the pain can sever you from your very core, from every emotion, and how it can prevent you from forming new connections. It's an agony that you never really recover from.

I am proof enough of that.

I squeeze my eyes shut for a moment, allowing the sentimentality to pass. There isn't room for that here, but it is a good reminder for moving forward.

Tearing my eyes away from the happy family memories, I study the other side of the large room. The entirety of it hosts one giant bed. It is as massive as mine, but the frame seems more regal, timeless, as if it was built for a king and queen centuries ago.

I run a hand across the plush white blankets, allowing my fingers to graze the furs at the foot of the bed.

Only one wrinkled pillow looks as if it has been slept on. The others are full and over-stuffed, as if they've never been used.

A quick peek inside each nightstand shows that only one is full, of course, with more books about plants. I roll my eyes. At least he has a hobby, though not one that will be particularly easy or fun to bond over.

The other stand is empty, and I can't help but feel the smallest bit of satisfaction that he doesn't seem to be secretly hoarding mistresses in here.

I glance through his closet anyway, just to be sure, but nothing there indicates that there is another woman either.

I linger for only a few moments longer, disappointment seeping through me at how relatively little is here. I may have some small bit of knowledge I lacked before, but I'm not much closer to understanding the man than I was before I came.

Khijha mews and sprints randomly across the room, pawing at a tapestry on the wall. I'm quick to scoop her up before her metallic claws can do any damage.

Just as I turn back to the passageway, a draft tickles the back of my neck. I glance back in time to see the tapestry moving ever so slightly, as if a breeze is coming from behind the art piece.

"Good girl," I say, scratching the top of the cub's head as she purrs in satisfaction.

I toy with the idea of following the draft to see where it leads. Reluctantly, however, I decide to save that for another day. We're pressing our luck enough as it is. And I have a feeling that whatever is behind that wall will require more time than I have at the moment.

Chapter 15

If I expected to wake up feeling rested or refreshed, I am, once again, disappointed. If anything, I feel worse than I did yesterday, my head pounding and my stomach roiling.

Worst of all, I feel weak.

I gather just enough strength to plop the chalyx unceremoniously onto the floor. If he did give her to me as a tool to use against me later, I don't want to let on that it has been successful.

I've yet to see him be physically violent, but I'm not willing to risk Khijhana being hurt.

She's still glaring at me grumpily when the king stomps his way into my room, as usual.

At least he doesn't seem any moodier than he was yesterday. Last night's excursion remains a secret, then.

Sigrid's now-familiar knock sounds in time with Khijhana's squeak of surprise as Einar scoops her into his lap. I barely resist the urge to narrow my eyes at him.

The tiniest arrogant tilt of his lips has me thinking he imagines he's stirred up some jealousy within me, so I lay back down and resolutely ignore him.

I realize that my behavior isn't mature or productive, and that I should be working to make things better between us, especially given my revelations about him last night. But it's too early, and he's too smug, sitting there with my cub and a cocky grin on his face, so I refuse to give him the satisfaction.

He chuckles under his breath as I pretend not to care. And I don't care. Not really. I don't have time to dwell on it for long before Sigrid sweeps into the room, filling the open space with the sheer volume of her presence.

Judging by the huff beneath her veil as her head moves from facing the bed to the king's chair, she isn't terribly happy with either of us this morning.

I reluctantly pull myself from the covers to join my husband for breakfast, wrapping a robe around my sheer nightdress. It's warm and alleviates the cold seeping into the soles of my feet from the frozen floor.

I tuck my icy legs under me as I take my seat at the table where Sigrid has laid out our breakfast. Einar watches me, his eyebrow quirking, but says nothing.

The older woman clucks her tongue lovingly at Khijha, and she springs from Einar's grasp, running to a saucer that Sigrid sets on the floor. She is oblivious to the rest of the room now, focused only on what appears to be milk and honey.

I can't imagine that is good for her, but I'm too tired to voice that thought aloud.

Besides, given the sickly-sweet smell wafting from what I can only hope is Einar's breakfast this morning, I'm beginning to think this is how the woman feeds everyone.

Except for me. I notice with no small amount of gratitude the flat, seeded bread, two medium-cooked eggs, and a steaming cup of tea in front of me. I should at least be able to stomach this, if I don't watch my husband eat his own ridiculous breakfast.

Once Sigrid leaves, the only sounds in the room are Einar's obnoxious chewing and Khijha's gentle lapping of the sweet milk.

My head is pounding, and each crunch or slosh of milk grates on my already well-worn nerves. I guzzle down the glass of water before me and fill it again, drinking the entirety of it in one go. Nothing seems to help the dryness of my mouth or the ache in my bones that never goes away.

I stretch and start in on my breakfast when Einar finally decides to speak up.

"You didn't come down for dinner last night," he says, rather than asks, around mouthfuls of sweet cinnamon-filled rolls.

"I had my meal sent up."

Einar sighs. "Yes, I noticed." He shovels in another bite. "I suppose I was wondering why."

I take a moment to decide how much truth to give him and settle for the easiest answer.

"Well, I've never been much on forcing others to watch me eat while their own meals grow cold. I figured it was simpler this way." Who knows? Perhaps he'll finally explain the masks.

"And yet, you have no problem making the servants walk three flights of stairs to bring you your meal?"

Touché.

I tilt my head and narrow my eyes at him before settling on another bite of my meal instead of responding.

He studies me under his furrowed brow but doesn't say anything more as he dives back into his sickly-sweet breakfast.

"My apologies, I didn't realize you had missed me so much," I tempt after a moment.

"I just found the room had entirely too much joy for my liking, without you there to drain it away." He speaks without inflection, but I don't miss the slight tilt of his lips.

I startle myself by laughing.

"I'm glad I could oblige you this morning, then," I respond.

"As am I." There is something curiously close to warmth in his tone, and I take it for what it is.

If not an apology, at least a truce.

When our meal is finished, he isn't as quick to leave my room as before. He, instead, stays to play with the chalyx and read next to the hearth while I bathe. I finish my bath quickly, all the while wondering if he'll be gone when I return, but he's still here, sitting in the same spot.

I pull another gauzy, impractical dress from my trunk and a matching array of jewelry. An emerald-encrusted nose ring replaces the pure gold one from yesterday, and I pair it with a similar ear cuff. After deliberation, I connect them with the gold chain again.

No one here knows its meaning, anyway, and I've always liked the look of it. A teardrop-shaped pendant graces my forehead, hanging from a chain woven through my hair.

I consider adding a set of bangles to my wrist, but I don't want him to think I am trying to hide the intricate artwork he is too uncultured to appreciate.

By the time I finish dressing, I still feel out of breath and lightheaded, but I ask anyway.

"I'd like to see more of the castle today, to finish up that tour." I would like to see more of this place, but also, a do-over would help to further our unspoken truce.

He eyes me for a long moment before answering.

"You don't appear to be up to walking anywhere."

"Are you implying I look unwell?" I raise an eyebrow at him.

"I'm not implying anything. You look like hell."

If by "hell," he means the circles under my eyes are turning a deep shade of blue, then fine. But I'm not the only one.

"Well if that isn't the pot calling the kettle haggard," I quip, gesturing to the signs of exhaustion on his own features before adding, "You know, some women might be offended by that kind of bluntness."

"But you're not like most women, are you?" There's an undercurrent to his tone that makes me doubt myself for a fraction of a second, but I push it away.

I hold his eyes with my own, refusing to look away or answer him directly. Finally, I make my way to the door, resting my hand on the knob in a challenge. "Are you coming?"

Khijhana is quick on my heels, and we wait for his answer.

He looks me up and down for several long seconds, then shakes his head and stands.

"So be it." He opens the door for me and gestures for us to lead the way.

"That's the spirit," I add, and I swear I hear the masked guards outside the door chuckle.

Any truce or good humor that I may have imagined in the beginning of our tour is cut short when we reach a staircase leading to the West Wing.

"Maybe we should wrap things up for today." Einar hedges, turning away from the steps.

"But why?" My curiosity is piqued. "Don't you want me to know my new home?" I have to force that last word, sure I will never view it as any such thing.

"This wing is reserved for the staff and guests only. There isn't anything to see." He proffers his arm and tries to lead me away, but I press on with a light-hearted tone.

"Oh, come now, let's just --"

The sounds of glass shattering and a cry ringing out from the top of the staircase cut me off.

Einar pales and dashes up the steps without hesitation. I move to follow him, prepared to help in any way I can. My heart is pounding in my chest, while I envision what could have caused the sound, who might be in pain, injured, or even being attacked.

"I said no, Zaina!" His booming voice echoes off of the tall ceilings and bare walls. "Go back to your rooms." His words stop me on the second step. They are final, his command clear.

He doesn't wait to see if I will obey, only motions to the guards nearby. They walk toward me to enforce his order.

Khijhana growls, and her ears go flat as the men approach. They hesitate for only a second before I pick her up, forcing her to obey as I have to.

I clench my fists around her fur in an attempt to fight down the panic and fury rising inside of me. The guards are thrumming with tension. Whether it's for the person who cried out or because of the king's raised voice, I can't tell. They silently lead me back to my rooms, exchanging a few hushed words with the guards who stand watch by my door.

Khijha paws gently at my face, her claws retracted, as she tries in her own small way to comfort me. I scratch her behind her ears, and she purrs, but it offers me little consolation.

My head is spinning, and my heart is thundering in my chest. I'm not sure why I expected this tour to go any differently than the last one, but at least it taught me some things that I didn't know before.

One. The king has no trouble raising his voice to women or humiliating his own wife.

Two. He would rather keep things from me than accept any assistance I might have to offer.

Three. I need to know what is in the West Wing.

If I am going to begin to unravel any of the secrets that shroud this sands-forsaken castle, it will undoubtedly start there.

CHAPTER 16

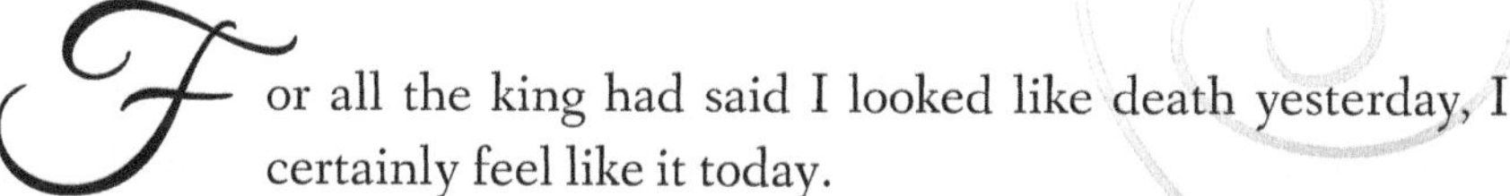

For all the king had said I looked like death yesterday, I certainly feel like it today.

My mouth is constantly dry, and my bones always ache. It seems that no matter how much rest I get, it's never enough.

I'll be damned if I'm in bed again when he flounces in with his superior expression, though, so I force myself to stand.

Besides, I know him well enough from our brief encounters to know he will pretend nothing happened yesterday, and I will not let that stand. Everyone has heard the rumors of the beastly king and the castle full of people no one has seen up close in years.

Now I'm here, in the midst of it, and it makes even less sense than the convoluted stories. Someone is going to tell me what's going on.

My steps are unsteady on the way to the table as it is, and Khijhana nearly topples me entirely in her haste to wait at the door for Sigrid. She's an intelligent little nuisance, I'll give her that. And she seems to be growing before my very eyes.

Surely, her paws weren't that big yesterday...

Sigrid arrives before the king, for a change. He is late. Worse yet, Sigrid has brought another of her horrid tonics.

With a sigh, I force the thing down. Every last salty, citrus tasting bit of it. I've already determined it's not actually poison, and it does help, just as it did yesterday.

"Shall I assume the king won't be joining me this morning?" I phrase it as a question, but I already know the answer.

She hasn't brought him a plate, and I'm not surprised he's avoiding me after yesterday. I am, however, curious to see what she has to say about it.

"You need be drink more water. Your body is hungry for liquid," she deflects, picking up the wooden pitcher and pouring me a large glass. "The mountain sickness, it sits with you."

"Sigrid?" I press, and she sighs.

"His Majesty has much things to do with the kingdom today." She is already moving toward the door as she answers, uncharacteristically eager to get out of this room herself.

"I thought you said he had nothing better to do than spend time with his wife?" I inject polite interest into my tone, but I doubt she is fooled.

"The things are come up," she answers.

Her tone has a ring of truth to it, but I can't let it drop.

"Things like what happened yesterday? In the West Wing?" I prod.

If I expect her to lie or hedge, she surprises me by doing neither.

"Yes," she says simply, her tone more accented than usual. "Things like that. I must get to them as well, Mistress, unless there is another things you need."

There is nothing I can think of that wouldn't be childish, and I can see I won't get any more answers from her. So, I shake my head.

"I won't keep you." The words have less warmth than I mean for them to, but Sigrid doesn't bristle.

If anything, she practically deflates on her way out the door, as though she's exhausted and disappointed all at the same time.

That makes two of us.

I lived most of my life in Madame's household, where it went without saying that someone was hurting at any given moment. It's no different here. Still, people suffer, and I am helpless to stop it.

I don't even know what *it* is.

I shouldn't be so concerned. That's not why I'm here, but I can't seem to help myself.

I had assumed Madame chose this kingdom because Einar is the only unmarried king this side of the Cerulean Sea, the quickest route to a throne. But perhaps it was more than that. Did she know they were weakened from within?

I heave a frustrated sigh.

It's clear no one else is going to give me any answers today, so I'll have to find them myself. Though only a handful of days have passed since my arrival here, it feels like a lifetime. It feels like more than long enough to live in a castle where I can't see another human face, save for that of the indecipherable king.

This has gone on long enough.

I dress in one of my many impractical gowns, this one a pale shade of yellow with sheer sleeves that drag along the stone floors, and I don my usual array of head jewels before leaving. Khijhana is at my feet, as impatient to escape this room as I am.

After yesterday, I wonder how the guards outside my door will react, but I stride out of my room without giving them a chance to doubt my right to be there. They let me pass, following behind me on eerily soundless footfalls.

I wonder if the guards rotate, if these could be the same ones I encountered yesterday. I only have small cues to go by when their faces are covered by the beaked masks, but I'm fairly certain they are different. One of their builds is a mite too thin, and the other seems an inch or two shorter.

My confidence in that assessment leads me to the West Wing, where I hope they won't know I'm not allowed.

It's a feeble hope, and one that I am rid of as soon as I spot the massive staircase with two frustratingly familiar guards posted at either side. They stand a little straighter when they see me, and I stop in my tracks.

"Are you lost, milady?" This from one of the two following me.

I never get lost, but I don't tell them that. Instead, I continue past the staircase like I had always planned on going this way.

Before I know it, I find myself nearing the room I had been drawn to on my first tour of the castle. The study is smaller than the other rooms I've seen here, the ceilings not quite as cavernous, allowing the roaring hearth to actually inject some heat into the area. The deep brown panels of the walls are as appealing today as they were the first time, and there are a number of plushy chairs situated in small clusters to allow for conversation, if I was not the only one present.

What calls me here, though, are the windows. High, curved structures that span nearly the entire height and width of the outward-facing wall, they overlook the back end of the estate where deep green, snow-capped cedars stretch as far as the eye can see. Beyond the trees are mountains that dwarf even the massive, imposing structure we are in.

I can imagine running through those woods, tiny glistening snowflakes settling in my eyelashes. The sight is so much freer than I will ever be, and I allow myself to sink into that feeling while I stand here, surrounded by the rare warmth of the crackling flames.

For the first time since I arrived at this place, I feel like I can breathe.

It's not a feeling I'm eager to let go of, so I search the room for something to pass the time until dinner. The far side of the study holds a small collection of books, but it's nothing I have any use for.

There are playing cards and wooden puzzles on a few of the tables, showing an interesting amount of use considering the vacant state of the room. There is even a small wooden chess board, pieces frozen in place halfway through a game. Finally, my eyes settle on an ornate grand piano in the corner.

My heart falters for a beat.

It's not my instrument. It never has been.

But it was my sister's.

I have never been away from Melodi and Aika this long, and the knowledge of what I left them to face alone is more than I can bear to think about.

I move toward the piano and settle onto the bench. My sentinels wait outside the door, but Khijhana follows at my heels, sitting between me and the doorway as though she is the one guarding me.

Hesitantly, I lift the lid that protects the ivory keys. I was brought up as a lady — we all were — so I know how to play, even though I generally choose not to.

There is sheet music here, but it is foreign and looks as bleak as the rest of this place feels. Instead, I let my fingers play along the keys an achingly familiar tune. It's not long before I am lost in the notes, lost in my own head.

It's warm on the balcony we share at the château, even with the late evening breeze rolling in from the water. Madame is in Bondé, and we are left alone for a rare change.

Aika plays her fiddle beside me, her shiny black hair whipping around with the intensity of her motions. She is tiny, shorter even than my shoulder, but everything she does is intense and fiery and bold.

Melodi dances along as if there isn't a care in the world, as if we haven't just watched a person be slaughtered for nothing more than a show of power. She is swept up in this moment in a way I am incapable of replicating, giving herself entirely to the music while her tightly coiled red curls spin nearly as gracefully as she does.

Mel begs me to sing, and usually I would give in. Usually, I can deny her nothing, but tonight I am playing the piano because Rose is sleeping. I can hardly begrudge her the escape I long so desperately for, not when she needs it so much more than I do.

Her golden waves and deep blue eyes are even more appealing than my own unique features, and that means nothing good here. At least she doesn't have to worry about that right now.

So, I am grateful, but I am jealous, too. Jealous of Rose's sleep, and Melodi's sense of self, and Aika's endless supply of passion...of every-

thing that allows them to cope with the unthinkable when all I can seem to do is disappear a little more each day.

There is no relief now that I'm here, now that I've left them to fend for themselves without even my dubious, haphazard protection. Besides, it's not as though I've escaped. Not really.

Not at all.

CHAPTER 17

I don't know how long I pound my fingers along the polished ivory and onyx before I finally force myself to stop. Missing my sisters, worrying for them — it solves nothing.

I am marveling at the rare feeling of a bead of sweat on my brow in this icebox when Khijhana lets out a low growl. Her ears fold back, and she lifts slightly off her haunches, as though she's ready to pounce.

I don't have to wonder long what's riled her up. Odger, the man from the feast with the silver star on his mask, glides into the room. His gloved hands are giving me a muted, polite clap, and I am nearly off-kilter enough to tell him exactly where he can put his praise.

But I still my tongue, because I may yet need him for information.

Instead, I rest a placating hand on Khijha's head and incline mine in gratitude.

"I didn't know our new queen was an aficionado," he says in his oily tone.

"Consort," I correct with a bland smile, as though I don't

remember him emphasizing the title at the banquet or don't realize that he is merely trying to flatter me now that we are in private.

"Of course." He feigns chagrin. "My mistake."

"Think nothing of it," I say, rising to my feet.

"Allow me to make it up to you over a game?" he gestures to a cup of dice at the nearest table.

He wants to play games, all right, but to what end?

Well, it's not as though I have anything better to do.

"That does sound nice, but perhaps you would indulge me with a different sort of game." I choose my words carefully and infuse my smile with more warmth this time, crinkling my eyes and allowing my lips the slightest pout.

"What did you have in mind?" He stalks closer, like the predator I know he is, and I fight the urge to cringe.

I point to the chess board.

"I haven't played in ages," I say truthfully, pushing back memories of the man who taught me to play. "But it could be fun."

He hesitates before answering.

"I'll go easy on you, I promise." His voice drips with charm, and I am certain if I could see his lips, they would be tilted in false self-deprecation.

"Well, if you promise." I glance demurely at him through lowered lashes and take my seat.

Khijhana stays glued to my side, never moving from between Odger and me, and it draws his attention.

He whistles.

"I had heard that he found you a chalyx, but I've never actually seen one in person."

Look at him, being useful already.

"I assumed they were common here," I respond truthfully as he sets up the board.

"They aren't common anywhere," he says. Then, he shakes his head, likely because he realizes he nearly complimented the king. "I'm surprised you chose this game. Most women don't play chess."

He means the words as a compliment, so I pretend to take them that way instead of acknowledging that his tone tells me he would feel the same way if I had told him Khijhana wanted to play.

"I suppose I'm not most women," I respond, the words a curious echo of my conversation with Einar. "Though, you hardly seem to be most men, either."

"Oh?" He stills.

"You seem to have almost no accent. Have you always lived here?"

He puffs out his chest before he answers.

"Jokith has always been my home, but I served as the king's ambassador for decades."

I shouldn't be surprised by his age when I know Einar's, but it constantly awes me how long the Jokithans live. It was a mystery of their lineage even Madame could never solve, one that seemed tied to the land itself.

Then, I register the rest of what he said.

"Are you the ambassador who chose me?" I ask, taking my time moving my knight directly into his line of fire.

He laughs, a sound that slithers along my spine.

"I would never have wasted your beauty on a man like Einar."

I pretend to miss the way he leaves out the king's title.

"You flatter me," I say, because I can hardly tell him the truth, that he revolts me.

We banter meaninglessly over a few turns, long enough for me to confirm exactly what kind of player he is. He's a coward.

He's all underhanded moves and defensive strategy, waiting for even an unskilled opponent to happen upon one of his many traps. It tells me all I need to know about how to steer this conversation. All I have to do is wait for the opening in his increasingly blatant flirtations.

"Surely, you didn't think I could let that move stand," he says, capturing the knight I've sacrificed for this very reason. "Of course, with a face like yours, I doubt you've encountered much resistance in the past."

I shoot him a saucy look.

"And what of your face, Sir? Surely, it's a travesty to hide it away from the world."

If there's any resentment toward the king on this matter, he'll be showing it right about now. Instead, he goes still. I think, perhaps, I've been too forward until he lets out a small sigh.

"Indeed, I long for the time when I can display my features before the world. But there are worse things, I suppose."

I don't think it's my imagination that his banal chatter is more subdued after that, or that he speeds up the game more than he might have. I don't push anymore, though, unwilling to lose the only person who has actually consented to talk to me.

Before he announces his win, my chalyx raises back up on her haunches, only this time, her head is cocked slightly to the side and her ears remain upright. This time, I have a feeling I know exactly who is on his way in.

CHAPTER 18

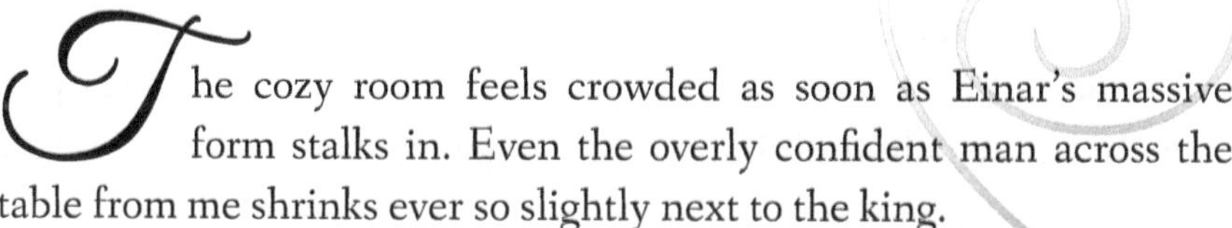

The cozy room feels crowded as soon as Einar's massive form stalks in. Even the overly confident man across the table from me shrinks ever so slightly next to the king.

Still, he doesn't turn to acknowledge the bigger man.

"Check mate," he tells me, his tone more intimate than the words require. "Truly, you played remarkably well, all things considered."

All things like my female anatomy, you mean?

"You're too kind," I say instead, managing the words without a trace of irony. "Perhaps we'll have a rematch soon."

Very soon, if I have anything to say about it. Even if I do feel like I need to scrub every part of my body the moment I leave here, like his personality left a physical residue.

I don't even glance at my giant brute of a husband as I stand up to make my way out.

Odger doesn't follow my lead, though. He stands up and looks the king squarely in his marble face before bowing several inches shallower than is appropriate.

"Thank you, My Lord, for allowing me the pleasure of entertaining your wife." He draws out the word pleasure, and Einar's face darkens infinitesimally.

The king looks to the spot where I have stilled to watch his exchange with Odger, then to Khijhana, who stands facing Odger with her features on alert. Finally, he turns back to the slighter man.

A slow smile spreads across the bastard's face, and I narrow my eyes.

Something amusing, dear husband? I don't ask, though, not in front of Odger.

"I'm sure the pleasure was all hers," the king responds.

The corner of my mouth tilts up ever so slightly. He believes he has read the situation perfectly well, that he's caught on to my game.

But I haven't even gotten started.

I close the space between Odger and me with two long strides, placing my hand lightly on his arm.

"Indeed, it was. I look forward to next time." I widen my eyes just enough that he believes it is the king being made a fool of rather than himself.

It works, if the way he struts from the room is any indication.

I turn back to Einar in time to see an irksome shadow cross his face, but he is already moving to the chess board.

"Care for a game that's a little more your speed?"

Why does it always feel like he's saying more than the sum of his words?

"What makes you think the game with Lord Odger was not my speed?" I ask, because two can play at double entendres.

"Just a feeling." He shrugs arrogantly, as if my answer couldn't possibly matter less to him.

My pride nearly has me walking out the door before my sense gets the better of me. Haven't I been looking for a chance to understand him better?

I take my seat across from him. He pulls a Jokithan coin out of his pocket and moves to flip it.

"Heads," he calls.

"Betting on your own face?" I quirk an eyebrow.

"It's the only one I can trust." There it is.

An undercurrent of anger, and, if I'm not mistaken, even jealousy.

I can't pretend I'm not pleased to have permeated his icy exterior enough to rankle him, but he isn't the only angry one. I haven't forgotten yesterday.

"And here I was about to say the opposite," I counter. "I'll take the wolf." It's the other side of the Jokithan silver.

He narrows his eyes but says nothing. The small silver coin lands with his pompous face staring up at us, and he flips the board so that the alabaster tokens are in front of him.

Though Odger had assumed I required the advantage of going first, I actually prefer to let the king make the first move.

He leads out with a pawn in a classic opening, one I get the feeling is intentionally neutral. I counter with a move just as bland, and our game begins.

We spend the next several turns in silence, each taking the other's measure, and neither gaining nor giving away the advantage.

Finally, he pauses with his nimble fingers hovering over his knight, the light catching on his silver wedding band.

"Am I to understand you meant to imply you would trust a wild animal over your king?"

It's an effective way to distance himself, though I hardly think of him as *my* king. He moves his piece, and I wonder if his question was as much to distract me as it was genuine.

I study the board. I see a solid dozen ways out of the trap he is weaving, but only a handful that would trap him in turn.

I know I should let him win, but something in me itches to play in truth, to pit my mind against his and see where it leads us. Besides, I've thrown one game today already.

Meeting his eyes, I slide my rook into position. The moonstones on my ring dance under the golden candlelight, like they're celebrating the small victory with me.

"Check," I announce, then respond to his question with one of my own. "Am I to understand you would blame me for such a notion?"

His glacial eyes don't leave mine, but neither does he respond. Anger rises in me, unbidden.

"Tell me, *my king,* how much trust you might have for someone who fills the space in their marriage bed with secrets and false niceties?"

He drops his gaze, features tightening with what I might have thought was remorse, if I could have believed him authentic.

"Everyone has secrets," he responds quietly, deftly maneuvering his king out of danger.

The hypocrisy of me arguing that statement is not lost on me, but I do it anyway.

"Indeed," I allow, countering his move before continuing. "Does everyone also restrict entire sections of their home from their wife?"

He opens his mouth to respond, but I barrel over him.

"For that matter, does *everyone* bark orders at a woman they barely know in a room full of those who are strangers to her? A woman who, if anything, he should show more than the usual respect for?" I don't expect him to apologize, but he can damned well acknowledge what he did.

His face turns to stone again, but he isn't too distracted to make another move.

"*Everyone* does not have the responsibilities that I do."

So much for remorse.

Whatever else had happened in that wing, he had no problem with the way he belittled me, the way he shut me out of everything that was going on in this castle, like I'm some random intruder instead of his wife.

"I see." It is an effort not to shake with the ire now trembling through my veins.

Khijhana presses herself against my leg, and I soak in her warmth gratefully, trying in vain to ground myself. I don't speak again until I've countered his move.

"I suppose that's all the reason you need for your behavior. I would hardly expect a man in as lofty a position as your own to lower yourself by offering explanations to a woman who will never be anything more than your glorified whore." I manage to keep my voice remarkably calm, but I spit that last word out all the same.

He rears back as though I've slapped him.

"I've never touched you!" The way he says the words with blatant disgust doesn't help his overall case of being an arsehole, but that was never the point.

He could have given me a hundred titles if he didn't want to make me Queen, but there is an ownership associated with a consort. He may as well have snapped a collar around my neck for all the pride he has afforded me, and I know it shouldn't matter. I remind myself of that constantly.

But it does, and it's not the only thing I can't get past.

"It doesn't matter what you do once you call me that, a fact we are both well aware of. So, tell me, my king, my master, just how your consort should view you now, so that I may follow that order as well."

His face is red with fury, his mouth opening as though he genuinely has no idea how to respond. If that's the case, he's the only one who's short on words, because I can't seem to stop mine.

"Is that why you wouldn't permit me to bring my own ladies or maids along? What need does a prisoner have of companionship?"

His flinch is barely perceptible, but I notice as he leans forward, no doubt to defend himself. Still, I don't stop.

"Perhaps you could force me to wear a veil as well." I am as close to unleashing the carefully cultivated threads of my temper than I have been in years.

"Or have you already commissioned one? How much fabric do you think it would take to obscure the hideousness of my own features from Your Majesty's untainted gaze?"

I have moved subconsciously closer to him with each word until we are mere inches apart by the time I stop speaking. This close, I can see that his eyes aren't really blue — at least, not entirely. They're flecked with silver, like jagged shards of ice. His lips are parted in acrimony or something I might interpret as desire on anyone else.

We sit like that for another heartbeat, frozen in time but for our furious breaths. Then he swallows, closing his mouth and backing away from the charged moment.

"I would never force a veil on anyone, let alone my own people." He delivers the statement without inflection, his attention solely on the queen he is now sliding slowly across the board. "There are things beyond you here, things you don't understand."

I take a deep breath, studying the minute changes in his features. The slight furrow in his brow, the vein pulsing in his neck.

To the untrained eye, he could appear emotionless, but there is something there brimming below the surface, something I can't quite name. None of it makes sense, though. If he doesn't force his servants and guests into masks and veils, then why speak so sharply to the girl cleaning the slime that day?

And why hide their faces, if not at his command?

"How can I possibly understand something you refuse to explain?" I finally interject, but he holds up a hand.

"You can't understand, but you can look outside the bubble of your own making to acknowledge that much before jumping to conclusions, something you have clearly not bothered to do." He stands up in a single, fluid movement, not breaking eye contact with me.

"Check mate."

I look at the board in disbelief, but he isn't wrong. And for once, I wasn't pandering. He's outwitted me.

By the time I glance back up, he has swept out of the study, leaving the room feeling even emptier than it did when I arrived.

Chapter 19

I turn our exchange over and over in my mind, dissecting it piece by piece, yet still, I come up wanting. What was said and all that wasn't is spinning in my head like a carousel that never stops.

I am already tired of playing this game. Of waiting for him to soften or change or to explain anything about this horrid, frozen, soulless place.

Weeks go by, and Einar doesn't join me for breakfast. I've taken all of my meals in my room, alone but for Khijhana.

Even Sigrid has been keeping her distance, though the way she gingerly helps me dress and insists on brushing my hair tells me there is no ill-will between us. There's only a wall of secrets that neither of us can seem to breach.

I groan for the millionth time, and Khijha rubs her massive head against my neck, nearly knocking me backward on the bed.

The chalyx never stops growing. In just the few weeks that have passed, she is now the size of a full-grown wildcat. Her purr practically rumbles through my bones, and I allow myself to take comfort in her for a moment.

Today is another echo of each day since I argued with the king. Sigrid draws my bath while I sip the special tonic she makes me each morning. Then, breakfast. Then, I am left to my own devices until lunch, and the same from the span of lunch until dinner and all through the night.

I return to the study most days, but neither Odger, nor Einar makes an appearance. And I don't touch the piano again. My emotions are precarious enough without another trek down memory lane. Instead, I pass the time by staring at the endless mountains and wishing I was anywhere but here.

Khijhana and I are on our way back to my rooms after one such visit when I turn a corner and stop dead in my tracks. A man is walking from the direction of the king's rooms. It takes me a moment to realize that it is, in fact, the king. His face is concealed by a black silk mask, but his arrogant posture and his solid footsteps are impossible to hide.

Unlike the doctor's masks of the guards flanking him, his is fashioned after the head of a wolf. He freezes when he spots me.

Several seconds tick by while we stand only strides apart, facing each other without a word until I finally decide to speak.

"Have you decided you'd like a taste of your own medicine? Is this penitence?" I gesture to the face covering.

"I am holding Court today." As usual, he responds without actually answering my question, but he has revealed something even more infuriating.

"So, you do allow people in the castle? Just not for the sake of your wife?"

The guards shuffle uncomfortably, but the king only sighs.

"I allow those in need to petition their king for a short period of time every other week." His tone drips with condescension. "I wouldn't expect you to understand the difference, as that would require you thinking of someone besides yourself."

I stare down at the faded markings on my hands, so he won't see the truth in my expression.

That I despise him.

This is at least the second time he has called me selfish, and it doesn't sting any less when coming from a man who essentially had me shipped here like I was little more than livestock, a man who couldn't begin to understand that I have spent my entire life at the expense of someone else's.

He hasn't moved, but he is impossible to read, even when his face isn't hidden.

"I think I prefer this face," I say at last, gesturing to his mask. "The beast. At least there is honesty in that." I walk around him without another word, giving him a wide berth and holding my head high until I reach the relative safety of my chambers.

He is better at avoiding me after that.

Khijhana is at least my constant companion, speculating and observing at my side. Even now, her ears twitch in warning.

I listen for the telltale footsteps in the hallway. They pause just in front of my door, their shadow stretching under the frame for several seconds before he decides to move on.

I'm not sure if the way my heart thunders within my chest is from relief or disappointment. Either way, his retreat is the sound we've been waiting for.

I ease out of the bed and into my slippers, careful not to allow a single floorboard to creak, in case he or a guard is listening. Tying the plush robe tighter around my waist, I ease open the panel in the wall and usher Khijha through before following her. I slide the hidden door back into place and pause, waiting to be sure Einar hasn't decided to venture through the passageways this evening.

When I hear the scrape of his desk chair on his floor, I feel safe enough to creep down the hall in the opposite direction.

Many nights of this routine have taught Khijha and me the ins and outs of most of the castle. I've even found a door that leads to a back entrance of the castle. It's solidly locked up, but only from the inside. I think I have come close to exploring all of Alfhild.

All except for the West Wing. There must be a passage somewhere, but I have yet to find it.

Khijha purrs and presses her body closer to mine in a gesture of comfort. I know she can feel the tension rolling off of me in waves, just as she is curiously in tune with all of my emotions. I've never had a pet, but the ones I've observed haven't appeared to be nearly this intuitive.

Once I solve the list of mysteries this castle has to offer, I plan to learn more about chalyxes and why they are so rare.

We continue down several corridors, winding our way through the shadowy silence.

It's somewhat unnerving how much I prefer the dark, hushed passageways to the light of day and interacting with people with murky motives. The shadows are illuminating, in their way, while the light offers so much brightness to hide behind.

Sadly, while my spying has revealed some information, it's not the sort I was hoping for.

There seems to be an illness spreading through the castle. Many of the staff have taken to their beds; some of the courtiers as well. Maybe it's a good thing I'm not allowed in the West Wing. I can hardly afford to fall --

The sound of whispering voices stops me in my tracks. Khijha doesn't need to be told to be still. Her glowing eyes peer up at me expectantly, while her tail curls around my ankle.

I find the small opening in the stones, just wide enough to allow me to peer through if I squeeze one eye shut. I still my breathing, straining to listen carefully to the quiet conversation being held.

"...unimaginable." A man's voice comes from the other side of the kitchen.

It isn't until the other speaks that I finally see them, two beaked forms.

"I know, I know. But what is he to do now? They're already

married." This from the taller but far skinnier figure. His voice is deep, with its own sort of built-in echo, as if he is perpetually speaking in a cave.

The broader figure huffs. "Maybe. I heard they haven't even consummated yet."

Gossiping cowards.

My pulse beats a heavy rhythm in my temples while heat floods my cheeks.

"If you don't consummate, the marriage can be annulled." The smaller man continues.

I clench my fists. They aren't saying anything I don't already know. We are nearing a month as it is, and I am no closer to the king now than I was before I got here.

"How he copes with being married to such a spoiled brat is beyond me."

"I agree. Too good to even leave her rooms, much less speak to anyone."

"He doesn't deserve the likes of her. After all he's done for us, all we wanted was someone who would make him happy."

Another reminder that I seem to be the only person he chooses to unleash his ire on. Well, me and Odger. *A duo I'd prefer not to be part of.*

"Here, here. She's nearly as bad as the other one --"

"I beg your pardon!" Another more familiar voice echoes off of the walls, causing the men to freeze.

Leif. His limping form comes into view, and the other two men give a slight bow in greeting.

Interesting.

"We do not speak so cavalierly of *that woman.*"

Somehow, I don't think I'm the one he means, unless he, too, holds a deep level of loathing for me. I sigh inwardly. Perhaps he only hides it better than his king does.

"I would think the two of you had more to do than gossip like schoolgirls," he chides.

Both beaked faces sag toward the floor.

"It just isn't right, Sir. After everything, that he would get stuck with *her*. And after we all pushed him into this." This is from the wider one, his tone dripping with remorse.

Leif heaves a sigh and puts a hand on each of their shoulders.

"You're good lads, but you're young yet. Marriage is hard enough for anyone, let alone with a whole castle weighing in." He allows a moment for that to sink in. "Give them their time, especially the girl. It can't be easy for her."

So, I hadn't read him that badly. Between Leif and Sigrid, at least there appeared to be two decent people within these walls.

They bow again, and he nods before turning to leave the room. All is quiet as the two men finish their cleaning until Khijha sneezes and it catches me off guard. I jerk away too quickly from the wall and crack my forehead against the stones.

Sirens!

If they hadn't heard her already, they most certainly heard that.

A hush falls over the men.

"You shouldn't say such things so publicly!" the taller one whispers more quietly, while glancing around the room for the intruder.

"Me? You had just as much to say as I did, to be sure."

They continue in this vein for another minute or so before the dishes are done and they vacate the kitchen.

I rub the aching spot on my head. It stings, but not as much as their words had.

I think back to the king's words about how I am the only reason the people are unhappy.

All this time, I thought I was doing them a favor by keeping away, by not forcing my awkward, foreign company on what was already clearly a complicated situation, but apparently, I had done quite the opposite. They despise me.

They despise me, yet love their king? The beast of a man who yells at women and forces — *allows* them to conceal themselves from the world. Or, at least, from the rest of the castle.

Something pricks at the back of my mind, and a new train of thought rushes in unannounced.

Maybe they're hiding from me.

The very idea is unnerving and, if I'm perfectly honest with myself, disappointing.

My chalyx paws at my legs, and I take her cue. I've learned enough about the castle and the people in it for one evening.

Chapter 20

When I awake the next day, I decide to do things differently. Sigrid fusses over the scrape on my forehead and applies a pungent ointment that she swears will help.

It's certainly vile enough to rival the tonic she gave me for the mountain sickness, so I can at least trust in its efficacy.

After my bath, I sit down to breakfast alone, but I'm not quite ready to let Sigrid leave.

"I was wondering if you might be able to help me with something?" I begin.

"Mistress?" Her voice is just a hair on the hesitant side, bringing home the unwelcome realization that I'm considered a wild card here.

"It's been too cold for me to stray from my rooms very much," I explain, realizing full well how feeble my excuse is. "But I was thinking, if I had warmer clothing, that I might be able to get out more. You know, around other people."

Sigrid stares at me silently, her veil concealing her features. I'm not sure exactly what she thinks of what I've said until she closes the gap between us in three long strides, takes my face in her gloved hands, and presses her veiled face to the top of my head.

"You make me so happy, today," she says, her voice lighter than it has been in weeks. "I have just the things for you. Come."

She grabs hold of my hand and pulls me to the wardrobe where she placed all of the clothes I brought with me.

Moving aside the gauzy dresses, she pulls open the lid to a chest within the wardrobe, one that I had no idea was even there, and removes several articles of clothing.

Laying them out on my bed, she fusses until I can see the full outfit.

White and gray fur-lined pants accompany a long-sleeved fitted top of the same material. What had looked barbaric on our wedding day appears somehow softer now, more welcoming and practical in a way that appeals to my own pragmatic nature.

It must have just been the man wearing them who made them so off-putting before.

What catches my attention and nearly steals my breath is the hooded cape she has provided. Not only is it a practical solution for the chill I can never seem to shake, something no one has yet thought to offer me, but it's red.

All this time, I've felt so...distant, so unseen, so very different from the rest of the castle. But Sigrid saw my wedding dress and the rest of my wardrobe and, instead of trying to force me into the dreary gray way of life here, she infused that gloom with color. My favorite color. And she made it feel like mine.

I run my hands over it, studying every inch of the stunning garment. Deep shades of crimson and ruby and garnet form an abstract pattern of roses in the soft crushed velvet. My breath hitches at the harsh memories and the constant reminder that the flower brings to mind.

The whole glorious thing is offset by bright white fur lining, lending the gorgeous cloak even more warmth.

Even if I can never gaze at the cursed flowers without seeing my sister in their every stem, petal, and even each thorn, I will wear the clothes with pride.

I will imagine her at my side, lending me her endless well of optimism, her own brand of strength, in a world with far too little of it.

I swallow, taking in the matching boots and thick, warm socks that my toes can hardly wait to wiggle into.

"Thank you," I say, choking back the emotion that has come unbidden, as I hold the items close to me to compare the sizes.

"I am have them made when you get here. But when you stay in your bed so much, is no use."

Normally, her chastisement might chafe, but I am too grateful to focus on anything else now. Besides, she's not wrong.

"I know. I'll be better."

"You will." She says it in that tone that's half encouragement, half command, but she definitely has to swallow a couple of times to get it out.

"I thought I might start with dinner tonight..." I bait the idea to see what reaction I will get.

"Yes. Wonderful!" She says the W like a V, and her excitement would be contagious if I didn't know it would be another evening of other people watching while I eat.

I want to ask why they even meet for dinner, but she is so happy and there is no tactful way to phrase the question. So instead, I nod my head.

"Perfect. It's settled, then. Will you be there, too?"

"Not this night. I rest. You go."

Unexpected nerves assault my stomach like the persistent flies down by the wharf, the ones that never leave you alone. But I've already decided this is the best course of action going forward. There's hardly any sense in backing down now.

Chapter 21

I walk down to dinner, feeling stronger than I have in weeks. It's amazing the difference it makes, being dressed for the occasion. Now that I've stopped shivering, it's easier to focus on everything else.

Like how very badly I've gone about all of this.

My cloak, I wear like the armor I believe it was intended to be. In it, I am impervious not only to the cold, but to the judgments of everyone in this castle. Including *him*.

I refuse to think about the discomfort of sitting next to the king at dinner when I've only spoken to him once in weeks. It hardly makes a difference, I suppose, whether he's ignoring me from behind my door or across a table.

But when I stride into the room with Khijhana at my side, my steps somehow weightier and more confident in the velvet boots than I had managed in my sheer, soundless, slippers, I realize I have no cause for concern.

No one is ignoring me, least of all the king.

A hush descends the moment my name is announced. The room

has been rearranged so that the thirty or so courtiers gather around a single large table.

Every veiled and beaked face turns toward me in a unison that is almost unnerving. The face I'm looking for is neither beaked, nor veiled, but he wears a mask all the same, one that conceals far more than the silken ones of the court.

Even now, even after a lifetime of studying men for their motives, I cannot guess at what lies in his pale blue eyes. The rest of the court stands when I enter, but the king has not moved his body any more than his unreadable granite gaze has left my face.

There's a subtle commotion. I realize the man next to him — Leif, according to the silver wolf sewn into his mask — has kicked him under the table. I'm sure I wasn't meant to notice, and it looks like I'm the only one who has. Einar shoots him a wry glance and reluctantly gets to his feet.

For the sake of his people, I'm sure. It certainly isn't for mine.

Nonetheless, I dip my head at him as though I appreciate his belated empty gesture and take my seat beside his, Khijhana wedging herself on my other side.

I may not have understood before, how important it was that I play this part, but I do now. And sands-be-damned if I'll let my pride — or his — stop me.

Though, his pride is a tricky thing to nail down. He is, after all, dining next to a servant this evening. Einar gives me a single, assessing glance before diverting his attention to Leif without a word.

"It is good see you this night, Con - Lady Zaina." A timid voice comes from behind a veil with the insignia of a ship.

She stopped herself short of saying "consort." Has someone explained that it's an offensive term in the common tongue? Odger had certainly known that from the start, and I suspect the king had as well.

It would be good to *see* her as well, but I can hardly say so without being rude, so I settle on a thank you. She turns back to her food, clearly embarrassed, even if I can't make out her features.

There's another shuffling noise to my right, and I can only surmise Leif has once again given the king a nudge toward propriety when Einar opens his mouth to speak.

"Indeed. How kind of you to join us." His tone is so perfectly neutral, I can't be sure if he's being genuine or if it's a jibe at the fact that I hadn't before now.

I decide to pretend it's the former, beaming a bright smile in his direction for the sparsely filled table to see.

"Well, Dear Husband, I figured I had left you in want of my company for long enough."

The table can assume I meant at dinnertime, but Einar knows perfectly well that I'm referring to his noted avoidance of me these past weeks.

His brow arches ever so slightly, but he doesn't respond, only motions for the servants to bring the first course.

It's another evening of eating our meal while the scant few guests at the tables wait. It's just as upsetting as it was the first time. But while I was concerned about offending Sigrid, I have no such compunctions about the man sitting next to me.

"Why do you insist on dinner when they can't eat?" I ask him when the conversation swells enough to cover the question.

His jaw clenches, like I knew it would. No matter, I'm not here for him.

"I don't insist," he growls.

"Then why --"

"Because dinner is about more than food," he says shortly.

Leif clears his throat, and I realize our voices carried more than I intended.

"If I may," his deep voice interjects, and again, I notice the way he seems to linger at the end of each syllable before moving on to the next. "It may seem strange with so many people, but it is not unlike any other family dinner."

I blink, trying and failing to imagine such a thing in Madame's household. Had my birth family eaten together? Those memories are locked away so tightly, I can't seem to dredge one up.

I hide my horrified expression a moment too late. But instead of the way Einar is close to crumpling his fork in his irritation, Leif asks patiently, "What were they like, in your home?"

The word *home* is nearly as foreign as the concept of a family dinner, and the lie Madame told is more than enough to keep up with, so I settle on the truth.

"We didn't have family dinners." I force a smile I don't feel, like the answer doesn't matter.

The table around us is still engaging in low conversational tones; Leif and Einar both go still. Then, Leif nods, almost more to himself than to me.

"Then it's a custom we will be happy to teach you," he says, and the kindness in his voice unravels something coiled tightly within myself.

"And I would be glad to learn." It's impossible to be anything but kind in return.

Besides, it may be the truest thing I've said all evening. I *would* be glad to learn in a life I'll never have with a man who actually loved me. As it is, I focus on enjoying small things about this moment, like how excited Khijhana is when I sneak her bits of roasted fish.

The more peaceful I feel, the more relaxed the atmosphere grows around us. The woman who spoke earlier asks if she can feed the giant cat as well, and I oblige. Nearly everyone at the table laughs when Khijhana, clearly having understood the meaning, practically sprints the couple of seats to the mild woman.

It isn't long, though, before the arduous voice of Lord Odger slithers across the table.

"Consort Zaina." He certainly remembers my title today. "How lovely to see you enjoying your meal with such...pleasure."

I fight not to gag on the last bite of vegetables, trying to speak up before Einar can. He's tense beside me, the energy radiating off of him practically feral.

For all that he doesn't seem to want me, he certainly does give off the impression of jealousy.

"Yes, Lord Odger," I respond. "My compliments to the chef."

"Wait until you try the glazed snowbird legs at the festival tomorrow." He says the words just a hair too innocently, like he already knows I'm not aware of any festival.

And I have a choice. Play into his hands and further prove to the room that I am ill-matched for their precious king...or cover for him.

I swallow my pride and do the latter.

"Einar -- His Majesty," I feign the intimate slip, and in the corner of my eye, Einar's gaze narrows slightly, "was just telling me about it. I'm so looking forward to finally seeing more of my new home and sampling... Oh, what was it you were telling me I simply had to try, dear?"

A hush falls over the room, and the king's eyes widen. He manages to wipe the baffled look off of his face in time to respond.

"The Sterling Eiswein. It's the jewel of the festival, made from our --"

"Icicle berries," I fill in, picturing the deep purple oblong fruit depicted in one of the books in the study.

He raises his eyebrows, and I turn back to Odger.

"But a glazed snowbird sounds delightful as well."

He nods, but the disappointment is evident in his lack of response.

The king's knee presses against my own, sending every neuron in my body on alert. He is thanking me, I realize, having discerned Odger's motives as well as I did.

And it may not be much, but that simple gesture feels like a victory.

CHAPTER 22

Einar shows up for breakfast the next morning as though he does so every day. Only this time, he comes through the front door.

I'm not expecting him, so I'm in the middle of teaching Khijhana to pick an object hidden in a cup. Her brilliant eyes follow the three upside-down cups with interest as I rotate them around on the table.

After a moment, I space them evenly apart and back up. She looks at me, then the cups, before nudging the one on the far right with her nose. It clatters over, revealing the feathered toy I have hidden inside.

"Good job, Khijha," I praise her, scratching the fur under her neck as she purrs in delight, while we wait for the king to make his purpose in being here known.

I don't have to wait long. He strides across the room until he is a respectable distance away before speaking.

"I'm glad I found you," he begins, but his tone is too polite for me to take him at his words just yet. "I have good news for you."

"Oh?" I ask, suspicion overtaking me.

"Yes. I thought you might be pleased to know that Sigrid has found a willing owner for the chalyx." He nods at Khijhana, and something between fury and panic seizes my chest.

Then, I catch the teasing glint in his eyes and realize I am giving him the exact reaction he wants even before he speaks again.

"You know, since pets are frivolous and all..." He leaves his sentence dangling like a question.

I feign a yawn instead of taking his bait.

"Khijhana wouldn't like that, I'm afraid. She's grown accustomed to my presence, whether *I* wish it or not. Besides, from what I've learned about the beasts, they can be rather temperamental when they don't get their way," I say in as nonchalant a tone as I can muster.

He cracks a small grin.

"Indeed. Well, I wouldn't want to enrage any temperamental creatures." His gaze lingers pointedly on me before sliding over to Khijha. "So, if you're certain it's not too much of a sacrifice, I'll have Sigrid let the person know it's not necessary."

"Very well," I reply, even though we both know there is no 'person'. "Did you come all the way here just to tell me that?"

"No." He stands up a little straighter and clears his throat but doesn't say anything else.

"Then, to what do I owe this rare delight?" I prompt him, smiling to show him I am teasing. Somewhat.

"Last night, at dinner." He peers at me like I'm a riddle he can't quite solve. "You covered for me."

"I did," I confirm without offering an explanation.

"You could have let Lord Odger undermine me."

"I could have," I agree, mostly to annoy him.

It works.

"Why would you do that?" he finally asks outright.

"Why wouldn't I?" I fight to hide my amusement.

"I've hardly given you reason to." He looks distinctly uncomfortable, and it's an effort not to laugh when I respond.

"Is that...an apology? Sands, I do believe I shall need to make use of the fainting room again."

He narrows his eyes, but the corner of his mouth lifts up.

"Kings never apologize," he replies in a carefully bland tone.

"Of course not. How silly of me," I muse. "I accept, nonetheless."

He gives a couple of prolonged blinks, opening his mouth as if to speak, then closing it again. Finally, he shakes his head, but I don't miss the sparkle of laughter warming his eyes.

"If you truly wish to accompany me to the festival, we ride out at midday."

He turns to leave without waiting for my response, like the imperious ass that he is.

I try not to let the relief show on my face that we'll be taking horses instead of another vomit-inducing carriage ride, but my smile does turn more genuine.

"Noon, it is."

When I spot sight of the king, I realize that, once again, my relief has come too quickly.

We aren't taking a carriage, that much is true, but we are also not riding anything I am familiar with.

I stand several yards away from a small sled attached to a team of what can only be wolves, though they are at least three times the size of any wolf I've ever seen.

I glance between my beast of a husband, my ever-growing cat, and the larger-than-life wolves before me.

Is everything in this kingdom massive?

Einar beams at his lead dog, one with midnight fur and gleaming amber irises, roughly scratching its ears and grinning like a child.

His silver-blond hair is pulled back into a knot, accentuating his high cheekbones, square jaw, and glacial eyes. His beard is a bit shorter, freshly groomed, and he donned the same shades of green that I wear now. The sunlight catches on the glint of silver around his neck and on blade of the axe strapped to his back.

By all appearances, he looks more like a warrior than a king. However, the way he plays with the giant wolves brings out a boyish charm in him that I haven't seen before.

The canines range in color from deep charcoal to a shimmering shade of pearl, and they appear to be somewhat tame.

Not that Khijhana cares. She hisses, bravely standing between me and the dogs.

The king laughs, and I am struck by the way it rings pure, unlike his mocking chuckles in the past.

He loves this, I realize. The blustery outdoors, the sled, maybe even the festival itself, but he's happier than I've ever seen him. Only now that the fatigued lines around his face are minimized do I realize the weight he carries with him the rest of the time.

I find myself wanting to draw closer to the warmth of his laughter, like a flame in this endless sea of ice. Before I know it, I'm halfway to the precarious-looking sled, my black and white, fur-lined boots making dainty footprints next to Khijhana's round ones.

Snowflakes are falling all around us, and I can barely even feel a chill through the fur-lined pants and tunic. The cloak is exquisite, the color of pine trees and the darkest parts of a forest.

I pause a few feet away, unsure where I fit into this mechanism. Einar stands in the fairly small space between two raised handles. There is no seat and nowhere else to stand, only a flat section of gleaming polished wood between him and the wolves that I assume is for cargo of some sort.

Einar registers my hesitation, and he takes a small step back, gesturing to the space in front of him. When I still don't move, he holds out a hand, as though it's my balance I'm concerned about.

"It's tradition," he says, but his outstretched hand feels like more than the empty gesture of custom.

It feels like a second beginning I'm not entirely sure I want at this point. I war with my emotions for only a split second before I place my slim, gloved hand in his colossal one and let him lead me into my place on the sleigh.

Riding a sled isn't the most dangerous thing I've ever done. It's not even close. But, taking his hand in that moment feels like something else entirely, something that sets my nerves on fire and sends adrenaline coursing through me.

I push down the feeling, removing my hand from his, and call out to Khijhana. She takes a moment to decide if she'll join us or not before reluctantly climbing aboard the cargo hold of the sled. She doesn't look pleased, but I get the feeling she has no intention of leaving me with these wolves on my own.

Once she's situated, Einar settles in behind me. The heat he seems to carry around with him spreads from every point of contact. I realize this is the closest I've been to him since the day he stopped my fall on the stairs, and it's strange how I am so unaccustomed to his closeness. Stranger still how tempting it is to relax back into him, to steal some of his warmth and laughter for my own.

His breath is hot when he leans down to talk into my ear.

"Lean into the curves."

I give a sharp nod, and he calls out an order. The hounds take off, jarring the sled with a motion that sends me hurtling backward into Einar, who doesn't so much as falter. They move as one, their long legs crossing the snow-covered hills in quick, graceful strides.

I glance back at the castle as we leave the grounds. The stained-glass window is once again what stands out the most, but this time I notice the small difference in the shape of the petals on the mosaic. They are not rounded or soft like a normal rose. These have sharper edges with a subtle hint of silver in the middle.

I must have let myself be distracted by the ominous portrait, because I hardly notice when we come up on a curve. I feel my balance slipping and hear Einar's chuckle as I whip back around.

I lean into the rest of the bend and focus on the journey ahead of us. The wind whips around us, but I barely feel it. I'm firmly caught up in our smooth glide across the terrain, nothing like the bumpy, nauseating carriage ride from my arrival. When I close my eyes, it's easy to imagine that we're flying through the air.

It's easy to imagine that I'm finally free.

CHAPTER 23

As we near the festival, he whistles for the wolves to slow. His body, so carefree only minutes ago, is now thrumming with tension. It takes me a moment to figure out why.

Heads turn in our direction. It starts with a handful of people, then spreads outward until the entire crowd is focused solely on us. It's surprising to see so many faces after so long in the castle, but hadn't the people of Colby been maskless as well?

They continue to stare, and I wonder if it's the wolves, but the way they look at Einar... It's more than that. Crown or not, he is every inch their king.

The sudden, piercing blare of a horn sounds, and the people bow in unison.

It's a curious sight, dozens of villagers with pale-white or deepest-brown skin, men and women alike taking a knee. I can't see Einar's expression, but I feel his breath whoosh out of him in relief. Had he doubted his people's response to him?

Still, his hand tightens around the steering bar.

The people rise with varying degrees of speed, their expressions ranging from excitement to disbelief and even confusion. More than one eyes us with suspicion, or even anger. The former wave, while the latter stand stoically by.

I do my part and wave back, beaming and leaning into Einar in a show of intimacy. He squeezes my hand in thanks before stepping off the sled. I turn to face him, and several of the people move to approach us.

"Where are your guards?" I ask in a low tone, always hyper-prepared for a situation getting out of hand.

"They're already here." He pauses, arching an eyebrow. "Why? Are you worried about me?"

"Worried about myself, you mean." My response is dry, but he smiles.

I don't mention that it is completely unheard of everywhere else for a king to ride into a crowd without the safety of his guard.

"My people are loyal," he answers in a more serious tone. "Even if they're angry, they respect their leader," he adds confidently. "Besides, the axe I carry isn't just for show."

Then, he takes a deep breath, and I realize that, for all of his bravado, he is still nervous. Maybe it's not for his safety, exactly, but the anxiety is there.

Einar plays his part better than I do, gallantly holding out a hand to help me off of the sled, then keeping his arm firmly around me even once I'm safely on the ground.

The crowd edges in around us, and I have to focus to keep my breathing steady in a sea of humans who tower over me.

Congratulations are offered. Questions of the castle's welfare are asked, and evaded smoothly for the most part, I note.

Some people make passive comments about not having seen him in years, their suspicions and even judgment clear in their tone, and Einar is nothing but diplomatic about it all.

When there is finally space to breathe and the crowd dissipates a bit, I move back toward Khijhana, who has successfully stayed away from the mob, but has been unsuccessful in her attempts to extricate herself from the sled.

"You haven't been here in a while?" I ask tentatively.

Einar sighs and looks around at the winter festival. Booths and snow-covered hills. Torch lights and the smiling people.

"No," he offers after a moment.

"Why not?"

He breathes out, and the joy that I saw on his face as we were leaving the castle is shadowed by sadness and resignation.

"It felt wrong to enjoy the festival when my people could not."

Could not? I mull over his words in my mind, but before I can ask for clarification, another man comes up to greet him.

I decide to let the subject drop for now. As much as my curiosity wants me to push the issue, I also don't want to ruin whatever semblance of peace we've managed to wrangle between us.

A man comes to see to Einar's wolves, but I intercept him before he can venture too close to Khijha. She's trembling as it is, eyes wide, while her claws bury into the woodgrain beneath her.

I'm still coaxing her off the sled when the sound of children laughing reaches my ears. I glance up to see a group of them throwing balls of the fluffy snow at one another.

One dives for cover behind the sled near Khijha and me, sending a sheet of snow flying up into our faces.

Khijha shakes her head irritably, letting out a low growl, and I bite back a laugh at her uncharacteristic grouchiness.

"I have sorry, Lady," the boy says, eyeing me with the same wide-eyed fear and curiosity he gives my chalyx.

His cheeks are rosy, and he's panting from the excursion of their snow battle. The simple act of a child being a child with no strings attached both fills and breaks my heart at the same time.

A smile stretches over my mouth, one that is far more authentic than any of the others I've offered recently. It's one that reaches my eyes and down to my very soul.

"It's all right." I lean down to help him up before wiping the icy water from my lashes and hair.

He gives me a toothy grin of his own before running off to return to his friends. I wave at them while they giggle and whisper to one another.

"If I didn't know any better, I would suppose you were almost enjoying yourself." Einar's deep voice rumbles through my center as he approaches from behind.

"Well, I shan't accuse you of ignorance in such a crowded place," I murmur back.

I'm only half paying attention to him, my concentration flitting from snowball fights to ice sculptures. It amazes me, the way these people have found a million uses and entertainment from the one thing in their kingdom they will never be short on.

"Indeed," he allows, and I look up to find him observing me closely. "My mistake. I see that now."

I don't know what to feel about what he sees in my expression, so I turn the conversation around.

"If I didn't know any better, I'd accuse you of smiling. That is, if that rabid animal on your face would move long enough for me to actually be able to tell."

Although, I can see now how common it is. If anything, Einar's beard is a bit shorter than those of the burly men around us. He strokes the thing protectively and feigns offense.

Before he can respond, someone calls his name from across the snowy field. They're holding two pints and gesturing toward him with one.

"Go on. I'll catch up with you," I assure him.

Truthfully, I could stand a moment to collect myself. It's a lot. This crowd, standing at the king's side, the way he and I are almost...getting along.

He hesitates for a brief moment, his lips parting slightly. Then, he nods at a man in the crowd and back at me before walking away.

The towering man he gestured to has dark skin, and his hair is silver and pulled away from his face in a half knot. If he's the guard Einar was referring to, I can't help but wonder why he doesn't have to wear a mask while the others do.

A tall woman who looks nearly identical to my guard falls in line behind Einar. *He keeps a female guard? Is she more than that?*

I shouldn't care, but it's hard not to wonder when I look around. The Jokithan women are, as a whole, nothing short of stunning. Strong, buxom bodies that move with a blend of confidence and grace. Was this what he always pictured himself with?

And, if so, what made him look outside his kingdom for a bride who was so very far from what he wanted?

I push the thought away. We're getting along today, and that is rare enough that I hardly need to borrow problems. Besides, it shouldn't make any difference to me.

It doesn't. Of course, it doesn't.

The smell of roasted nuts and meats wafts up from the center of the faire, beckoning me closer. I set out to explore with my guard following close behind.

People call out from the booths, showing me scarves or foods or cloaks. Some have simple jewelry, sweets, or even weapons. Others have gear for animals, artfully made leads for the dog sleds and the largest saddles I've ever seen.

I would probably be freezing even in my warm clothes, but there are raised bowls of crimson stones emitting waves of heat.

It's overwhelming after being cooped up in the castle for so long, but I can imagine my sisters would love it. So, I smile in spite of myself, determined to enjoy this small moment for them.

I meander slowly through the shoppes, stopping a few times when something stands out. A tiny flame earring catches my eye. As I'm examining it, thinking to send it home to Aika, one of Einar's guards steps up, the one who had been trailing me.

"I am Gunnar, Lady Consort." His voice is deeper than I was expecting, his teeth a sharp white contrast to his skin. "My sister is Helga." He gestures to the woman with the king. "The king has sent funds for you." The gesture is well-intended, but it makes me feel like...a kept woman.

My title of Consort doesn't help that.

I take the coins, trying not to notice the scrutiny the booth teller sends my way. I can hardly blame her. Curiosity abounds for the foreign bride with her exotic pet as we stand out like a blood-red rose in the pristine snow.

CHAPTER 24

"Here." Einar strolls toward us holding out what looks to be a large turkey leg. "It's a snowbird. You promised Odger that you would try one. We wouldn't want to disappoint him, would we?"

For how territorial he is in the man's presence, he doesn't seem too concerned about my actually enjoying Odger's company. I can't help but mess with him a little.

"I wouldn't dream of it. Then what would we have to talk about the next time we play...chess?"

Einar's eyes narrow, but he speaks with a deliberate casualness.

"You plan to play lots of games with him?" A loaded question, if ever I heard one.

"It's what I live for." I meet his eyes to let him see the sarcasm in mine.

Einar grunts, but I don't think I mistake the relief in his eyes. He masks it by taking a bite of his own giant bird leg, while thrusting mine at me.

It's so heavy, I nearly drop it.

"Why does everything in this place have to be so large? Aren't there any normal-sized things, foods, or people here?"

He stares at me for a moment, laughter in his eyes.

"Most women aren't disappointed in that sort of thing. It's when things are too small that it's a problem."

I roll my eyes and look down, trying to hide the flush in my cheeks. Gunnar and Helga laugh freely.

"It's nice to know some things don't change," I remark drily. "No matter what kingdom you're in. Men everywhere, king or not, are little more than debauched teenage boys."

The king shrugs, not bothering to deny it.

"Eat your food, *wife*." He smiles around another mouthful.

I can't deny that the glazed poultry looks and smells divine. I pull a piece off with my fingers, as the warm juices drip down my hand. Khijha is practically drooling, licking the drops of grease from the snow near my feet.

When I finally pop the small bite into my mouth, my eyes practically roll to the back of my head.

It's delicious. Savory, with a hint of sweetness, but I don't even mind. Each of my tastebuds are grateful and over-eager as I continue tearing chunks off with my fingers, refusing to eat the leg in the same manner as my brutish husband, no matter how tempting it is.

We walk as we eat, and I look up to find we've wandered into a section with games and contests. Men and women alike arm wrestle, shoot bows, or throw things at targets.

"Care to give it a try?" Einar's wry grin is a challenge.

"After you," I allow. "Didn't you say that axe was for more than show?"

I tell myself I am using the opportunity to size him up, to learn more about him. Khijha nudges me with her head, and I wonder what she senses from me in that moment or if she's only asking for food.

I decide it's the latter and slip her the giant bone with some meat still on it.

The king's smug smile is his only reply before he makes a beeline for the axe throwing booth. I follow, and of course, Khijha trails along, her tail straight, a proud gleam in her eye while she carries the snowbird leg. Even if people would have crowded their king, they give the chalyx a wide berth.

"His Majesty cares to try his luck with the axes?" The woman who mans the booth announces this loudly while she sets down three axes in front of him.

Despite the cold, the cloak she wears over her tight-fitting dress opens to reveal a triangle of cleavage. Her smile is brash, and she eyes the mammoth of a man standing next to me without an ounce of shame.

I can't help but glance at Einar to see if he is returning her look, but he has eyes only for the axes. Breath whooshes out of me in what is most definitely not relief, just in time to see a massive crowd gathering around us.

Gunnar and Helga ensure they keep their distance, though the mood seems to be good-spirited. Still, I place a hand on Khijhana's head to keep myself from being overwhelmed by the boxed-in feeling.

Einar's face, however, is pure excitement, his eyes practically lighting up when he meets mine.

"It's not luck if you've got the skill," he counters loudly to the crowd, but his eyes don't leave mine.

The people laugh and cheer, and the king's grin is broader than I've ever seen it. He throws the first axe, and it sinks squarely in the middle circle of the target.

The crowd roars, and the woman gives a throaty laugh.

"Anyone can do it once, My King, but you've got two more!" She is clearly enjoying the show she puts on for the onlookers, and the king takes it in stride.

"Fair enough, my good woman." He picks up the second axe and brings it over his head.

This one, he throws with a flourish that almost makes me laugh. The game-master isn't the only one playing to the crowd. I wonder if I will ever be that comfortable with so much attention on me.

Another cheer goes up when the axe meets its target. The king looks at me, and I give him a begrudging applause, though I can't help the smirk tugging at my lips.

Finally, he reaches for the third axe. He turns to face his adoring fans before he throws this one.

"If I win this one, what shall I claim as my reward?"

Suggestions are thrown out from ale to eiswein, trinkets, and more than a few lewd ones. The king listens and laughs before pointing with the axe toward the side of the crowd. I blanch, knowing full well what comment was just called from that direction.

"A kiss from the lady it is!" he roars.

He very pointedly does not look at me as he raises the axe over his head and turns to throw it in one fluid movement. Without even the barest of a second to aim, he hits the center solidly.

The onlookers shout 'Huzzah!' and laugh, but I curse internally. Wasn't one public kiss enough for the man, for his people? My face is heated, from anger, obviously. I try to keep my expression neutral for the sake of our audience and likely fail.

He turns to look at me, his eyes shining with a mirth I don't feel. Then abruptly, he sinks to one knee.

"Well, my lady?" he says to Khijhana, putting his cheek directly in her face.

She hesitates only a second before obliging him, dropping her bone to slide her rough tongue against his cheek before picking her treat up again.

Laughter breaks out among the crowd, and I marvel at this man who has never so much as given a genuine smile in my presence, entertaining half a festival's worth of people with his antics.

It's more than that, though. All day, Khijhana has received reverent glances, and terrified ones as well. Now, the people smile in her direction. With one calculated move, he has changed the way they look at both of us.

And suddenly, I am equal parts impressed and wary of the man who sees so much more than I gave him credit for.

"Now, it's your turn." Einar looks at me, and I feel my features go tight.

Is he going to kiss me in front of all these people, after all?

But he gestures to the booths around us after only a moment.

"Choose your weapon, My Lady," he says loudly.

I narrow my eyes at him, because I know he was off-footing me intentionally, but again, I realize he is playing to the people. They look at me with more warmth in their curiosity already.

There is something refreshing in the way they take women and weaponry in stride, something that emboldens me more than it should.

Axes are out, because I could never outdo him there. I am unlikely to win in an arm-wrestling match, and my skill with a bow is mediocre, at best. That leaves knives and throwing stars. I mull over my choices for a moment before heading toward the stars.

The crowd gives us a wide berth, but they stay gathered to watch my performance.

"The stars are harder than they look," Einar warns, but the challenge hasn't left his gaze.

I shrug my shoulders innocently and stride over to the booth, my fingers already itching for the familiar cold steel.

"Why this?" His voice is quieter now, the question only for me.

They're easy enough to maneuver, versatile and light enough that there is no real danger in missing. But I give him a different answer.

"They remind me of my home," I tell him in a low tone. *Or, at least whatever semblance of home I had with my sisters.*

Why did I admit that? Aika loved any weapon she could throw, and she has been on my mind today, but it's more than that. Somewhere between his challenge and his performance, a feeling of recklessness is seeping in.

I should ignore it.

But I don't.

"The King's Lady at the stars!" the man at the booth announces, though the horde of people around us could hardly grow any larger.

I instantly like him for saying Lady instead of Consort. The king hands over a small coin, and the man lays out three silver stars, each uniquely engraved and freshly sharpened.

I pick one up on the pretense of examining the detail, but I use the opportunity to take its measure, the weight and balance, before I aim for the target.

I throw the first one in the most basic fashion. A light, overhand toss that spins toward the middle of the target.

Applause rings out behind me.

"Beginner's luck," the man announces, but his smile is kind.

The crowd's response isn't as rowdy as it was for the king, but they are loosening up toward me.

The second one, I barely take time to aim. I throw it sideways and it hits closer to the center, just across the bullseye from the first.

This time, the reaction is more exuberant.

"Oho!" the man exclaims. "Let's see if she can finish strong!"

I turn to look the king straight in the eye, and for a fraction of a second, I let my mask slip. I let him see the fire that burns through me in an answer to the challenges he keeps throwing out.

He raises his eyebrows, and it's like he's daring me. A long-hidden part of me rears up in answer.

Without breaking his gaze, without taking even a second to aim, I pluck up the last star and throw it with a flick of my wrist. Silence descends in the fraction of a moment it takes to sail toward the dead center of the target.

Einar and I both turn to see the result. The final star wedges itself between the other two, sinking a solid inch deep into the sturdy wood.

Raucous approval meets our ears, but I have eyes only for the king. For the expression that is tinged with awe, with satisfaction, even, but not the slightest hint of shock.

I should be worried, but I am high on the energy of the crowd, the win, the way that for the first time in as long as I can remember, I didn't have to hold a part of myself back to make someone else feel larger.

"What does the lady claim as her reward?" the grizzled man in charge of the booth asks.

The people's enthusiasm is contagious, and that's the only excuse I have for what I do next.

"I think a kiss from the king should just about do it."

They roar their approval, and I tell myself that's why I did it. For the people, for the show we've put on all day, to gain favor with them and him both.

It's not because I see myself mirrored in the man across from me. Not because I think he sees it, too, and isn't shying away from it, isn't emasculated by it. It's certainly not the way he looked while throwing that axe.

Besides, surely this gesture will be as empty as the first.

In the end, I tell myself a thousand different things, but I know every one of them to be a lie.

I meet his gaze with the same challenging expression he always has for me.

Your move.

The cocky look he gives me is all the warning I have before he puts his enormous hands around my waist and pulls me toward him, lifting me up until our faces are level, then pressing his lips heartily against mine.

I have a second to register that they are the warmest thing at this entire festival, warmer even than the raised bowls of stones, before he sets me down again.

"To the king and his lady!" The man at the booth leads a cheer, but I hardly hear it.

All I make out is Einar's voice in my ear.

"Your cheeks are red."

"It's freezing out here," I murmur back, though we both know the temperature hasn't changed in the last minute.

"Of course. How silly of me to not have noticed the sudden gale," he calls me out.

I open my mouth to deny his implication, but then I see something that makes me freeze in my tracks, effectively eradicating every last vestige of amusement.

The face turns to disappear before I can look twice, but it doesn't matter. My heart drops to the pit of my stomach.

No.

But the denial sounds weak even in my head, because I would know that shaggy black hair anywhere.

I try to follow the figure with my eyes, but he is a master of blending in, better even than the sister who has been on my mind so much today.

The villagers have come to congratulate Einar, and though they are becoming accustomed to me, it is their king they wish to see. It's an easy matter to slip away and make my way through the rapidly dispersing crowd.

I weave through the people in a zigzag fashion, both to better spot the man and in an effort to lose Gunnar. When I still don't spot him, I duck behind tents and booths, in between the large carts of the vendors, but all of my efforts are fruitless.

He's gone.

Khijhana mews, as if she's wondering why we're chasing after a shadow.

Part of me is wondering the same. Surely, if it was *him*, he would've made himself known.

"Is everything all right?" Einar's deep voice sounds behind me.

I don't miss the underlying worry in his tone, so at odds with every interaction we've had for weeks, and I turn to face him.

Something in his eyes unnerves me. The way I want to be honest with him, and the way he makes me feel like I could be. But it isn't real, not any of it. When we get back to the castle, I'm sure he will be back to being his usual ass, and I'll just be the unwanted bride he was shackled with for reasons I still don't understand.

I shake my head, forcing a smile while I wrap my arm around his.

"Of course. I was just exploring a bit. There's so much to see," I say with more animation than I feel.

Whether or not he or the guards behind him believe me, he plays along as we walk around and take in more of the festival.

By the time we leave, I've almost convinced myself that I was imagining the familiar face. But even *I* know that would be too easy.

Damian is here. And that means none of us are safe.

Chapter 25

By the time we arrive back at the castle, I am frozen solid from the evening snow and my shaken nerves, and Khijha looks no better. She irritably swipes away some snow that has settled into her whiskers, and I stifle a small laugh at her expense.

The feeling of freedom from earlier had disappeared in the wake of Damian's appearance, and all the reminders it brings. I am here for a purpose, one I am actively not fulfilling. It is one thing to soften the king, but another entirely to allow myself to be softened.

I shake my head, unreasonably furious with myself.

Einar watches me with an expression that is too probing, too insightful, and though I know I should thank him for the day, I find myself walking away from him with a hurried, "I'll see you in the morning, then."

I am only a few footsteps away when his voice follows me.

"On the second day, the people usually stay past nightfall to welcome in the lights."

"What lights?" I turn, curious in spite of myself.

A slow, mysterious smile spreads across his face.

"I suppose you'll have to go back to find out." He is teasing me, but it's more than that.

I believe he genuinely wants me to come.

I have a mission, one I can't fulfill if we aren't getting along. I tell myself that's the only reason I dip my head in agreement before turning to shuffle up to my rooms.

When I arrive, Sigrid has a bath waiting for me. Since our first disagreement over the water, she has never filled it more than a hand span high, for which I am grateful. I splash the warm water over myself, letting it slowly thaw me and trying very hard not to think about the last source of heat I used to warm myself.

It's one thing, doing what I need to do. But life has taught me better than to let my feelings get involved, even with a man who is, technically speaking, my husband.

When the king joins me for breakfast, I am already awake and dressed for the day in another of the outfits that Sigrid has provided for me. Today, the accents are the same deep purple as the outside of the berries that make the eiswein. Amethysts sparkle on my nose and upper ear, connected by my usual gold chain.

The jewelry helps to ground me when little else in this place does.

Between that and the fact that I have finally started to wake up at my usual hour, I'm feeling a little more like myself each day. Not that feeling like myself is anything to be excited about. But physically, I'm feeling stronger and more energized than I have in quite some time.

For his part, Einar looks much the same as always. If he feels any differently about me today than he did before our outing to the festival, it doesn't show in his carefully guarded expression. Though, his eyes do linger on my face a little longer than usual, and I can't help but notice the way he angles his chair more toward mine at the breakfast table.

When Sigrid comes bustling in this morning, she surprises me by bringing more than food.

"The post comes not as much far out here, but these letters come today." She holds out two envelopes addressed in handwriting I know as well as my own.

Aika's messy, hurried scrawl is on the top envelope, where she hasn't even bothered to put my full name, let alone a title. It just says *Zai*, and I shake my head a little, grinning, before looking at the second.

Melodi's patient, careful hand has written out my full title, even the part I hate. *Lady Zaina, Consort to King Einar of Jokith.* I laugh a little at her unflinchingly straightforward nature.

I can feel Einar's gaze on me, and I force the expression from my face.

A small, selfish part of me wants to keep their letters untouched, unopened and exuding the essence of everything that makes my sisters who they are. If I don't open them, if I don't read them, then I don't have to hear any dreadful news they may contain.

But the wondering would kill me all the same. I have spent my entire life protecting them. I could no sooner turn off the part of me that worries than I could stop breathing.

The king is still studying my expression, so I set the letters aside as though it doesn't physically pain me to do so. He raises his eyebrows.

"I should give you some privacy to read your letters."

But there is an undertone there, and I wonder if by making him think I wish him to leave, I will undo some small bit of the progress we made yesterday.

"That's not necessary." I wave my hand as though it's silly, as though I wouldn't love nothing more than a moment alone to read these snippets of my sister's voices. But he already looks at me like I have something to hide, so I pick up Aika's letter first.

I note with some interest that it was postmarked ten days ago from a post office in Bondé. She's still in Corentin, then.

. . .

To my favorite older sister,

I'm her only older sister, I think with a pang. It's so like her to write such a thoughtless line, though.

You've always been difficult, but tracking you down has been something else entirely.

Madame always played her cards close to her chest, so I'm not surprised Aika hadn't known her plans, but I can't deny a small tightness in my chest unfurling at having it confirmed. And for all her blasé nature, she clearly went to a lot of trouble to find me. Something in me warms at the gesture. I feel a little less alone if my sisters at least know where I am.

I continue reading.

My life hasn't been nearly so exciting as yours has been, though I'm starting to suspect the boy is hiding something from me. Not that I care, obviously.

Obviously, she does care about the only person in the world who can best her at cards, and I wish I was there to tease her about it. I resist the urge to rub the sudden ache out of my chest.

Anyway, I hope you're planning a trip home soon. We are all starting to miss you, Mother in particular.

Instead of a signature, she has merely drawn her trademark flame on the bottom of the page.

My mind flashes back to the man in the marketplace today. Not for the first time, I curse this blasted castle being so far from everything I have ever known, so far from the people who are trying to get in touch with me. To warn me.

I glance over at the king, who is pretending to be busy with his book, though his eyes have not moved in a few seconds.

"It's only my sister. She misses me," I add with a forced smile.

Only when the uncomfortable expression crosses his face, when I belatedly identify it as remorse, do I realize that he will likely take that comment as a jab because he is the one who has forbidden them from coming. Not wishing to put him on the defensive, I quickly cover.

"She's just bored because the social season is over."

But his next response tells me I have blundered again.

"I thought you didn't have any siblings." His brow furrows.

Whether he asks from suspicion or polite interest makes no difference. It takes everything I have to keep my expression neutral, to force air into my lungs and back out again as though his simple question is not all it takes to send me into an outright breakdown after the events of the past few weeks.

"Not by blood, but yes, I grew up with three sisters." I want to take the words back as soon as I say them.

He doesn't ask why I have three sisters but only two letters, and I am absurdly grateful for that. I practically tear the next letter open in my haste both to escape the conversation I am in and to see what my more practical sister has to say.

Dearest Zaina,

Please forgive me for not writing sooner. Your whereabouts were only discovered this very morning.

I rarely worry for your safety, even half a world away, but I hope you'll grant me leeway just this once to tell you that I worry for your spirit. I know you are shaking your head right now, that you have always felt that it was your job alone to worry. But I can imagine it would be easy to lose yourself with no one there to ground you.

So, for my sake, remember that you have family. You are loved. And you have hope. The darkness won't last forever, sweet sister.

I know, too, how much you hate talking of such things, so I will move on now.

Things here remain unchanged, as they always do. Although with Aika out so often lately, and you not here, it feels markedly bleaker than before.

Your absence is felt keenly, by none so much as Mother, I think.

Indeed, she grows more anxious by the day. I hope that we will see you soon. I hope that you can feel my love even halfway across the world, and I hope that you do not allow yourself to become as frozen as the vast tundra around you.

Sincerely,
Melodi

I squeeze my eyes shut against the truth of her words. It's always been like this, though, my worrying for Mel's safety and her worrying for my heart.

If Aika worries about anything, she keeps it well hidden.

I turn my attention back to the king only to find his expression has gone hard and he is rising from his chair.

"I apologize. I hadn't meant to ignore you --" I begin.

"Not at all," but the words sound oddly monotone. "I have a few things to attend to before we can head to the festival. I will meet you just past midday." With that, he sweeps out of the room.

I might have believed him, was I not so adept at discerning another person's lie. I glance at the table where his mug of tea is still steaming and his sugary breakfast remains uneaten.

Even Khijhana stares after him suspiciously. I force myself to finish my own breakfast as though nothing had happened. After all, if I let every one of the king's ever-changing moods affect my own, I would likely never feel sane again.

CHAPTER 26

By the time I meet the king in front of the castle, all traces of whatever mood had overtaken him earlier have disappeared. Once again, I note how much more carefree he looks out here than within the confines of the castle walls. His posture is more relaxed, his expression less guarded.

I take a step toward the sled, intending to stand where I had yesterday, when he holds out a hand out to stop me.

"I apologize for not thinking of it sooner, but I wanted to make sure you have this today." His tone is still casual, but his expression has closed off ever so slightly, enough that I can't tell exactly what he is thinking when he holds out his other hand.

In it, he holds a sizable coin purse. It is made of white, supple leather and tied together with a black velvet string in a decidedly feminine design.

I hesitate before taking it from him. I have been showered with valuable gifts before, but I can't recall ever being handed over the freedom of coin, something I can spend as I see fit.

"I noticed you eyeing a couple of the booths yesterday. I assumed it went without saying that the castle's coffers are yours for use, but I thought this might be an easier way for you to get whatever you desired." He is babbling, I realize with no small amount of amusement.

"Thank you," I interrupt him to put his mind at ease, taking the weighty purse.

Though, truthfully, the words feel inadequate to express what I am feeling. While money may mean nothing to him, he has given me more than something valuable. He has given me choices, something I have never had before.

My dresses have always been ordered for me, most of my accessories gifted. But never chosen by *me*. I am reminded of my feelings yesterday while shopping. Had my guard been paying that close of attention to me? Had he noticed the way I resented him paying for everything? Or had the king genuinely forgotten before, and was merely correcting his oversight?

I doubt he realizes what this means, since it is unheard of for a lady to care about these trivial sorts of things, but I appreciate the gesture, nonetheless.

I press the purse against my chest, my nimble fingers tying the strings around my left hand with my right, and it isn't until I notice him watching that I remember that isn't something most people can do.

More knowledge that was forced on me, tying and untying knots with one hand.

Blasted sands...

This isn't the first time he's caught me off my guard, and I realize I am slipping too often lately. I force a laugh.

"Well, you try to wrestle yourself into some of those dresses without help."

Whether he buys my excuse or not, the smoldering look in his eyes tells me that perhaps he's thinking more about wrestling someone out of clothes instead of in them.

I should look away, but I don't. I hold his gaze with each step nearer until I'm standing directly in front of him, and only then do I finally spin around, grasping the bars in front of me.

He settles in behind me, stepping closer than he had yesterday.

Is it my imagination, or is he exuding even more heat than usual?

Chapter 27

This time when we arrive, there are rows and rows of people to greet us, and their smiles are contagious. Einar and I wander through the crowded passageways and alleys, taking in the sights and reluctantly enjoying one another's company.

I tell myself that it's just for show when he holds my hand as we walk, just as the other couples do. I tell myself that it's all right to pretend to enjoy the way it makes me feel to be so close to him.

Something in the distance catches my eye, and we make our way to the outskirts of the festival to examine it. People are crowding around and building a dome-like structure out of snow, solidifying the creation with cold water that forms an icy glaze around each snow brick.

There are several more further down the hill, but this one sits a little further back and looks a bit bigger than the others.

Einar notices me watching, captivated by the strange creations.

"They're called igloos."

"Igloos?" I ask, trying to recall if I've ever heard the word before in my studies of the country.

"Yes. They are basically natural huts that the villagers camp in for the duration of the festival."

"Aren't they cold?" I ask, trying to imagine how miserable it would be to sleep in a frozen room surrounded by snow and below-freezing temperatures.

Einar chuckles. "No, it's actually quite enjoyable."

"Sure, it is." My brows twist in disbelief, and he laughs again.

It's difficult not to completely lose myself in every sight and sound and smell. It would be so easy to become attached to this place and these people, if I could only let myself.

A vendor calls out and beckons us toward him, pulling me from my thoughts.

"Eiswein! Eiswein for Your Majesties." I don't miss the plural in the titles.

Einar doesn't correct him, either, and I mentally tuck that away for later.

When we approach the vendor, Einar speaks the common tongue.

"Henrick! My good man!" Einar clasps wrists with the man, their grins stretching wide. "What's it been, forty years since I last laid eyes on you?"

Henrick laughs and hugs the king tightly.

"I think this to be so, Einar," he answers in the common tongue as well, his accent thick and endearing. "Though, I have been back to here for two year. You have just not been coming to festival to know this. In fact, I hear it has nearly been twenty years since you are come to festival."

Einar sighs, but before he can respond, Henrick places a hand on his shoulder and smiles.

"I figure you must be going through phase. You were so young when you become the king. You are still young, my friend. It would make the sense if you needed a few decades to learn more about who you are."

I swear I see a small flush in Einar's cheeks at the words, but my mind is spinning. Finally, Henrick looks at me and introduces himself.

"I am think this is more than phase." He laughs again, but bows to me, placing a kiss on my hand. "It is pleasure to meet my friend's bride. Welcome. You would try the *Eiswein*, Lady?" he asks, holding out a delicate wooden stein with intricate carvings and details of a winged woman with pointed ears next to a tree.

"I would be honored, Sir." I happily take the mug, examining every gorgeous detail.

Henrick offers one to Einar as well, and they clasp hands again, speaking Jokithan and catching up on what has been happening in the years since they've seen one another.

It's one more thing that's strange to think about with these people. And how young Einar is by comparison. *A phase, for twenty years?*

I catch a few statements in their conversation that nearly bowl me over entirely.

The man was his father's best friend. And while his dark skin is smooth, his eyes full of life, I nearly choke when I realize that he is well over one-hundred-and-fifty years old.

I take a tiny sip of my wine, testing it while I wait for them to finish catching up. It is smooth with a hint of spice, but the aftertaste is sweet. Far too sweet not to be suspicious of, but I can't deny that part of me wants more, if only for its famed warming properties.

After a few minutes, I take another slightly longer taste and notice how it feels ice-cold at first, but quickly warms on my tongue, almost like the heat of tea. The texture is smooth, and while sweet, it has a kick similar to whiskey when it burns at the back of your throat.

It's unlike anything I've ever tried. The complexities in the flavor and temperature are baffling. I take my time drinking it while the men catch up, but by the time they are finished, I have downed the entire cup.

The vendor notices and gestures to refill my stein, but I decline.

"As tempting as the offer is, I believe I should hold off."

His face falls slightly as if I have offended his generosity.

"But, if it's alright with you, could I have some bottled for later? I would love to purchase this stein from you as well. It's such magnificent craftsmanship."

He beams and nods, happily filling several bottles of the wine for me.

"I thought you didn't like sweets," Einar says.

"I don't usually. But alcohol doesn't really count."

"I see. Maybe we'll have to find something that makes you change your mind then," he says, inching closer to me.

There is something predatory in his eyes, the way he looks at me when he says it, that makes me wonder if he's even talking about food at all. I glance away from his intense gaze, not able to endure the million different ways it makes me feel.

The kind vendor hands us a leather bag with four bottles inside. When I go to pay him for the stein, he shakes his head, insisting that it is his gift to me.

I dip into my purse and dig out a couple of the heavier coins. I don't look at them too closely, because it's still bizarre for me that they hold the face of the man standing next to me.

I press the coins into the vendor's hand, not wanting his kindness to go unpaid, and he takes them graciously. Einar watches wordlessly but shoots me an inquisitive glance when we leave.

"I thought it was more than worth it to finally feel a little bit warm." I shrug as though it was nothing for me to be able to give that man something for his trouble.

And indeed, I already feel markedly less frigid, like tiny embers are being stoked within me to warm me from the inside out.

"Perhaps I should go back and buy several more jugs since you seem to be in a constant state of freezing at the castle," he offers, a hint of teasing in his gaze.

"Perhaps you should. Or better yet, we could line every inch of my rooms in these glorious thermal rocks." I gesture to the pits spaced evenly all around us.

The king laughs.

"Those are usually used to heat vast outdoor spaces, specifically where they would be safer than a fire, but also because they would be stifling in a smaller area."

"It's a chance I'm willing to take so that I might be able to feel some of my extremities on occasion." I wiggle my gloved fingers for emphasis, giving him a wry smile.

He huffs out another chuckle, but it is drowned out by a decidedly louder huff nearby.

I glance around him for the source of the noise, only to find another tent, this one larger than any we have seen so far. The wooden sign hanging from the open doorway has Jokithan words and the image of a horse engraved on it.

"Horses," I say aloud, angling myself toward the tent. I have to admit I am curious what would merit them being brought to the festival.

"You could say that," the king mutters as he trails behind me without objection.

Khijha growls in protest at the smell of the animals inside, but I press on anyway, knowing she won't stray far from my side.

Ten stalls line each side of the tent. Most of them are empty, save for a few.

The horses they contain, much like everything else in this kingdom, are larger than the average steed. They have thick, long white hair, like that of cows I'd seen once in the countryside. Their hooves are taller, wider, and denser than normal as well, no doubt to survive in this icy region.

Their manes are locked in knots instead of braids, the same way many Jokithans wear their hair, and they all seem well-behaved and tame — placid, even.

All but one.

At the far end of the makeshift stables is a stallion covered in the warmest chestnut-colored coat with a white blaze. He bucks and bites at his handlers in an effort to be rid of them. Each time he raises up, I can see the white stockings on each of his legs.

He doesn't belong here.

The thought harkens back to my own presence in this place, and I can't help but feel a kinship with the creature who so clearly feels trapped by his circumstances.

The horse, if you can even call it that, towers over the Jokithan handlers by several feet.

So, naturally, when I approach, they fear I will be flattened by the anxious beast. The king makes no move to intercept me. In fact, he leans against a pole in the center of the tent, as though he doesn't have a care in the world. Maybe he doesn't, for that matter. Maybe I would be doing him a favor if I got knocked out by this crazy horse.

Though, I don't think he's crazy. Not really. Just discontent. I move closer, shushing him and clucking my tongue, which does a good job of getting his attention.

"Get back, Lady. It is too dangerous," the women tell me while throwing another rope around the horse's neck.

Even Khijha hisses in warning, attempting to stand between me and the behemoth.

I ignore them all. The steed locks eyes with me, and I can sense his fear, his anger. He is a kindred spirit, wild and untamable, locked into a fate he didn't choose.

"How much?"

The trainers look at me as if I've lost my mind. Maybe I have, but I ask again anyway.

"You do not want this one, Lady. Let us show you better hestrinn. Ones that not try kill you."

Ah, so that's what they're called.

"I appreciate the offer, but I want to know how much for this one."

"Lady, this one is mutt. It is no good for you. It is no good for anyone. We take him to the dragon."

I assume something has been lost in translation since dragons have been extinct for centuries, and I push again, impatience quickening my movements.

Taking out a fair amount of the gold pieces in my purse, I present them to the handlers.

"Is this enough? Or shall I ask the king for more?" I add flatly.

Regardless of whatever this *dragon* is, I can only surmise that this hestrinn's fate is not promising.

Vaguely, I gesture to where I know the king still stands, silently taking in this scene. I can't decide if I am gratified or frustrated that he doesn't bother to step in, but I know that reminding the handlers of his presence will stop their objections in their tracks.

Sure enough, the handlers look to the king, then exchange only a single glance with one another before nodding.

"We will have him brought to castle for you, Lady. But we do not think this is so good idea."

"Thank you," is all I say, handing them the coins before walking away, the king at my back.

Khijha hisses and growls to remind me of her disapproval, so the king remains the only one not to have made his opinion known.

Strange.

His long strides are at my side within a couple of steps, and I peer sideways at him only to find him studying me intently. I raise my eyebrows, inviting him to ask what's clearly on his mind.

"Why that one?" His face is inscrutable.

"You disapprove?" I ask, immediately on the defensive from the interaction with the handlers.

"I didn't say that. I was just curious why you chose that particular one out of the bunch." He is careful to leave out his opinion and avoid singling my purchase out as the worst in the lot.

My guard subsides a bit when I realize he is genuinely asking. I turn his question over in my mind, trying to give him an answer that's real.

"He is wild and spirited. But just because he isn't bending over in submission as their captive doesn't mean he shouldn't have a chance to live a different sort of life." I glance back at the tent where he had been tethered to such a short lead, where he would have lived out the rest of his life like that until they fed him to this 'dragon' of theirs. "You never know what he could be capable of without those chains."

CHAPTER 28

The sun is falling behind the mountains, and I realize this is the first time I have seen a sunset since arriving in Jokith. I can't deny that it is uniquely beautiful, reflecting off the pristine white snow and bathing the treetops in a golden glow.

The igloos around us have multiplied, and it occurs to me that it's a lot of work to put into something temporary. The people don't seem to mind, though.

"How can they see whatever lights these are from inside the igloos?" I asked the king, noting the solid roofs of the dome-like structures.

He chuckles.

"They can't. We gather outside for that."

"Then why..." I don't finish my question, because the answer seems painfully obvious now. They stay the night in these tiny igloos. And likely, we are expected to do the same. I'm not sure what expression flits over my face, but the king takes note of it.

"We don't have to stay," he says in a low tone. "It isn't generally safe to travel at night, but I suspect your usual terrifying expression will be enough to frighten anything that would think to attack us." He throws his head back and laughs.

"Indeed. If not, I'm certain that thing on your face would finish the job." I gesture to his beard with a small laugh of my own.

I see the townspeople shooting as surreptitious glances, and I know I have only one real choice here, despite his words.

"You want to stay, don't you?"

The corner of his mouth stretches upward as he exaggeratedly shrugs his shoulders. It tells me everything I need to know, and I laugh.

"Then we shall stay."

He smiles, his eyes brimming with unspoken thoughts.

And for all my natural skill and careful tutelage at reading the nuances of human emotion, I can't for the life of me discern his right now.

It's well past sundown, and I haven't seen any of these alleged lights we are all waiting on. Something in my expression must show how I am feeling, because the king shakes his head with a soft laugh.

"I think it's safe to say patience is not one of your many virtues," he comments.

"I'm flattered you think I have many virtues," I respond with a soft laugh of my own. "All I'm saying is, these lights must be very impressive to be worth all this effort." I gesture around me to the hundred or so logs that have been set out around the subtly glowing warm rocks. And beyond that, to the igloos that outline the entire festival.

"Oh, they are unlike anything you have ever seen." Not for the first time, he looks at me when he says that, as though he's talking about something else entirely. Then, he glances around at the camp and up to the sky. "Of course, it's not just the lights. We also come for the dragon."

This is the second time a dragon has been mentioned, and I can't deny that my curiosity is piqued. I raise an eyebrow.

"You don't believe in dragons?" he asks me.

"You have to admit, it does seem a bit far-fetched..." But even as I say the words, my eyes flit to Khijhana, the giant tiger-like animal that grows twice as fast as anything in nature should. I think about the king's wolves, nearly as tall as I am. The Jokithans themselves with their unnaturally long lifespans. And even the Mayima, the race of people who live in the water off the coast of Delphine.

I realize my skepticism is probably misplaced.

"All right," I allow. "Let's assume I do believe in dragons. What would make this one so special?"

He looks around before taking a breath.

"Legend has it that this area used to be filled with dragons, but as the humans came in, the dragons began to leave — or were chased out or eradicated, no one really knows — but of course, the first version is the more romantic tale, the one that has made it down through history."

I find myself nodding along, already caught up in his unlikely skill as a storyteller and unwilling to break the spell of his carefree and open disposition. It's so unlike his usual closed-off personality.

"No one knows where the majority of them went, but there is one in particular who makes an appearance during the old moon." He gestures to the sliver of a crescent left in the sky.

"He -- or she," he adds, seeing my expression, "is especially active when the lights are strongest, like during this very festival."

I cling to each word; whether or not I believe him is irrelevant. I find that I could listen to him talk this way for as long as he is willing.

"It is said that this dragon has the ability to tell a true soul from a tainted one," he continues. "And that there was a time when the villagers would track it to its cave with their intended to see if they would pass the test."

By now, I am beyond enraptured.

"What happened if they...weren't pure?"

He pauses, arching an eyebrow, his expression full of mischief as he takes another long draught of his eiswein.

"They were eaten," he finally says as if it's the most natural answer in the world and not at all gruesome or awful.

I let out a surprised trill of laughter at his nonchalant tone.

"Oh, is that all?" I say between chuckles. "Perhaps I should have brought you there then," I intend the words as a joke, but they sober me up quickly.

The more I learn about the king, the more I wonder if he would've passed the test. Whereas, I know beyond all shadow of a doubt that I would be little more than dinner for a dragon.

If the king notices my disquiet, he doesn't comment. He only chuckles along.

"That would certainly have been one way to get out of this marriage," he allows.

"There's still time," I grant, trying to pull myself back into the amusement of the moment.

He stiffens, his expression morphing from contented to something else entirely.

"Do you really want out of this so badly?" he asks, his tone taking on a more somber note.

I pause, unsure of how to answer for both him and me.

He shakes his head, but doesn't press for a response, looking around again at the rest of the villagers. I look with him when something that has been nagging at the back of my mind once again occurs to me.

"What about the people in your castle?" I ask, changing the subject.

"You mean, have they gone to the dragon?" He lifts an eyebrow.

I almost smile in response, but I think of how many times he has avoided this line of questioning so far.

"No. I mean, they seem to know plenty about the festival, but they aren't here. You said they couldn't enjoy it." I leave that thought dangling in the air between us, hoping he will respond to it without having to ask a direct question.

He doesn't, of course, so I probe further.

"Are they not allowed to come to the festival?"

He takes a deep breath and lets it out slowly, resignation painting his features. He lifts his eiswein to his lips and takes a long swallow before he finally turns his head to face me again.

"As I told you before, I don't put that kind of restriction on them."

"Then why aren't they here?"

"They don't leave the castle."

I know that the couples and families around us continue to converse, some in low tones and some in loud, slightly inebriated voices. But it feels like a tangible bubble of silence descends with his statement. His words feel so final.

"Ever?" I finally clarify.

He nods.

"For how long?"

He is quiet for so long that I begin to think he is refusing to answer. Finally, he takes another drink, staring straight ahead into the glowing embers of the strange stones when he speaks.

"Seventeen years."

I fight to feel something besides horror. Seventeen years in that castle. That's almost as long as Melodi has been alive. Suddenly, Sigrid's sadness when she tells me that she knows what it is to be away from the people she cares about makes so much sense. There are many things that make more sense and so many more that don't make any at all.

But where the king had been carefree only moments ago, sadness is now etched into every line of his face, and for all that I am a monster, even I cannot bring myself to ask him more when he has finally revealed so much. This night means something to him. And though these are answers I have wanted, I suddenly hate myself even more than usual for putting that expression on his face.

The visceral emotion frightens me, because he is far from the first person I have hurt, and I doubt he will be the last. Why should his pain matter more than anyone else's?

But it does.

So instead of questioning him further, I find myself stretching out my hand and placing it over his.

"Thank you for bringing me here tonight," I say quietly, and he entwines his fingers with mine.

The sky is growing darker, and couples are scooting closer to one another as we wait for what will happen next.

"So, why did you come this time?" For reasons I can't explain to myself, I hold my breath for his answer.

"Well, you did announce that we were going to my entire court." He raises his eyebrows.

"Is that the only reason?" It has been half a lifetime since I let my curiosity get the better of me this way.

He studies my face for a long moment, but he is saved from making a response by a gasp going through the villagers around us.

He flips his hand over to encircle mine and squeezes it, his open eagerness almost childlike in this moment as he gestures for me to glance to the sky.

When I follow his gaze, it steals my breath away. It's like the sky is putting on a show for us. Subtle at first, then sharper in clarity. Lights brilliantly twinkle in a pattern I can't guess at. Bright, shining columns of green fading into a purple that is more subtle but no less breathtaking.

The lights flow like waves on the sea, gently swaying but far more striking.

A quiet settles over us like a blanket, while everyone watches in awe at nature's spectacle.

This may easily be the most beautiful thing I've ever seen.

That is, until the dragon appears.

CHAPTER 29

A shadow grows in the distance, sailing toward us as if it is following the movement of the light above it. I squeeze Einar's fingers, my mind running wild with the possibility that I might see something as mythical as a dragon.

Sure enough, the closer it gets, the easier it is to see the silver and pearlescent scales reflecting the soft glow of the torch light and fire stones around us.

Its large wings beat more slowly as it attempts to land nearly fifty yards away, sending a strong breeze through our makeshift camp.

It lands near the edge of the hill where several villagers have thrown raw meat and carcasses for its meal.

I stare, mouth agape, and watch it devour every last ounce of their offering, wondering how easy it would've been for the dragon to make a feast of us instead.

Everything about it is captivating, from the glowing embers in its nostrils to its shimmering white teeth and steely blue eyes.

Even Khijha is in awe as she observes the mountainous creature, her tail swaying softly, her eyes fixated.

It isn't until the beast is finally flying away that I realize I have been squeezing Einar's hand tightly the entire time. I relax my stiff fingers and applaud with the rest of the villagers once the dragon is headed back toward its home in the mountains.

Einar's deep laugh sounds beside me, drawing my attention back to the moment.

"Amazing," he says softly.

"It was. I've never seen anything like it." I glance at him. "Jokith just keeps on surprising me."

He nods, and a smile tempts the corner of his mouth as he hands me his stein of eiswein.

I debate for a split second before deciding to go for it. If ever there was a time to celebrate with a drink, it is on a night like tonight. Besides, it may be fascinating, but it is still freezing.

We lay there under the lights, watching them dance for us for several more hours.

The lights never fade, but they grow even brighter and more spectacular, as does the canopy of stars behind them. Some people around us eventually make their way into their small huts for the evening, while others continue to sip their wine and enjoy the heavenly phenomenon.

It isn't long before I'm yawning, my eyelids becoming too heavy to appreciate the beauty above us any longer.

"Come, wife. We should sleep." Einar stands and, with no notice, lifts me up onto my feet next to him.

My heart beats a heavy rhythm in my chest, and I blame it on how quickly he moved me.

Khijhana yawns and stretches next to us, then heads into the small igloo without any coaxing.

Einar scratches his head and chuckles. "She's a smart one, isn't she?"

"Indeed," I add with a smile.

He holds out a lantern and gestures for me to follow her into the small frame. While I'm warm enough with my fur-lined clothing, I'm not sure sleeping in the snow is sounding all that appealing...until I see what's inside the small frozen hut.

While the exterior is pure snow and ice, the interior is something else entirely. The lantern shows a small shelf where our eiswein has been stored and a small basin of steaming water with a bar of soap for cleaning up. It is being heated by a single tiny crimson rock.

I marvel at the detail of the engravings on the dome above us. The lantern's subdued flames highlight a story that has been carved into the icy snow.

People gather to watch a dragon soaring through the stars. If I follow the story around to the other side of the igloo, it appears they are begging for its blessing and finally receive it at a cave in the mountains.

An infinitesimal part of me wonders if these designs are in every igloo here, or only ours. It warms my heart that whoever made this hut for us was thoughtful enough to show me the history of the festival. History I was able to be a part of tonight.

An ache in my chest forms at the thought, and I push it away.

Several furs and pillows lay at the center, forming one gigantic bed. Or, it would be if it was only for me. I swallow hard, realizing it will be the first time Einar and I have slept in the same room, let alone the same bed.

Images of our first night together come rushing back, and I'm grateful for the fading light. Red floods my cheeks as I remember standing only inches away from him, naked. I could feel the heat radiating off of him then just as it is now, and I wonder if he's remembering that moment, too.

Though, I also vividly recall the rejection from that night.

Does he regret that now? Do I?

Khijha paces back and forth before settling on the spot directly in the entrance. I can't be sure if she's standing guard, watching the lights, or giving us privacy, but her distance leaves only the two of us on the makeshift bed that is far more comfortable that it appears.

Einar lays back with a sigh, his bulky frame taking up more than half of the space. His hands are resting under his head, and his eyes are closed, but he can still somehow sense my hesitation.

"I won't bite. Not hard anyway," he assures me, and the corner of his mouth tilts up.

Heat floods my entire body from what has to be embarrassment...

"I'm not altogether certain I believe you."

"That's fair," he adds with a sleepy sort of laugh that makes my chest tighten. "But what if I promise?"

I bite my lip and shake my head in resignation before deciding to settle in next to him.

"Fine. But just know that I bite back," I say as he pulls the blanket over us, his arm lingering around my frame.

"Oh, I'm counting on it." His words are barely a whisper, his warm breath tickling my ear.

My body tenses and tingles as my head spins. I barely had any wine tonight, but I am completely intoxicated in this moment. His fingers graze the curves of my hips, his hand stilling as it cups the swell of my thigh. The anticipation of what will happen next runs wild through every inch of me.

After a moment, he chuckles and removes his arm, resting it against his stomach instead.

I stifle either a groan or a laugh, I'm not sure which. He knows full well what he is doing, and I almost call him out on it when I hear the soft rhythmic sounds of his even breaths and realize he's fallen asleep.

What. A. Bastard.

I shake my head slightly, trying to calm my racing heart and still the embers within me that are begging to be set ablaze.

Taking several deep breaths, I put out the lantern and try my best to fall asleep.

It doesn't take long, for a change, but I'm haunted by dreams of my sisters. Rose-colored blood pools at my feet, and I cry out, but there is no sound. I'm helpless and trapped and too far away to protect them, as a voice I know all too well repeats over and over, "You have failed me again."

I thrash and kick, trying and failing to let out a scream when a heavy, comforting weight settles over me. A gentle shushing sounds in my ear, and the images go black. All is calm and still again.

Any peace that was found in the night, any respite from those nightmares, however, is completely gone by the morning.

I wake up shivering, despite being covered in furs. Einar is gone and Khijhana has resumed her pacing.

I stretch and am about to make my way out of the igloo to find my husband when he pushes his way in instead. Something in his stance immediately puts me on edge.

His back is ramrod straight, his expression etched with anger. He moves toward me, tension radiating off him like the air just before a thunderstorm.

Khijha is quick to move between us, her eyes wide and her haunches raised. I reach out a hand to touch his arm, and he glares at it as if it's offensive.

"What's the matter?" I ask, pulling back my hand.

He stares at me, searching for something in my eyes before grunting at whatever he sees there.

Suddenly, I feel like I am standing bare before him again. But instead of the feelings the memory brought on last night, I feel only the sting of rejection.

"Einar --"

"It doesn't matter." He shakes his head. "I have things to attend to before we head back. I'll meet you at the sled in a few hours." With that, he turns to leave.

Any sign of the cold I felt upon waking is gone now. I thought we made progress last night, that we might have even drawn a little closer, but these walls he's thrown up again in the light of day remind me why I never wanted that to begin with.

Once I'm finished furiously washing my face, brushing my teeth, and smoothing my hair into a braid, I decide to head back out to the festival. Though the last thing I want to do is be in a crowd, it's not like I have much of a choice unless I want to spend my day hiding in this tiny space and giving the people even more cause for judgment.

As soon as I emerge from the igloo, several shop owners call out to me, displaying their wares and begging for my attention.

I know Einar told me to spend all of the coin to help out the villagers, but I can't help the inclination to save some back, just in case I may need it later.

I politely thank the vendors and keep walking, my thoughts running rampant. I hate seeing the disappointment in their faces, but I need to be smart.

It isn't until I am walking away from the last tent that I hear a raised voice and the whimpering of a young woman.

On high alert, I glance around until my eyes settle on one of the vendors who I had refused. A young girl was trying to sell grooming gear for hestrinns, and I had brushed her off, too lost in my own thoughts to pay her much attention.

Her father, or employer, is now berating her. He raises his hand to strike her, the blow landing before I can even cry out. He's careful, though; he thinks he's hidden from sight behind their tent and between the rows of other vendors.

It's too much to take.

I stalk toward them, willing myself to be calm as I approach, but under the surface lies a roaring blaze of fury.

"Pardon me?" My tone is more forceful than the words imply.

The abuser feigns innocence, pasting on a genial smile as he nods. "Is there anything I can be help you?"

The young girl behind him is doing her best to wipe the blood from her nose before turning and forcing a painful smile.

"Yes, this lovely young lady had shown me some of the grooming equipment and even a few of the saddles for a hestrinn. At first, I told her no," I pause as if I'm mulling it all over, "but I recently acquired one of my own. I want to be sure I have everything I need for him."

I gesture to one of the saddles and the table full of decorations for an animal I know nothing about.

"How much for all of this?"

The man's mouth nearly falls open, but his eyes gloss over with the lust of coin. "You are want *all* of this?"

I nod, and he gives me an exorbitant amount that even *I* know isn't worth it. But I agree anyway.

"Perhaps the young lady," I pause, waiting for them to supply her name.

"Sarah Agnes," she offers quietly.

"Perhaps you would visit me at the castle, Sarah? And help me with his care and grooming? I'd love to see what you could do with his mane with these." I pick up a few of the beads and strips of fabric.

Tears brim in her eyes as she looks fearfully to the man who just beat her.

"I know that the king would consider it quite a favor if you would be so willing to help his new bride," I add with a slow blink of my thick lashes.

"Of course." The greasy man bows. "Anything for His Majesty."

I crack my gloved knuckles and memorize each line of his oily face. I have no tolerance for those who use their size or position to break another person's spirit.

"She can be come on the next day," he adds, motioning for her to pack up the items.

Sarah blanches, and I speak up before I can help myself. I know that look. That fear.

"Actually, it would be a great favor to me if I could have her come sooner. You see, I could use someone trustworthy to oversee his transport back to the stables and his settling in. I would be willing to pay more for this, of course."

I dump the remaining money from my purse on the table.

The man smiles, the expression all wrong on his repulsive face, before nodding and greedily counting the coins I've laid out for him.

An uneasy feeling forms in my stomach as I tell her which stable number she will find my hestrinn in.

I know it's thoughtless to invite her to the castle right now. Sands know what Einar will say when I let another person intrude on his palace of secrets. I will deal with that later, though. I couldn't just pass her by. I've been in her boots before, and what I wouldn't have given to have someone pull me from that position.

The disquiet continues to grow, however, until I realize the feeling is coming from another source. Someone is watching me.

A predator.

I've hunted and been hunted enough to know the feeling.

The hair raises on the back of my neck as I look around, searching the crowd. Einar is nearby, but the feeling isn't coming from him, nor does it abate when I see him.

It's something else.

I continue to scan each person until I catch sight of the familiar face again. Dark brown eyes stare at me from his chiseled olive-toned face. His signature coal hair is tied back by his neck, and a matchstick rests between his lips.

He is right next to their tent.

Watching. Waiting.

This time, he doesn't run away. He wants me to see him. He smiles before pulling his hood lower and slowly disappearing back into the crowds.

This time, there is no question that it is Damian.

My heart drops to the pit of my stomach, and I want to be sick. This time, he wants me to see him, to know that he's here, and there's only one reason he would do that.

Because my time is already up.

Chapter 30

I try to collect myself, but I know Einar notices. He doesn't comment, though. The only words he has spoken to me since we met back up at the sleds, were to say that *the girl* can sleep in the stables and is not permitted within the castle walls.

I don't bother arguing. I know enough about him now to see that there is no getting through to him in this mood. At least Sarah Agnes will be safe until I can help her figure something else out.

Despite the stormy disposition of the man behind me and the appearance of Damian at the festival, it's hard not to lose myself in the feeling of the wind racing by as we take the dog sled back to the castle. The wolves pick up speed, catapulting me just a bit further back into Einar's arms and his warmth for a fraction of a moment before he stiffens, backing away from the contact.

He dismounts the moment we are in front of the castle doors, and I follow suit, coaxing Khijha to my side. We stalk away from him without a backward glance, and he doesn't bother to follow.

Perfect. I try to tell myself how little it matters, how little I care in the grand scheme of things. I try to busy myself with one hundred other things, grateful that we have arrived well after dinner and I won't have to suffer his presence in the dining hall tonight.

But by the time I finally make it back to my rooms and fall into bed, I can't lie to myself any longer. Khijhana is warm, but she is not the warmest thing I have slept next to lately. I hate how my bed feels stupidly empty without him next to me. But mostly what keeps me awake well into the night is that I have never been more furious with myself.

Finally, I fall into a sleep even more fitful than last night's was.

By the time the king arrives for breakfast, I am awake and dressed, no sign of last night's lack of sleep marring my features. I am practiced in nothing if not putting on a face.

Since I have no plans of venturing outdoors today, I have dressed in a simpler outfit. Citrine stones at my nose and ear bring out the pale blue embroidery on my silver velvet gown, not that Einar seems to notice. I'm not sure why he has graced me with his presence this morning only to stare stone-faced ahead, nibbling at the breakfast Sigrid left with a decided lack of enthusiasm.

Finally, I lose whatever fragile hold on my patience I had to begin with, the façade breaking along with my desire to play coy.

"One might think that sharing an igloo with your wife was the worst thing to happen to you all year, dear husband." I don't look at him as I say the words, but my ire is clear, all the same.

He, however, sets his book to the side like it's the opening he has been waiting for. He looks straight at me before he responds.

"You talk in your sleep." He says the words like he is pronouncing a death sentence.

I will the blood to stay in my face, in my extremities, to not let him see how that pronouncement terrifies me. Racking my brain for the details of the dreams I had that night, I try to figure out what I could have given away.

“Is that what you’re so upset about?” I ask, mostly to give myself a moment to think. “Tell me, Your Majesty, is that an offense punishable by death, or shall the king grant me a pardon, just this once?”

If I expect to goad him into acknowledging his own ridiculousness, I am immensely disappointed. He glares at me as though he fails to see the humor in his complaint. Then, he narrows his eyes, studying me as though there’s something he can glean from his perusal before he speaks again.

"You spoke of a rose."

I blink, even my usual quick wit abandoning me as I realize I have absolutely nothing to say. His eyes squeeze shut in something like pain, and he shakes his head.

"So, you don't deny it, then?" he asks me.

"Deny what? That I talk in my sleep?" It would appear I have found my voice at last, though not to say anything particularly useful.

"How peculiar, what appears to be on your mind. A rose." He says the word again, enunciating each sound. His eyes burn with fury and accusation, and I know I have no choice but to give him the truth.

Or at least *a* truth.

"Rose." I repeat his last word, but I say it like an argument.

His eyebrows lift, and I clarify further.

"Not a rose. Just Rose." I can't seem to make myself say anything else.

"Would you care to explain the difference?" He says it in a tone that makes it clear he does not see a difference. But to me, there is every distinction in the world.

"You asked before about my sisters. I told you that I had three. Yet, only two wrote to me." I haven't put the pieces together for him, but he surprises me by not interrupting.

Something in his expression tells me he had already been curious about that and reminds me what a fool I would be to underestimate the man who bested me at my own game.

So, I continue, treading carefully.

"Melodi is the youngest. Aika is only a year older than she is. And

Rose," I stumble over her name, it's been so long since I said it out loud. "Rose was two years younger than I am. She would have been 20 this month."

His face crumples in sympathy, in remorse, and it's more than I can take from him right now. All at once, I am done, with this conversation, and with this king, and with every sands-blasted bit of this kingdom.

He opens his mouth, and I'm sure the next words out of it will be an apology, but it's one I can't bear to hear.

Without another word, Khijhana and I flee the room and all of its unsettled emotions. I don't know exactly where I'm going, but I know that the walls around me feel more suffocating than anything. I have to get out of this castle.

Chapter 31

The guards outside don't wear masks, so whatever the reasoning on that, it only seems to apply to those within the castle walls. It's a stark contrast to the isolation of being within the castle, but their expressions are just as impassive as the covered faces indoors.

They walk the grounds, keeping an eye on me from a distance as I find my way to the stables, despite never visiting before. When I left the castle doors, I didn't stop for directions. I simply left, and no one cared to stop me.

The sun is high above, casting a soft warm glow, but it does nothing to heat my frozen skin. I was too angry to grab my cloak, and too prideful to return for it.

Instead, I take a deep breath of the icy air, allowing it to burn my lungs, bringing pain to some other part of me than the constant agonizing throbbing in my heart. Khijhana presses against me, lending me some of her warmth until we get to the stables.

Then she stands in the doorway, watching over me but declining to come closer to the hestrinn.

Examining the stables proves to be interesting all on its own.

Every other type I've seen in the past isn't nearly as accommodating as this one is. Maybe it's the colder climate, maybe it's the adoration for animals that the Jokithan people seem to possess, but either way, the stables are more of a luxurious home for the steeds and their caretakers than anything.

Not a bad alternative to the castle for Sarah, I think, grateful that she hasn't been uncomfortable out here.

The inside is heated and sealed off from the harsh elements of the constant winter. There are special quarters for the handlers and groomers and even breeders. Apparently, the castle prides itself on having one of the finest and purest lines of hestrinn in the northern region.

At least, it did until my latest purchase. I smirk.

My anger dissipates, and my curiosity grows as I stroll through the stalls and watch the groomers carefully at work. So far, everyone in here is also maskless. I have to wonder if they have lived their lives in the same stasis as the rest of the castle, or if they have been able to move about more freely.

One of the hestrinn huffs behind me, her muzzle appearing over my shoulder. I laugh a little as she lips at my hair and ear.

When I pull away, she reaches toward me again with her giant head, and I stretch out an arm to rub her neck. She happily leans into my touch, whinnying in delight.

As I continue my stroll through the aisles, I can't help but marvel at how exquisite they all are. To call these magnificent beasts *horses* feels dishonest. They are more like a distant relative of the species. A cousin that you can see some family resemblance in but only if you look closely.

They stand at least twenty hands, maybe more, dwarfing their smaller relatives. The handlers are all far taller than me and still have to stand on small ladders to brush the tops of their coats.

Their coats are a glimmering silver or shining onyx with alternating long manes, many of which are artfully braided. For as much as I had begun to hate the lack of color here, I am beginning to find the beauty in it as well. Because it isn't a lack, so much as a perfection of these two shades in particular.

I run a hand over another one of the hestrinn's muzzles when he dips it down to greet me. His long hair is silky and smooth. He's a gentle giant, and it's easy to see the love that has gone into them from their caretakers.

It's truly awe-inspiring to see such docile animals being so tenderly cared for. That is — until I make my way toward the back of the stables where sounds of frustration are coming from.

Young Sarah's fair skin is flushed red, and her silver tresses are slick with sweat as she tries and fails to climb the ladder to brush the hestrinn's mane. Each time she gets close, he lifts a leg and kicks the ladder over, causing her to fall to the ground.

"*Andskotinn kúkalabbi!*" she curses as she wipes the sweat from her brow.

I can't help but laugh and immediately regret it when she hears me.

"Beg pardon, Lady. I have sorry. I do not mean to speak so freely." She bows and nearly loses her balance again.

I hold up a hand to stop her, moving closer to her and the beast, who is obviously amused with himself.

"No, forgive me for laughing. He seems like quite the *andskotinn,* indeed," I say, grinning.

She blanches at my understanding of her language before nodding in agreement with a smile of her own.

"He is, Lady. He is mad with me now, because I will not give more frosted sugar. I keep have to go out the side door when he gets too angry."

I notice for the first time how my hestrinn's stall is conveniently placed by a back entrance, making it far easier for her to make a quick getaway if he decides to kick.

"Frosted sugar?" I echo back. "What is that?"

Sarah Agnes smiles and opens a bag to reveal small wheat flakes coated in sugar.

"He likes these?" I ask, taking one out to examine it.

The hestrinn breathes out hard and looks at my hand eagerly. I hold up the treat for him, and his lips are covering my fingers immediately, threatening to take my whole hand into his mouth with the snack.

He makes an awful sort of chomping sound, his lips smacking loudly as he devours it.

We both laugh, and, while the noise is disgusting, somehow it also just endears me to the creature more. Once he is compliant again, we are able to brush and groom him with ease.

"I have want to ask," Sarah speaks up after a moment. "Why do you choose him? There are so many better hestrinn here for you." She tilts her head to the side, genuine curiosity in her features.

I reach to place a hand on his mane, and he leans into my touch as if he understands what I did for him.

Or more likely because he knows I will cave and give him more sugar.

"Because no one else would," I answer simply, and she nods.

We finish grooming him in silence, and he seems happy with the two of us paying him so much attention. When we're finished, we offer him some more frosted treats, and he once again devours them.

We can't help but laugh at the sucking sounds he makes as he savors each piece. Drool comes pooling from his mouth, and he snorts in delight when he's done, shaking his head and sending the droplets everywhere.

"Well, that was disgusting," I say, thoroughly amused as I wipe the spit from my cheek.

"Aye." Sarah laughs as well. "You chose crazy one, Lady. But it appears he is good sort of crazy."

"Why does everyone keep saying that?" I finally ask. "Apart from the obvious mannerisms and temper he displays, everyone else seemed to know he was crazy from one glance."

Sarah nods and wipes the sugar remnants on her pants before pointing to the white rim around his eye.

"There. That is sign he has crazy. When you see this, you stay away." She studies me for a moment before continuing. "But not you. You invite him home. You are good to him. That says something about you in here." She points to my chest.

"That I invite drama?" I ask playfully.

Sarah shakes her head.

"No. That you love deep, and you save helpless." Her smile fades. "You save me, too. Thank you."

My eyes begin to sting as I take in her words. I can't be vulnerable here. Not here, not anywhere.

"No, you saved me," I finally say. "I needed someone to help with this guy, and it was a favor you were doing me. That's all."

The corner of her mouth tilts up in understanding and she dips her head.

"Even this, I am never going back to him. I cannot."

She doesn't need to say anything else.

"You will always have a home here," I add quickly, making a promise I shouldn't. "I could use some help reining in his crazy, if you don't mind staying on."

She nods and begins braiding his hair to match the other hestrinn in the stables.

"I suppose we should give him a name," I muse aloud.

"Yes, he is needing something to match his personality."

I chuckle and agree, running through a list in my mind before landing on a name I heard ages ago.

"What about Gideon?"

Sarah puzzles it over, repeating the word to get a feel for the pronunciation. "I like it. What does it mean?"

"Bruiser. Or destroyer."

The girl throws her head back in a fit of laughter before adamantly agreeing, pointing to the few marks he has already left on her body.

"Bruiser. I like this. It suits him."

Chapter 32

The fresh air and time with Sarah and Gideon have served the purpose of calming me down somewhat. That, and the reminder that I have at least done a single decent thing in my life.

The horse is safe, and she is safe, and it's more than I can say for most of the people that I care about, certainly more than I can say for myself. But it's something.

I'm not ready to go back to my rooms yet, so Khijhana and I find ourselves once again in the study. It is vacant, as usual, and the king's words from my first week here come back to me.

Despite my efforts, the people are definitely still avoiding me. It's clear this room has seen plenty of use, and with the newfound knowledge that they have been here for seventeen years, I am sure they are all familiar enough with the castle to feel perfectly at home utilizing its many spaces.

Whether it's personal or it's about their secrets, it's clear that I am the reason for the emptiness in this wing of the castle.

I sigh, pausing near the piano, running my fingers gently over the keys.

None of it matters. It feels as if I spend half of my life reminding myself how little anything here should affect me lately.

I am still pacing the room, trying to thaw from my venture outside, when footsteps sound from the entryway. I freeze in my tracks, but don't bother to turn around. They are familiar enough to me by now, having heard them outside my room every night for weeks.

Khijhana casts the king an irritable look, and I am absurdly grateful for her support. He says nothing, neither to her, nor to me. He only walks in his usual cadence, confident steps that border on arrogance.

He has never had to doubt whether he is wanted in a room, has never had to mitigate himself for the sake of others.

I still refuse to face him, but I hear the sound of chair legs scraping against the stone floor. From the distance, I can surmise that he is sitting at the table where we played chess before.

Finally, his voice rings out behind me. It's deep and, for a change, contains the emotion he so rarely infuses into it.

"I thought we might play another game."

I spin around before I can cover the resigned expression on my face.

"Don't we play plenty of games already?" I ask him flatly.

He studies me for a moment, taking in more of me than I want him to see, as usual.

"A different sort, then." He gestures to the chessboard.

I think about the man I saw at the festival and the way the time is slipping through my fingers so precariously, and I want to say that it's for all of those reasons that I agree.

But I know what a liar I am.

Because mostly, I just want to know him better, to explore the inner workings of his mind. So, I take my seat across from him. Once again, he flips the coin.

"I'll take your head this time," I say with the barest tilt of my lips.

He doesn't respond verbally but proceeds to flip the coin and show me the wolf's head. His move, then. I feel a satisfied smile tug at my lips, and he narrows his eyes.

"If I didn't know any better, I would swear you were playing to lose."

A small, sad laugh escapes my lips.

He doesn't know how right he is. How it feels as if I have spent my entire life with little choice but to play to lose. How there is no real winning here. No real winning for me anywhere.

But he's also wrong, because in our last game, he beat me fair and square, which is something that few men can boast. So, I say nothing.

We take our turns in a tangible sort of silence, the kind that feels louder than conversation would. The kind that says more than words do.

It isn't until we are at least twenty minutes into the game that I hear his voice again.

"There is a sickness in the castle." The silence shatters into a thousand scattered pieces. He has broken it to tell me something I already know, and that isn't like him. So, I wait him out.

He makes a move, and I counter. Back and forth we go until he speaks again.

"It isn't new. But it is getting worse."

I turn his words over in my head, flip them around, and study them for the answers I have wanted so desperately.

"What do you mean, worse?" I press.

Einar rubs his temples, pretending to study his knight even though we both know full well that he only has one viable move if he wants to protect his king.

"It's progressing, and they are...suffering," he says reluctantly as he forms a castle.

It isn't just his move that makes the pieces he's given me and the ones I've observed click together in my mind. His people haven't left *this* castle in seventeen years.

I wasn't allowed to bring anyone with me, and I have encountered so few of the staff or courtiers except from a distance, across a vast dining table. None of their families visit. They are closed off behind their gloves and veils in their own private wing of Alfhild.

"That's why they wear the masks?" I phrase it as a question, but it isn't, not really. It's the only thing that makes any sort of sense. He meets my eyes, nodding.

"And yet you seem concerned neither for my safety, nor your own." I gesture between our clearly unmasked faces.

"You are not at risk," he says firmly. His pupils don't change in size, and his gaze does not waver.

The truth, then.

In a much quieter voice, he answers the second part of my question. "And neither am I."

Guilt overtakes his features, and I wonder at that statement. He doesn't appear to be lying, but there was a small note of falsehood as well. And then, there's his disproportionate remorse.

Did he cause this sickness somehow?

I open my mouth to ask him, when a flurry of footsteps interrupts what I was about to say.

Sigrid sweeps into the study without preamble. I reluctantly pull my attention from the king to the woman who is shuffling much faster than usual to reach me.

When she draws closer, I notice the large ivory envelope in her hand.

My heart races.

I know who it's from before I catch sight of the address. But I stall anyway.

"I thought the post did not run often here?" I strive and fail for nonchalance in my voice.

Sigrid steps beside me, and I wonder what is in my tone or my expression that causes her to place her free hand on my arm with concern.

"It is not, but this letter is from private courier."

She doesn't have to tell me how expensive something like that would be, how extravagant, how very rare it would be to pay for such a service without an urgent need.

But she does not know the unnecessary excess with which Madame fills her life. The king's lips begin to form a question of his own.

It's a question I don't wish to answer, so I reach out with fingers that have gone numb from lack of blood flow, fingers that feel nearly as leaden as my insides, and somehow manage to grasp the envelope.

I don't look down. I can't bear the sight of her seal, a conch shell pressed into crimson wax that drips around the edges like rivulets of blood.

I think I mutter an excuse to the king before I clamber up from the small table, heading straight for the room I was so desperate to escape only hours ago. It's not subtle, but it's all I can manage. I shut the door behind me and tear open the cursed envelope, heart thumping out an accusation with each thunderous beat.

To my most valuable daughter, she has begun her letter. Not cherished. Not loved. Valuable. Given no less and no more weight than one of the many priceless, pretty things she has draping every surface of the château.

I trust everything is going well, though, I confess, I had expected to hear from you by now.

I know how you still mourn your sister, especially this time of year. It pains me to think that if you go too long without checking in, something may befall one of the other two before you have the chance to see them again. These times are so uncertain, as we both know.

My fingers tremble so violently, the letter falls to the floor and I scramble to pick it up so I can finish reading whatever vile things she has written for me.

Of course, they are perfectly fine at the moment. And I am sure with as resourceful as you have always been, you will find a way to ensure they stay that way.

See you soon,
Mother

. . .

Footsteps sound behind the panel to the passageway, and I throw the letter into the fire on instinct. It gives me no satisfaction to watch it burn, though, not when I know nothing can rid me of that woman as easily as I destroy her letter.

I think of what my sisters wrote to me, of how her anxiety had begun to heighten even weeks ago.

I squeeze my eyes shut just as the passageway creaks open. I want to acknowledge the king's presence, to pull myself together before he sees me this way, but all I can see are golden curls soaked in a pool of blood.

Solid, steady hands cover my own, but even the king's significant warmth is not enough to chase away the chill that I can feel deep in my bones.

I force myself to breathe, in and out again, while my brain races through a thousand possibilities. Like the fact that she has set me up for failure and how she will enjoy punishing me for it.

Like how every lesson in my life up to this point has taught me not to let my emotions get the better of me, yet here I am.

"Zaina." The king uses my name so rarely, it pulls me out of my stupor.

I open my eyes, and he is so much closer than I thought. His eyes are peering down at me with none of his usual guardedness, only a look of real concern.

"What is it? Have you received bad news from home?" His voice is so soft, it threatens to break me.

I open my mouth, then close it again. I'm not sure what the right answer is. I'm not even sure what the truth is. All I know is that I'm so cold, and he is so warm, and his lips are inches from my own, and I never seem to know what's going to happen next in my life or when the next tragedy is going to strike.

I don't think. I close the space between us, pressing my lips against his. And for all the times he has rejected me in small or large ways, I don't worry about that this time.

Nor should I. He wraps his massive arms around me and pulls

me closer, opening his mouth to deepen the kiss. I take his invitation, running my hands along the broad chest I've wanted to feel under my fingertips since that first day I saw him.

And for all that I have teased him about this thing on his face, his beard is rough against my skin, contrasting with his soft lips, and it is perfectly him. Perfectly us, I amend.

Isn't that all we are? Rough edges around smaller, softer pieces of ourselves?

He picks me up, and I wrap my legs around him while he walks us backward until he is seated in the middle of my enormous carved bed. His hands go for the buttons at the back of my dress, and I lean into him to allow him more room to maneuver.

All I want in this moment is my skin against his skin, to leach away some of the heat he carries around with him when every part of me feels so very cold.

He unfastens one button and then the next, and I am coming undone as surely as my dress, each ragged breath coming faster, mingling with his in the tiny pockets of space between our frenzied kisses.

His mouth moves down to my chin, and then my neck, and I arch my back to allow him easier access. An animalistic sound I never thought to hear from my own lips escapes me as his tongue flits across the side of my neck.

Then I see it, out of the corner of my eye, the envelope I forgot to toss into the fire along with the letter it contained. The blood-red conch shell — a promise from across the continent. And I remember what happens to the people who get close to me.

I scramble back from him, too off guard to hide my carefully honed agility. His arms stay frozen in the air for a fraction of a second before he lowers them to his side, blinking his eyes against whatever haze he is still in.

"Zaina? I'm sorry, I --"

I throw up a hand to stop him, because if there is one thing I know, it is that I cannot handle an apology from him right now.

"Just go."

He opens his mouth to argue, and I feel my resolve crumbling.

"Please," I add, realizing it is probably the first time I've ever spoken the word to him. I can barely get it out past the tightness in my throat.

His expression shutters, and whatever he was thinking is now as much a mystery to me as it ever is. Without another word, he goes to the passageway and shuts the door quietly behind him.

I wish he had slammed it. I wish I could slam it. I wish I had some outlet for all of this rage and panic and frustration. Hell, I even wish I had a bottle of that eiswein in here right about now.

Anything would be better than this sinking feeling, like I am deteriorating before my own eyes and am powerless to stop it because I know that I have no choices going forward.

This is the cycle my life will take, protecting the ones I love at the cost of literally everything else

Chapter 33

Khijha makes a pitiful sound as she follows my pacing through the room. I want to scream. To cry. To allow myself the emotions that everyone else has a right to, but me.

"I've messed it all up," I say to the empty air around us. "I've ruined everything."

"Ruined what, dear?" Sigrid's voice is startling, though it is softer, sadder than normal. Much different from her usually plucky tone.

I see red as unbridled flames of fury fill me. Fury that I hadn't heard her, hadn't noticed another person's presence or heard the door open or close. Fury that I had let my guard down and that every time I turn around, I make mistakes that I cannot afford.

"Do you never knock? Am I not allowed a sands-damned moment of privacy or peace in this place? Do you all think you have a right to me, that you own my time and attention?" I am yelling, something I never do, and it's almost a relief to finally vent an emotion until Sigrid clutches her heart.

I close my eyes, instantly regretting that I have hurt her. She doesn't deserve my ire. Whether anyone else does is a different story, but she certainly doesn't.

"I'm sorry. I didn't mean --"

The sight of her crashing to the floor stops the words in my mouth. Her head cracks loudly against the stone floors, echoing through the room.

"Sigrid?"

She is limp and unmoving, aside from a small twitching in her gloved hand.

"Sigrid!"

I rush to her side, unsure of where to touch her, of what hurts aside from her head. Pained breaths come from beneath her thick black veil, and I don't even consider what I'm doing until my hands are on the gauzy material.

Einar flies through the panel in the wall. His lips are still swollen from our encounter, and worry is etched deep into each line on his face as he takes in the sight of Sigrid lying motionless on the floor.

My fingers are still grasping her veil, and I continue to pull it up when he shouts for me to stop and runs toward us.

But his words are too late.

I gasp in horror as I get my first glimpse of what she has been hiding all this time.

Her face is covered in white feathers, with a strip of black ones from the bridge of a red beak-like nose back to her scalp. They grow from open wounds, some scabbed over and some very fresh. Whatever transformation is happening to her, it is not painless, and it breaks my heart.

Her small round eyes are red-rimmed and unblinking as her pupils contract and expand repeatedly, and the wheezing sound that escapes her mouth has me terrified.

"She's barely breathing!" I cry out to Einar, who has begun removing her gloves.

Sigrid's slender fingers cringe and twitch in what appears to be pain as sleek black feathers slowly sprout from her knuckles, drops of blood dribbling from the wounds.

"What is this?" I ask, horror-stricken.

"The illness." The king's voice is gentle as he answers without hesitation.

There isn't any urgency in his movements, just anger and a hint of sad acceptance of this horrible situation.

But she seemed so healthy.

No sooner does the thought cross my mind than I realize that's not likely true. I think on how she's been more absent than normal lately. Her touch, softer. Her voice when she entered, I had thought I'd heard sadness, but I realize now that it was frailty.

She wasn't well and hasn't been, and I've been so caught up in my own selfishness that I didn't pay her enough attention.

"What do we do? How do we help?" Tears burn in my eyes, but I refuse to let them fall.

Now is a time for action.

"Tell me what to do," I demand.

Einar looks at me, and there is no wall concealing his emotions this time.

Shock, anger, fear, and even something like hesitation war within his gaze

"You're not...disgusted?" he asks hesitantly.

I squeeze my eyes shut for a moment and quickly shake my head in disbelief.

"I'm not a monster." I wonder if the insistence in my tone is more for his benefit or for my own. "She's been my only friend here, my only friend in a long time. She's in pain and we have to help her."

Feathered fingers wrap around my own as Sigrid acknowledges that she can hear us. The gesture nearly undoes me entirely.

"What do we do?" I ask again, more resolutely.

The guards helped move Sigrid to my bed, and the castle physician has come and gone, giving her an elixir to help with her breathing and overall pain.

Einar paces as he waits for the courier he's summoned. He left the room only once to grab writing materials and scribbled furiously on them, cursing everything under the sun as he glanced back at Sigrid every other sentence.

Despite his knowing that this *illness* has been here for so long, it pains him to see her suffer. To see them all suffer. That much is clear.

A knock barely sounds at the door before the guards open it and Leif enters.

"The courier is here," he says with an anxious tone before casting a glance my way, his beaked mask lingering on Sigrid's helpless form.

Einar doesn't hesitate or take the time to respond. Instead, he thrusts the sealed envelope into Leif's gloved hands, and Leif quickly hobbles from the room to deliver it to the waiting messenger.

Einar still refuses to make eye contact with me, and he hasn't said a word in the past hour.

Not that I am trying very hard to communicate, either. I am more focused on Sigrid, propping her up with several pillows in my bed and trying to get her to drink a bit of tea. She tries to shoo me away, but she can barely even lift her hand for the gesture.

I level her with a stern look.

"None of that," I say, insisting on her taking another sip. "You have spent weeks waiting on and being kind to a perfect stranger, all while your own health deteriorated. You will let me do this now."

I push away the images of what Madame would have done to me and any servant she found me acting so familiarly toward. Though her reach seems to have no end, she is not in this room, and she has already left me so little room for kindness in my life that she will not rob me of this as well.

I feel Einar's gaze on me now, but he doesn't comment.

He speaks only to Sigrid.

"Is there anything else you need?" He stokes the fire with a poker, as though she will get better if only he can make her warm. "Anything at all?"

"No, Ùlfur." It's the second time she has called him little wolf, and it almost makes me smile. But one look at the state she is in effectively rids me of that notion.

Then she thinks again and asks the king to have someone bring her to her bed.

"No," I break in without thinking, ignoring the disbelieving look Einar sends my way.

I am sure he provides well for his servants, but I doubt even Sigrid has a bed as nice as mine, and I'm not certain I trust that anyone would be capable of carrying her so far. This *thing* they have could attack them, too, and they could wind up hurting her if they fell.

"You can recover here for the time being." I squeeze her feathered hand gently. "Just rest, please."

Leif returns, this time without knocking, and he moves a chair to Sigrid's bedside, grasping her other hand in his.

She nods at me weakly, and I stand up, pulling the thick covers a little closer around her shoulders before finally lifting my eyes to the king's.

He stares at me with an expression I don't have the energy to try to decipher.

I gesture my head toward the panel, and he follows my gaze before letting loose a sigh, his shoulders falling slightly with the movement. He nods.

I know the feeling. Truthfully, I would rather stay in this room with Sigrid if it was not for the fact that I'm certain it would only be to watch her die. Something I am not willing to let happen if there is another way.

Besides, I am no fool, and the king has been doing more than keeping secrets. Once again, he has been lying.

Chapter 34

We are standing in the middle of his room, the silence filling the space between us as I watch his chest rise and fall with each grieving breath he takes.

He's leaning against one of his bookshelves with his head tipped toward the ceiling, and the quiet continues to stretch on.

Part of me wants to reach out and touch him, hold him, be held by him. Only hours ago, we were locked in a moment where nothing else existed, and I can't deny a selfish part of me that wishes we could be in it again, feeling only each other and drowning out the world and its problems and its pain.

But that won't make them go away.

So, I try very hard to ignore the oppressive presence of his massive bed, even larger than mine. I try not to remember how I felt the last time I was in a bed with him, or the way his lips felt against my bare skin, or how he tasted like cinnamon and honey.

I try to ignore the traitorous part of me that just wants to crawl back there with him, even if we are just a couple of liars.

I shake my head to clear those thoughts, looking him straight in the eye when I call him out.

"An illness?"

He says nothing, his gaze settling slowly on the bed as well, and I can feel the tension stretching between us like one of Aika's fiddle strings about to snap.

"Funny," I pull his attention back to the conversation at hand. "It's like no sickness I have ever seen. In fact, if I didn't know any better, I might even think she had been --" I stop before I finish my sentence, unabated horror washing over me.

"Think she had been what?" Einar's voice is reserved, curious, as he moves away from the bookshelf and angles himself toward me.

"Poisoned." I breathe out the word through lips that have gone numb.

All at once, I feel like an idiot, like even more of a pawn than I have always been.

"And what would you know of it?" He narrows his gaze, cocking his head to the side.

It isn't hard to summon the anger I need to lift my chin, my own eyes burning with rage when I respond.

"Only that it is like no sickness I have ever seen, nor heard of. Or would you like to double down on your lie and pretend that it is some rare Jokithan plague?"

Instead of so much as a flicker of remorse crossing his features, indignation widens his eyes.

"You wish to speak to *me* of lying?"

I distantly register that his lips aren't moving exactly as they should, but my mouth outpaces my mind when I answer.

"And what have I lied about?" Plenty, but I mostly want to know which of them he has figured out.

But he doesn't answer. He only looks at me with a waiting expression, like he expects me to deduce the answer on my own. And belatedly, I do.

Because we aren't speaking the common tongue.

I realize now what his sharp glance in my room had meant. Not because I had refused Sigrid what she had asked for, but because she had been speaking Jokithan when she told the king to have her moved.

Inwardly, I curse my thoughtlessness. Outwardly, I remain calm.

"Are you expecting me to apologize for picking up some of your language in the several weeks I have lived here? Would you rather that I remain ignorant of my own people?"

"Your knowledge would suggest far more than *picking up some of the language*," he shoots back at me, using my own phrase.

Again, I pull from the substantial supply of rage and injustice swirling around in my mind and infuse it into every one of my features, my posture, and my voice when I speak.

"If you'll recall, I had very little else to do when you brought me to your castle, alone, then refused to see or speak to me for weeks."

Shame crosses his features, just as I had hoped it would.

"None of this is helping Sigrid," I add in a softer tone. "Why don't you tell me what you know, so at least I can better care for her. Maybe I can help."

He sinks into his armchair, letting his head fall into his hands.

"There's nothing anyone can do to help." He gestures around at the books, and I realize that this is the first time he is aware that I have been in his room.

I take a moment to study it ostensibly.

"What's all this?" I asked.

"Research. Seventeen years' worth. I've been looking for an antidote, and I am no closer than I was when I started. And I'm running out of --" He cuts off, looking at me sharply.

Seventeen years.

"Running out of what?" I prod him.

"Time," he says at last, his fingers tugging at the chain around his neck that he never takes off.

I suppress a scowl. He might be running out of time, but that's not how he had planned to end that sentence.

What is he running out of?

He is still keeping secrets, though probably not as many as I am.

Before I can ask anything else, a loud knock sounds at the paneled door.

"Enter," Einar says, his eyes still locked onto mine.

"We've had word," Leif says, limping toward us to hand Einar a rolled-up piece of parchment.

"Already?" I ask.

Though, in a country with dragons and magically growing fantastical cats, I'm not sure why I'm surprised.

The king quickly unfurls the letter, his eyes scanning its contents before he nods.

"Right. He's close, then. I'll be leaving immediately."

Leif nods and opens the main door to the king's room to signal something to the guards before heading back to Sigrid.

"Who did you write to?" I ask while Einar throws a few of his journals and vials with various plants into a satchel.

"My ambassador. He has been helping me. Last I heard from him, he believed he might be on to an antidote, but that was months ago --" He pauses, sighing. "When they took a sharp turn for the worse."

I nod, but then something strikes me, and the room begins to spin.

Right before I got here. Right before I was sent here, last minute, more like it, by an ambassador. Like the one allegedly helping him.

He casts a sideways glance at the tapestry on his wall before turning away.

"I'm coming with you," I announce as he reaches for the door.

"The hell you are," he commands with finality before slamming the door shut behind him.

I feel frozen in a flurry of emotions. My pride makes me want to chase after him and insist. My fear makes me want to stay with Sigrid. My rage wants to shatter everything in this room. But Madame's voice in the back of my head is telling me something else entirely.

It makes sense now, why Madame had chosen this castle. How she knew it had been weakened from the inside. How many people in the world have the knowledge to turn a person into an animal, or even a version of one?

Haven't I seen her do this before, or at least something similar?

So many things are clearer now. I wish they weren't. I wish I could go back to when the king was just a cold bastard and I was just the bride he purchased. Because all of this knowledge and insight, even though it feels like it changes everything, it changes nothing in the end.

But when has wishing ever gotten me anywhere? That was one of the first lessons Madame taught after she obtained me.

After she *stole* me.

Khijhana presses herself against my leg as though she senses my despair, and I let her, because I lied before when I told Einar I am not a monster.

I'm just not nearly as much of one as the creature who made me. The one who plucked me from my home and molded me to suit her needs.

The one who poisoned this entire castle.

CHAPTER 35

It doesn't take long for me to decide to explore the passage in his room again. The way he looked at it before he left told me enough to know that it's important.

I must have missed something.

I push the tapestry aside and scan the wall before my eyes snag on the stone brick that sticks out just a bit farther than the others. I press it, and it gives way to reveal a solid stone door. I open it to the winding staircase, this time feeling the walls along the way for anything I may not have seen the first few times I was here, during all those weeks he left me to my devices.

Khijhana mews and tentatively climbs the steps while I slide the heavy door back into place. The motion brings Einar's words back to mind.

The hell you will as he slammed the door.

Slammed the door. Ordered me to stay.

He doesn't even realize the web that's being woven around him, and the stubborn bastard refuses to trust me, refuses to believe that I might be able to help him.

My blood boils as I make my way up the private stairs.

I don't even know who I'm so furious with. Einar for shutting me out again, or myself for deserving it. Or, most of all, Madame.

I can still help him, I tell myself.

I can't risk outright disobedience, though. Images of my sister's fair skin and golden hair reappear, as they always do when I contemplate the very notion.

The sound of her laugh. The way she smiled and followed my every move without question, for better or worse.

Worse, as it turns out.

I push the memory away. This is different. I wasn't given any direct orders about this.

Unless...I think about the second set of instructions I was sent with. It had seemed so trivial, weighed against marriage and a baby.

Steal something valuable and replace it with something worthless. He'll never know the difference.

A betrayal, but a relatively minor one, all things considered.

I have been so, so stupid.

Desperately, I focus on my surroundings.

What did I miss?

The staircase ends in a vast room with a domed ceiling and rounded windowpanes.

Each wall is full of books, plants, and alchemist's tools.

There are graphs on the wall of various plants and their anatomy broken down piece-by-piece with a small description of the medicinal or toxic properties. But most prevalent are drawings and notes on one flower in particular.

A rose.

The reminders of her are endless, even as the pieces of this twisted puzzle click horrifically into place.

Several vials line the walls with papers next to them. I had largely ignored them before, but this time, I shuffle through each paper.

1 Rose petal - 3 ml of lavenaia berry juice - claw of raven - *Turned to a combustible black substance.*

1 Rose petal - 7 drops puffin blood - stardust - *Boiling acid that rots flesh.*

1 Rose petal - 8 ml wolfsbane - tail of scorpion - *Promising at first - but seems to accelerate effects of poison.*

They go on and on in this way, all of them with slashes drawn through them, notes and warnings scribbled next to them. There must be hundreds of variations here that he has tried, and all have failed.

I hastily search the drawers and cabinets and vials for answers, but I come up empty. And the longer I'm here, the more I realize that I will only find what I need if I'm with him.

He's not the only one running out of time.

With those thoughts, I sneak back into my room and discreetly change into the warmest clothes I can find, packing an extra cloak in a small bag along with whatever food is left over from earlier, as well as a canteen of water. It isn't much, but it will do in a pinch.

The memories reappear.

I'm thirteen again. Rose and I are packing what few belongings we have to escape from the window balcony of the villa.

I had just arrived home and found her sleeping. Her eyes were red and swollen from tears. She knew I hadn't wanted to go. She knew I was scared.

It was the night I became a woman. It was the night that whatever was left of my childhood had been sold to the highest bidder.

'You're of age now. Let's not let this go to waste.'

When the first signs of womanhood appeared, the bidding started.

I had fetched a very high price — enough to pay for the burden of keeping me housed and fed. Or so I was told.

I couldn't allow her to do the same to Rose. Not my Rose.

I'm creeping past my bed when Sigrid's voice reaches my ears.

She motions for me to come closer, and I do, in spite of the time I've already lost. I ignore the voice in my head that tells me this may be the last time I see her.

"Where?" she barely croaks out, but I understand her meaning.

"I am going after him," I answer honestly, careful to keep the emotion from my face.

She swallows hard, and I help her take a sip of water.

Her frail fingers apply the slightest pressure to my hand as she nods in understanding.

"So...so many --" Her words are interrupted by a coughing fit, so I help her sit up for another drink. It isn't until she's laying back down that she finishes.

"--thorns, but less than before." She reaches for my face with a shaking hand, smiling through her pain while she touches my cheek.

This simple gesture nearly breaks me in two. I don't deserve her kindness, but I treasure it, nonetheless.

Her words are an echo of what she's said before. But this time, it's different. It's an unspoken understanding that there are layers to each of us. Broken pieces that make us who we are. And on some level, I get the feeling she understands me better now than she did then.

I'm just not so sure it's a good thing.

Leif clears his throat behind me, the physician at his side once more.

"I'll leave you to it," I say, quickly removing myself from her side and heading out the door without looking back.

CHAPTER 36

With all of the commotion in the castle, it doesn't take much for me to sneak away into the stables. Maybe the guards don't think I will actually leave, or maybe they don't care.

I find Sarah at Gideon's stall, where the latter is shuffling around impatiently. Khijhana casts Gideon another look that borders on disgust, clearly feeling that his behavior is beneath her. Her head reaches my elbow now, and I mentally amend my list of reasons why the guards didn't bother stopping me.

Sarah doesn't question me when I ask her if Gideon can be ridden, and she doesn't mince words or waste time helping me. She seems to sense my urgency, which isn't altogether surprising. How many times has she been desperate to escape a situation?

While she helps me saddle my hestrinn, a look of warning fills her eyes, and she speaks in hushed tones.

"He is good horse, Lady. But he likes to lead. Let him run and he will stay behaved," she cautions, showing me the best way to mount him and get back down again. She teaches me a few of her commands, easy ones that he is likely to follow, and gives me a final word of advice before I leave.

"He is fastest hestrinn here, faster than any I know, but he is wild. Listen to him, and let him tell you what he has need." I don't miss the worry in her voice, but I also don't have time to stay to learn more.

Gideon may be a wild card, but he is fast, and he is mine.

We head in the direction of the freshest horse hooves, toward the mountains. There are two sets of tracks, so he likely took one of the guards. At least he isn't completely reckless.

Gideon seems pleased to be free from the stables and running through the snow. Sarah wasn't wrong. He is fast, faster than even his size accounts for, faster than any horse I've ever ridden. If I was worried about the hour or so I had lost exploring in the king's absence, I'm not really nervous about it now.

Fortunately, the snow has stopped falling, so their hestrinn have left deep, clearly marked hoof prints in the blanket of snow, easy for even me to follow.

Gideon is remarkably easy to steer, as long as I let him set his own pace, and he soon seems to see that we are following the marks left by the other hestrinn. There is little for me to do but keep my seat, leaving my mind free to wander.

Which is never a good thing.

I held her small hand in mine as we ran down the beach toward the village. Every part of me hurt and felt dirty and ashamed. I fought back the tears and ignored the pain, because I couldn't let that slow me down. Not when we were so close to freedom.

I told myself that I would be back, though. I would find a way to save Melodi from this hellish prison, too. Even if her fate wouldn't be as awful as ours, she still didn't deserve to be stuck in this place with that horrible woman.

Rose tripped and fell so many times, her sleep-deprived body unable to keep up with my pace.

We were almost there, though. I could hear the lapping of the water against the wharf.

We turned a corner, and the cargo ship came into view. I had been eyeing it for months, but it was a risk, one I hadn't been willing to take until tonight.

We made it all the way to the loading bay before I saw him. Damian. Relief whooshed out of me. He had gone ahead to pay our passage. This was it. We were almost free.

But his expression was all wrong. A slow, malicious smile spread across his face. He opened his mouth to speak, but I knew what he was going to say before he got the words out. I had already lost.

"I've found them for you, Mother."

I'm not even trying for stealth, though I don't know what I will say when I catch up with Einar. Even if I could trust him with the truth, I'm not even sure what that is anymore.

Regardless, he doesn't get to order me around like one of his dogs and expect me to sit and stay where he tells me to.

As usual, it's easier for me to focus on my anger than any of the other thoughts competing for first place.

Gideon flies down a small embankment, pulling me momentarily out of my vicious thoughts. It is clear that he struggles with changing speeds. He is all or nothing, and we begin to slide and stumble more than we were before. The path ahead is getting steeper and slicker, and if I was on any other horse, I know we wouldn't have made it this far. Though, I'm not certain Gideon will make it much further, either. Or at least, not with me atop him.

My balance clearly isn't what it used to be, and I seem to be tilting or sliding far more than normal.

But in spite of all this and the incline, Gideon is undeterred and continues upward.

I lean forward as far as I can to lighten my weight in the saddle, which propels him forward even faster. My core and lower back burn from the strain, but I somehow keep my seat.

I turned to run, knocking on doors at random in a plea for help. But the islanders knew who we were. Who we belonged *to. They couldn't risk their lives for ours, and in the end, they sealed Rose's fate.*

We seem to be going in a nearly straight line northwest, toward the snow-capped mountains in the distance that already feel so much larger as we approach them. It makes sense why they don't bother with regular horses here. None of them could manage this terrain or the freezing temperatures.

With Gideon's thick coat, he doesn't seem even the slightest bit fazed. Even Khijha was made for this. She has no trouble keeping up, though I worry that we are making our presence too obvious.

If my hestrinn and cat are larger than life, then whatever is potentially lurking within this forest could be as well.

But they can't be any worse than other monsters I've faced.

By the time we were back at the château, my tears were spent. I was silently resigned to the punishment we would face. I held Rose's head to my chest as sobs wracked her body, assuring her that she wouldn't take any of the blame. It was my idea, after all.

We bolt around towering spruce and fir trees, up increasingly steep trails. I want to trust that Gideon knows what he's doing, as he has so clearly taken the lead, but I get anxious every time we come too close to the imposing trunks and branches. This is the last place I want to be injured.

I am neither weaponless, nor defenseless, but I won't pretend to know how to escape or kill any predator here.

And I haven't forgotten the dragon.

Gideon has not slowed even for a moment, though. He is spectacular, even with his eyes rolling around in his head a bit and the crazed noises he makes on occasion. I have no way of knowing how much faster he is than an average hestrinn and no way of gauging our progress, though.

All I can do is hope we are gaining on them and hope I will catch up to the king in time to get some sands-blasted answers.

CHAPTER 37

Nearly three hours have passed, according to the position of the sun, when Gideon starts to act fidgety. He even slows his pace without my tugging on the reins.

I am already nervous, because I've heard the sound of streaming water for the past half hour. I try to trust Gideon, try to believe that he won't come upon a river and stop so suddenly that I pitch forward, but my trepidation won't quite buy it.

I look to Khijhana, and she is fixated on a space beyond the trees, but not necessarily on guard. Have we caught up with them at last?

Sure enough, we follow the overgrown trail a few more meters and spill out into a small clearing with a narrow river running alongside it.

The king and Gunnar stand in front of it, their two hestrinn lapping up the water rapidly. Both men are facing me, weapons drawn.

The barest hint of relief washes over me, but I ignore it. I refuse to entertain the idea that I am relieved either to find him here safe or to find him in a man's company rather than Helga's. Or any other woman's. With everything at stake, it isn't something that should matter at all.

But with all the secrets he keeps, hadn't I wondered more than once if that was one of them? And who would he trust to make this journey with him when he so clearly did not trust me?

My reluctant relief is short-lived in the face of Einar's anger. He throws his axe to the ground, where it lodges itself in the frozen earth. Jaw clenched, he brings his fingers to the bridge of his nose, squeezing his eyes shut like he can will me away just by wishing it.

I tug on Gideon's reins, a little surprised and grateful when he actually stops. Despite Sarah's lessons, I struggle to dismount him with my stiff legs.

I know mounting him again will be even more difficult, but it's worth it to give my body a break. Once I convince him to drink alongside the other hestrinn, I finally look up at Einar.

The king's glance travels from my frustrated hestrinn to my chalyx, who is calmly removing debris from one of her paws, and finally to my face, which I have ensured holds not the slightest sign of remorse.

For all the times I have thought that his expression was inscrutable or difficult to read, I have no problem discerning it now. White-hot fury paints every single line of his face. From the corner of my eye, I can see that his companion is more flummoxed than anything, but I have eyes only for my husband.

The seconds tick by with only the whistling of the icy wind interrupting our standoff. Along with his rage, disbelief and what I could even swear is disappointment make appearances in his kaleidoscope of emotions.

But I don't back down.

After what feels like a lifetime, he runs a hand over his braided silver hair, acting for all the world as if I am nothing but an annoyance to him.

"Gunnar," he addresses the guard without turning his head. "Please ride ahead to the ambassador, let him know that I will be delayed --" He looks at me irritably. "For an indeterminate period of time."

"Right away, Your Majesty."

The man mounts his steed with a frustrating ease and gives a polite nod in my direction before he rides away at full speed.

I'm sure my husband would be thrilled if I would address him with the same level of easy acquiescence, but I'm afraid he has another thing coming.

Once Gunnar is well on his way, Einar begins pacing back and forth. The tension is rolling off of him in waves as he scratches his beard and shakes his head.

I roll my eyes before noticing that Gideon has stopped drinking and is staring at Einar's movements. His ears are flicking back and forth, and his lip curls up. I follow his gaze toward my husband's stomping feet making deep tracks in the snow and shake my head.

I remember what Sarah said about his disposition.

"You're making him nervous. You need to calm down," I say while stroking Gideon's mane, making gentle shushing noises.

Einar stops and stares at me, righteous indignation clear on his features.

"*I* need to calm down?" He laughs, and the sound is wholly without humor. "What do you think you're doing here?"

"I told you I was coming with you." I inject a little extra nonchalance into my tone, because he may be furious, but he is not the only one.

"And I told you that you were doing no such thing."

I have already been forced to give the control in my life over to one person, and I will be damned if I give a shred of what I have left to him, even temporarily.

Gideon continues to huff, and even Khijha moves to stand between us.

"You may command your subjects, but you do not command me." My voice is quiet, with a lethal timbre I rarely let anyone hear.

But then, he pushes my buttons in a way few people do, and I am already standing on an edge.

Einar only shakes his head.

"And we're back to this." He has the nerve to sigh. "Does everything come down to power with you?"

Spoken like a man who has never had to fight for it. I rear back at his accusation, having lived my entire life without a shred of power at the whim of a woman who wants nothing more.

"If, by power, you mean the basic dignity afforded to any adults," I spit back at him, "then yes, I suppose that it does. Did it ever occur to you that I might be able to help?" I add, mortified by the way my throat begins to feel thick on the last word, because honestly, my reasons for coming are jumbled in my head now.

His eyes widen in understanding, and I look away, because he doesn't get to treat me as though I am beneath him and then have the nerve to look like he cares.

And because he doesn't begin to know what it is he thinks he understands.

His voice is every bit as forceful, though, when he responds.

"Help in what way, Zaina? Unless you have some knowledge of poisons and cures, or some magical way to stop time, then how exactly did you expect to help?"

He barrels forward without waiting for me to answer, which is just as well, because I don't have one.

"You take off into a countryside you're unfamiliar with, handling an animal you know nothing about, one that could kill you if you're not careful. You're reckless and thoughtless." There are only inches between us as he speaks down to me. Gideon stomps his feet and paws at the ground, clearly upset by our argument. Einar backs away, taking a deep breath before he continues.

"Did it ever occur to you that I had my reasons for telling you to stay behind? That you have no experience riding a hestrinn, that speed was of the necessity, that I might have wanted you there with Sigrid for a reason?"

His pain and his worry seeps through on those last words. But I know how to spin emotions and use them to my advantage, and I will not be on the receiving end of that.

"I think it's clear that I was not a hindrance to your speed." I gesture to Gideon, who is already anxiously shuffling his feet in anticipation of our next run. "Sigrid had many capable and willing hands at her side when I left, as you well know. But if you had wanted me there as well for whatever sands-blasted reason, all you had to do was explain that --"

"There was no time!" He cuts me off, practically yelling now.

"There was no *need*, is what you mean," I correct him. "Because no one expects the king to explain himself to anyone, least of all his lowly *consort*. Do not pretend to me that the handful of seconds it would have taken you to ask me to stay rather than to order it would have perilously delayed your journey."

Einar opens his mouth to respond, then closes it. I have left him speechless, at least momentarily, though no less angry. We are both breathing heavily, angry white puffs of breath appearing and then dissipating in the air before our faces. Gideon backs away slightly, and I put a calming hand on his neck.

The king takes in the horse's fidgeting movements and Khijhana's otherworldly stillness, but he still says nothing. His face has gone carefully blank.

Finally, I speak up.

"For all that you were worried about your precious time, we are certainly wasting a lot of it staying here to argue." I am not without feelings. I can read between the lines and see that he wanted someone to be there with the woman who was obviously like a mother to him, and in another world, in another life, I would be the kind of person who could sit at her side and do nothing.

But I don't have the luxury of being that person. There is more at play here than I think either of us fully understands. One thing is clear, though.

I need to see this ambassador.

Chapter 38

I stretch to grab hold of Gideon's saddle, trying and failing to pull myself up. Before I can try again, rough hands grab hold of my waist, tossing me upward with such force that I nearly sail over the other side of my hestrinn. I grind my teeth as I situate myself.

Gideon stomps and paws at the ground until Einar finally moves away to mount his steed as well.

Einar doesn't agree for me to come with him, but he does not argue when I prod Gideon into a trot behind him.

In fact, he doesn't say anything at all for nearly an hour.

I can tell it is an effort for Gideon to let the king's hestrinn lead the way, and even more so for him to stay at this careful speed. He stamps his hooves and huffs every so often, shaking his head a bit in frustration.

I can't pretend I don't relate. I also don't have an easy time lessening myself for the sake of those around me.

Khijhana is happy to take up the rear, likely sensing that my anger at the king has ebbed away into something a little less potent. As the sun drops behind the mountain, I beckon her closer to me. I am grateful that she wants to protect me, but for all her size, she is still a kitten, and a domesticated one at that. I don't know what's in these woods that is bigger than she is, and I don't want to find out the hard way.

If the king is trying to ignore me, he is doing a poor job. His shoulders are hunched, and he tosses several half-glances over his shoulder. When the path finally widens, I let Gideon pull forward to ride at Einar's side instead of his back.

I am just debating whether I should bother to try to break the silence when he slices clean through it.

"I realized that as long as we've been married, we've never really taken the time to get to know each other." The words are innocuous enough, but his tone is all forced pleasantness, bordering on mocking, and I am immediately on edge.

"No," I agree. "That was never something you seemed interested in."

"An oversight on my part." His voice is darker now, and I know I won't like what he says next. "So tell me, where did you grow up?"

“I'm from the Eastern Lands, near the Mirrored Desert." I hesitate, still wondering what his game is. “But I have spent the better part of my life in Bondé, in Corentin.”

It's not a lie. "And yet, you speak the common tongue without the trace of an accent?" He startles me from my thoughts.

This is an interrogation — that much is clear — but his tone is polite enough that I can't call him on it without looking like there is a reason I don't want to answer his questions.

"I have a gift with language, as you have already noted yourself." I let my irritation show in my tone, hoping he will drop this line of conversation.

He doesn't.

"Don't sell yourself short. What you have is more than a gift. You speak my own language as though it were your mother tongue. Why hide such skill?"

An irritable sigh escapes me, sending plumes of smoky condensation from my nose.

"Perhaps a lifetime of suspicious and easily emasculated men has taught me better than to flaunt my particular set of skills." I eye him pointedly, though I don't actually put him in that category.

I need a moment to think, but he doesn't give me one.

"Exactly what is your particular set of skills? You throw stars, you play chess, you --"

"Do everything a man can do? Have I offended your sensibilities, or merely wounded your pride?" I shoot back, still trying to gain the upper hand.

"You're so good at flipping a conversation on its head, Zaina, and I might even believe you, except..." He pins me with a stare that has the blood draining from my face.

"Except what?" I say with all the false bravado I can muster.

"Why, if you were teaching yourself my language, would you refuse to speak to a sick woman — a woman you called a friend — in her own tongue? Unless you had something to hide."

I scramble for a response that makes sense, something that won't feel like a lie. Hesitation is the first tell, so I open my mouth before I'm even sure what I will say.

Just then, Gideon stamps his feet again, but this time, he doesn't seem to go any faster. If anything, he's moving sideways and even backing up slightly, his ears twitching.

"Something's wrong," I say, looking to Khijhana and noting that while she doesn't look exactly anxious, she is looking intently off to the side.

"Are you that desperate to change the subject?" Einar asks me sharply.

My jaw clenches, and before I can respond, Gideon whinnies and shakes his head, rearing up a bit as he moves toward the side of the narrow trail. Finally, the king deigns to look in our direction. His eyes widen, and he reaches out a calming hand toward my hestrinn, rubbing his own clearly better-trained one on the neck.

I don't understand the panic widening his eyes since he is looking behind me and whatever Gideon is backing away from is clearly up ahead.

But it's getting dark now, bathed as we are in the shadow of the mountain, and I have been more focused on the king than our surroundings. I realize my mistake a moment too late, when Gideon rears up again, backing up until his back leg slips down further than it should be able to.

The jolting motion makes me lose my precarious grip on his reins and my seat in the saddle. I've never been much of a screamer, but I let out a yelp as I sail through the air until my foot catches in one of the stirrups.

Gideon's feet are back on the ground, but now he's bolting down the trail, and it's all I can do to wrangle my foot out of the stirrup before he tramples me to death. I hit the ground hard before rolling back down the mountain.

My chest aches, and I can't breathe. The wind is knocked from me as I continue to flip and roll for what feels like an eternity.

By some miracle, I finally crash into a snowbank near the edge of the cliff, just before sailing clean over it.

I gasp and choke when air forces its way into my lungs. Stars line my vision, but I still see Khijhana's form taking hesitant steps toward me.

When the ringing in my ears stops, I hear Einar's voice in the distance, but I can't make out the words he's saying. He has dismounted and is waving frantically. I strain my eyes until they can focus a little more on his lips, which are moving emphatically and forming two words.

I roll to my side and try to sit up, my head still spinning, when I finally make them out.

"Don't move!"

The earth begins to shift beneath me, and Khijhana's eyes widen as she tries to back away.

A crack has formed in the snow around us, and, for all of her scrambling, she is now sliding toward me at an alarming rate.

Einar's face is panic-stricken as he races forward, his arms grasping wildly at the empty air. But he is too late. I am already falling.

CHAPTER 39

The side of the mountain isn't kind as Khijha and I fly down it. I can't focus enough to see how she is faring; instead, all I feel is blind panic as we careen toward the bottom of the cliff on a frozen slab of ice and snow.

Flurries race all around us, obstructing my vision in a blanket of white. With each glacial mass that is knocked free, our speed increases. We're sailing faster by the second, hurtling toward the base of the mountains.

I don't even see that we're nearing the bottom until I hit the ground with a thud, the several feet of snow beneath me barely cushioning the impact as it forces me forward now.

Khijha's growls ring out, and I let loose a breath, relieved that she's still alive and nearby.

I'm scrambling, digging my nails into any surface I can find, but my frozen fingers can't find purchase. They burn and ache, and I keep sliding until I skitter onto a sheet of pure ice.

A pop and snap ring out, and Khijhana's growl is cut off by the sounds of splashing and gurgling water.

I dart a frantic look toward the noise, even more terrified than before as the sound of more ice cracking echoes around me.

Falling to my death would have been horrific enough, but no, the world would never be that kind. I'm going to drown instead.

An even louder crunch sounds, and the ice beneath me begins to splinter as my momentum slows.

When I finally come to a stop, the fractures beneath me worsen, and icy water pools all around my frame.

There is nothing I can do, I realize with a swirling of varied emotions.

If I could force my aching body to move, I would crawl away from the danger, but the fissures stretch too far.

It wouldn't matter anyway. Or so I tell myself as the water deepens and the ice continues to thin.

Madame's words fill my head.

"You are such a disappointment, Zaina."

How many times have I replayed that moment? How many times has that memory haunted me?

The ice finally splits wide open, and I drop down into the arctic lake. I take a final gasping breath as it pulls me under, its biting tendrils stabbing at my skin as I thrash and kick and try to make my way back to the surface.

Everything around me is the deepest shade of blue, so blue it is almost black, save for the one fading circle above of rapidly dimming light.

The oppressing glacial temperature freezes each of my joints and muscles, slowing my movements.

The cold burns like fire, setting my skin aflame.

I want to scream out in agony, but I fight to hold the remaining oxygen in my lungs as I continue to sink even deeper to my watery grave.

"You are such a disappointment, Zaina." I hear her again, and images and scenes of those painful memories come rushing back.

Rose is lying on the ground. Bruises cover her face, and her once-golden hair is sticky with fresh blood pooling from her nose and scalp.

Her chest refuses to rise or fall, and her thick lashes are closed and unblinking.

The pressure in my chest is too much to bear. I've reached my breaking point. My mouth opens in a gasp, and the air rushes out of me while frigid water fills and chokes my lungs. I'm suffocating, just like all those people Madame punished.

It's pure agony.

My vision goes completely black.

I've never felt so much pain.

I deserve this.

The stabbing pains grow more intense, and it's as if knives are piercing my flesh. Then, there is nothing but the memory of the sister I once knew.

I tell myself that Rose is sleeping. Even now she is beautiful, the bruises unable to steal that from her completely. Part of me is relieved. My perfect sister will never have to face another day in this hell we were forced into.

She will never again have to miss the family she was stolen from. Her fate has been kinder, because she didn't have to face the true horrors that Madame had planned for her future.

Her sentence is over at just eleven years of age.

And now, mine is, too.

CHAPTER 40

I gasp, and water heaves and spews from my shaking body. I steal desperate breaths, eager to take in as much oxygen as I can.

My body works to expel the icy water, and every part of me throbs and writhes with the effort.

Once I'm finished, gentle hands cradle my head.

"Zaina? Can you hear me?"

I force my eyes open, but the movement is slow. Painful, even.

"Zaina?"

A blurred figure stares down at me. It takes several more moments to register that it's Einar who is holding me. I must say his name aloud, because a hushed prayer of thanks escapes his lips as he pulls me closer.

Even with the relative warmth emitting from the king and Khijhana's fur on the other side of me, I am racked with violent shivers. Einar manages to keep a hold on me, though, gripping me almost too tightly as he clambers to his feet.

"I need to get you to the caves," he says, and I'm not sure if he's explaining where we are going or asking for my permission, but I can't seem to make my eyes stay open or stop shivering long enough to nod.

I slip in and out of consciousness, cognizant of nothing but the jolting motions of my own tremors and the king's rocky trek through the snow. Khijhana lets out a noise between a whine and a meow, and it sounds far away.

I fade again, the world going black around me.

When I come to, the smell of damp earth fills my lungs and I'm lying on a stone floor.

My heart races, and I can practically hear the clinking of my chains and the screams of the prisoners in the other cells. Breathing is difficult, and I gasp and scramble until my fingers find something soft. Something that shouldn't be in the dungeons of Villa Paradís...

Khijhana?

I force my eyes open to see the chalyx pressed against me on a rock-hard floor. She doesn't seem to mind that my fingers are tangled in her silver fur.

Taking a steadying breath, I focus on the world around me, confident that I am not in Madame's dungeons. My muddled thoughts puzzle through the last thing I remember, and I come up short again.

I should be dead.

But instead, I am staring at the ceiling of a cave. I force my weary gaze to the right. Khijhana is nestled against me, blocking a significant portion of my view, but I can see the far edges of the cave walls and notice that they are bathed in a greenish glow.

Rather than flicker like firelight would, this light seems to shimmer and swirl on the walls, though that could just be the way my eyes still jump around from the jarring motion of my shivers.

The room smells like damp rock, like the stones near the beach by the château, only not as salty.

Vaguely, I register that it is warmer in here than it should be, warmer than I would think the shelter of the cave accounts for. Not that it matters, because the heat isn't penetrating my skin. I still feel like I am freezing from the inside out.

With some effort, I turn my head to the left side, and what I see makes me wonder if I have woken up at all, or if I am merely dreaming this entire bizarre scene.

The king is frantically stripping his clothes off, laying some of them out on the floor and putting others in a pile nearby. Again, I think how this cannot be real, because no one is sculpted as perfectly as he appears to be. Each chiseled muscle is accentuated by the shadows in the hazy green light, lending him an ethereal quality.

"What?" I breathe the word out through my chattering teeth.

He turns to face me wearing nothing but his silver chain, and I focus my eyes on the key dangling from the end, the way the light glints off of it, rather than his taut body.

Some distant part of my brain is absurdly grateful that my blood refuses to flow well enough to flood my cheeks. There is no trace of embarrassment on his features, though, only determination with the barest edge of fear around his eyes.

"We need to get you warm." He says it like it's an explanation, like somehow his nudity correlates to my warmth, and the whole exchange lends itself to the unreal quality of this moment.

But the sharp pain, like a thousand needles stabbing me all over my body, manages to permeate even through the numbness brought on by the cold, convincing me of how very real this is.

My eyes close again, and when they open, he is kneeling next to me. His hands go to the hem of my shirt.

"No." The word comes out weakly, but he stops and meets my eyes.

"Zaina, you have hypothermia. Your body is freezing, and if we can't get it warm, you will die. It is warmer in here than it is outside, but that will not be enough to save you." He says the words bluntly, firmly, and whether that's a compliment to the fact that he thinks I can handle it or he is trying to scare me, I'm not sure.

And I don't have the energy to explain to him how it seems that death is constantly courting me, seducing me, and pulling me under with its quiet promises of peace in a world where all I seem to know is pain.

"Zaina!" His tone is urgent, and I realize I have drifted off a little.

"Please," he says in a softer tone, and I think it might be the first time he has ever said that word to me.

Why is he saying it now?

He pulls urgently at my shirt, and I remember.

"Go ahead." I grant him my permission, telling myself that it's only because it's easier than arguing with him, that I know he will do this regardless, and not because a part of me wants to stay here in this moment with him, in this world with him.

He makes quick work of removing my clothing, and there is nothing sensual about it. His gaze rarely leaves mine, and if he has to glance down quickly to find a button or clasp, his eyes move right back to my face.

I don't know what to make of that, because I have not seen this side of a man before, but it feels like, for all I have accused him of not respecting my privacy or my wishes, perhaps in this moment he has lent me more respect than any single male who has come into my life since I was six years old.

Images assault me, like a portrait flashing before my eyes in between each violent rock of my body. A hand that lingers too long on my arm, another man's voice sounding in my hair, whispering crass and obscene things while his breath is too hot, too moist, and too close to me. Rough hands shoving me against the wall while a much larger body presses against mine. My sister's katana at the man's throat.

That last image almost makes me smile, and I feel my head loll.

"Stay with me." Einar's voice is less controlled than I have ever heard it, and it almost strikes me as funny, because I couldn't go anywhere now if I tried, but I can't stay with him, either. Not really.

All of these thoughts flit around my head like the wraiths my mother used to talk about, my real mother, the one I never allow myself to think about and will never see again. The one who probably doesn't even know that I'm still alive.

Or was, anyway.

"Please." He says that word again, startling me from my reverie, and I feel his arms come around me.

He lays me gently on the cloak he has spread out on the floor. He presses himself against me, his skin against my skin, and takes the clothes he has piled next to us. He puts something over our feet and another under our head, then pulls the cloak as tightly around us as he can, cocooning us inside.

So many times, I have noticed the way he seems to emanate heat from within, and that was through the fabric of his clothes. With his bare skin next to mine, he is a solid source of warmth, searing its way into my skin and chasing away the ice that has settled down into my bones.

Khijhana's weight settles in behind me, and I allow myself to surrender consciousness again at last.

CHAPTER 41

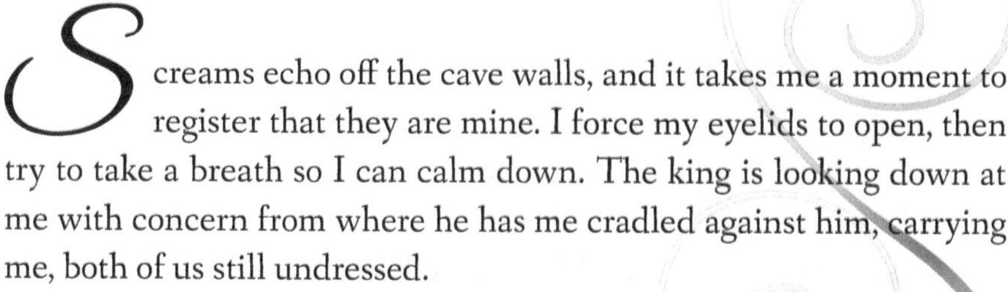

Screams echo off the cave walls, and it takes me a moment to register that they are mine. I force my eyelids to open, then try to take a breath so I can calm down. The king is looking down at me with concern from where he has me cradled against him, carrying me, both of us still undressed.

As soon as I am quiet, I am able to hear the other sounds around me, Khijhana's low growl and the king's murmured words of comfort.

I don't put the pieces together until I realized that my feet are wet.

Why are my feet wet?

Frantically, I look down only to realize that the king is standing hip-deep in a shimmering pool of water.

No, no, no.

I open my mouth to scream again, but I'm startled into silence by Khijhana's snarl and Einar's hiss of pain.

"Zaina, I need you to calm down before your chalyx gives me more than a warning bite," he says softly, fixing me with his pale blue gaze.

"No," is all I get out through my trembling lips.

What I want to say is, *No, I will not calm down. No, I will not go in this water*. Or any water, ever again. A pained expression flits across his face.

"You are warmer than you were before, but you are still shivering. It is not enough, and we have no way home without going back out into the cold. This water is warm."

Steam rises from the glowing pool, so I'm sure he is telling the truth about that, but my answer doesn't change.

"Please," he says again. "These are supposed to be healing waters, and you *need* to heal."

"No." I shake my head rapidly. "Out," I order him.

His face is resigned, but he turns and sits me on the cave floor.

"Khijha," I call, and she comes exactly where I want her, between myself and the king, her large furry body covering mine from his view. I don't need to feel more vulnerable than I already do.

I burrow my face into her side, taking deep, ragged breaths, fighting against the shivers that threaten to consume me.

"Zaina." Einar says my name softly, once, then twice, before I finally lift my face to meet his eyes.

There is worry there, and fear as well. Emotions I had wondered if he was capable of, let alone would bother with for my sake.

"What?" I breathe out.

"I know you don't want to go back into the water, but please don't make me watch you die." For the first time, his mask slips completely away, and instead of seeing tiny fragments of the emotions he tries to hide, I am hit by the full force of his anguish.

And I want to tell him yes, but I can't.

"I can't," I say that last part out loud. "I feel better now," I tell him, and it's not quite a lie.

He squeezes his eyes shut for a prolonged blink, then leans in closer to me. Khijhana lets him. She stiffens and settles protectively on my lap, her body covering my torso. Even standing in the waist-high water, he looms over my seated form.

"You can't go back out there like this." He shakes his head. "I know you don't trust me. Truthfully, Zaina, I get the feeling that you don't trust anyone entirely, and also that you probably have good reasons for that."

His stare burns straight through me, and I feel naked in more ways than one.

"But I need you to believe that I would never let anything happen to you. I need you to know that I meant what I said on our wedding day when I promised to protect you. Don't make me go back on my word."

He holds my gaze steadily, waiting for me to respond, but I have no words. It doesn't seem to bother him, though. If anything, I wonder what my face reflects, because his eyes widen a fraction in what looks a lot like hope.

"Do you believe me?" he asks me in a strong voice.

I find myself nodding, a single, traitorous dip of my chin.

Slowly, he holds out a hand.

"Then, please."

I gently tap Khijhana to move, and she is off of me in one quick, graceful movement. I am bare before the king, but my nudity feels like the least of it. I slide closer to him, one tiny millimeter at a time until my feet are hovering just above the water.

He moves slowly, broadcasting each motion as he places a massive hand on either side of my waist. I let him pull me toward him, never breaking his gaze.

I don't look down.

I don't trust myself to stay calm once my toe hits the water. All I see are the shards of ice in his eyes, how they remind me of the icicles hanging from the roof of the castle and the branches in the forest around us, a combination of beauty and danger that resonates down to my core.

I am knee-deep in the water now, and he is right. Already, it is the warmest I have been since my fall. Then, he lifts me with no effort at all, pulling me in until I am inches from him and the water reaches my waist.

I make the mistake of glancing at the surface, and that's when the panic hits. I scramble back toward the ledge, sure the water is already back in my lungs.

I can't breathe.

My lungs are burning, and my chest is tight.

I can't breathe.

Distantly, I hear Khijhana let out a warning growl. The king's hands disappear from my waist, and, for a moment, I am furious, panicked, betrayed.

Didn't he say he wouldn't let anything happen to me?

Why is he letting me go?

Then, his arm comes around me, and he pulls me until I am flush against him, using his other hand to steer my face gently until it is turned toward his again.

"You're safe. I've got you."

My cheeks burn with shame, and I hate him for seeing me this way. More than that, I hate him, because he has made it impossible to hate him, and in doing so, has complicated my life in a way he will never understand.

He takes one of my arms and pulls it until my hand is around his neck, then does the same with the other. It should be awkward, the two of us standing naked in this pool and staring at one another while I have a series of panic attacks, but I can't seem to care.

My chest is pressed solidly against his, and I focus on matching his steady breaths and the even rhythm of his heartbeat. My body finally begins to thaw. Even the pain in my throat lessens.

It takes minutes or hours of him holding me, breathing with me, before the last vestiges of ice leave my veins. As the panic finally subsides, a different sort of thought comes creeping in, the kind that makes my heart want to race for entirely different reasons.

He has been more of a gentleman than I would have thought possible, but my own intentions don't feel nearly so pure with his rock-hard body flush with mine, our faces so close that our breaths are merging into a single puff of air.

I know I should get out of this pool, should remove myself from him rather than break the propriety he has worked so hard for.

But good decisions were never my strong suit.

My lips part, and I let him see the wanting in my eyes. His mouth drops open in surprise, his pupils widening, and just as I am debating whether or not to close that distance, he makes the decision for me.

He moves with an agonizing slowness until his lips press against mine, more gently than I would have expected from him before today. But there is nothing tenuous or cautious about it.

He is taking his time, like he is determined not to miss a single sensation as he explores my mouth with his. He lifts me up until I am seated on the edge of the smooth cave floor, and it seems impossible that I have all but forgotten we were in the water, but there is no space in my mind for anything but Einar.

He tastes the way sunshine feels against my bare skin. He's sweet like spiced honey or warm mead on a winter's day. I could drink him down forever and never tire of the way his mouth feels against mine.

With my knees on either side of him, our faces are level for a change. I take his bottom lip in between my teeth, and his grip on my waist tightens. Awareness courses through every inch of my body, and there is no part of me that is even the slightest bit chilled anymore.

His lips skate from mine down the side of my neck and lower, his fingers roaming my body, leaving a trail of liquid fire in their wake. I tug on his biceps, and that's the only invitation he needs to come up out of the water.

He lays me back gently, his body over mine, and I am shocked by the force of my desire when I have spent my entire life avoiding situations like these.

"Are you sure?" he whispers against my lips, his blonde hair spilling down around his damnably handsome face.

"Yes." The word comes out as much of a plea as an affirmation, but I can't summon the energy to care, because there's nothing I want more in the world than to lose myself to him and this moment right now.

But as with everything else I have wanted in this world, it is not to be.

CHAPTER 42

Khijhana lets out a high-pitched sound and scrambles across the cave, startling us both. Einar pushes himself up, further away from me, already looking in her direction.

Before I can wonder what my chalyx is doing, a faraway voice reaches my ears.

"Your Majesty!" A panicked voice is calling for him, over and over again.

It's his guard.

"Gunnar," the king confirms. He squeezes his eyes shut, something between regret and aggravation passing across his features. I almost smile at the mirror of my own thoughts, but I am in too much shock from what I have almost done willingly, assaulted all at once by memories of the last time a man claimed that much and even more of me.

I shiver, a different sort of cold settling into my bones as the embers of my desire have morphed into something more like revulsion now.

I barely register when the king throws his cape around me to cover me, pulling on his own clothes and calling back out to the man.

He walks toward the mouth of the cave, Khijhana at his side, calling back and forth with Gunnar.

I wish I had something more than this cloak to cover me, but my own clothes are still damp, and I am in no hurry to revisit my hypothermia.

Einar walks back toward me, stopping a few feet away to pull on his boots.

"I'm going to meet him outside." He pauses, and I can sense that he's assessing me.

I nod, not quite meeting his gaze. He kneels down and cups my cheek in his enormous hand.

"Are you all right, Zaina?" His voice is quiet with concern.

"Yes. Just getting a bit cold again." And I do feel cold, just not in the way that he thinks.

I try for a smile, but it doesn't meet my eyes. I can tell he doesn't quite buy it, but he doesn't push me, either.

"Of course. I'll be right back." He presses his lips to my head before turning to leave.

I wrap his cloak tighter around myself and allow Khijha to comfort me as I test the feel of the water on my toes.

Forcing down the panic that comes, I remind myself of how different this pool was from the icy lake that tried to end me.

Images of people being lowered to their watery graves in cages intended to make them suffer as long as possible come to mind. I want to vomit, but I force myself to keep my foot in the warm spring anyway.

I need to do this.

The water is warm, and luminescent somehow. If I ignore my aversion, it is pretty. In a haunting sort of way. The sound of boots slapping against the cave floor startle me, and I jerk my foot out.

Khijha's ears flit and she cocks her head to the side in the opposite direction before she gets up and goes to inspect whatever is back there.

"Zola and Gideon found Gunnar," Einar says in a low tone. "And he followed my tracks here."

"Gideon is alright?" I interrupt him, realizing with everything that happened I hadn't even given my hestrinn a second thought.

"He's fine. Gunnar said they won't come any closer than the tree line, so he's going back to grab our satchels. I have a spare set of clothes in mine that we could make work for you, for now."

A pale imitation of a smile tugs at my lips, both at the image of me trying to make Einar's clothes fit and at relief for my hestrinn.

"Because we are so similar in size?" I glance up at him.

He gives me a tentative smile in return.

"I packed some spares as well, though," I tell him.

"Perfect."

We sit there in silence, both unsure of what else to say to the other. In the wake of what happened between us, any conversation feels strained and awkward now.

When Gunnar approaches with our things, I'm relieved for the chance to do anything other than think.

Einar blocks my body from view while he speaks with Gunnar, even though I'm wrapped in his cloak. The sounds of their voices fade as it strikes me that his clothes aren't frozen icicles as mine are, a fact I should've noted earlier.

We hadn't discussed what happened or how he found me, but this whole time, I had thought he was the one who pulled me from the lake.

I run fingers over the small cuts in my shoulder where some of the most searing pain had been felt. Two puncture wounds are on one side of my collarbone, and two matching ones are on the other.

The sound of Khijha's purring drifts from around the corner of the cave. Immediately, I remember the four gleaming metallic canines that she possesses, and I'm awestruck, if not confused. I rub my fingers over the puncture wounds, shaking my head in disbelief.

They are smaller than they should be, and already scabbing over. *Maybe the springs really are healing.* It would hardly be the strangest thing I've seen in Jokith.

Einar has dug my clothes out of my satchel, and he hands them to me as he and Gunnar turn away to give me a modicum of privacy to dress.

My body has been on enough display for one day, so I decide to take it a step further and travel around the corner where I know my chalyx is waiting. It doesn't take me long to don the new trousers, tunic, and boots. Then, I wrangle my tangled hair into a braid.

Despite hearing Khijha's purrs, she isn't in this corridor. I follow her sound further down and tentatively turn the corner, my path lit by the strange glowing water of the hot springs, when a warm gust of air comes wafting toward me.

Even more curious how a breeze made its way this far into the caves, I continue on. The purrs are growing louder as I turn another corner, and I am about to open my mouth to call for my chalyx when I come face to face with a different mythical creature.

It's the dragon.

Chapter 43

I gasp and skitter back to the wall, pressing myself flush against the rock, as if that will somehow prevent the creature from seeing me.

Khijha looks up in curiosity before she goes back to rubbing her nose and whiskers against the dragon's scales. I open my mouth to beckon her away, but no sound comes out.

I thought I knew fear — I'd faced my worst one when I was drowning — but this is something else entirely.

The dragon's eyes are closed and, each time it exhales, glowing embers alight in its nostrils and a gust of thermal air comes wafting toward me. It smells like campfire and is oddly soothing for a creature purported to eat the impure.

I shudder, but Khijhana continues to cuddle close to the giant beast while it remains asleep and blissfully unaware of our presence.

This close, it's the size of two houses stacked atop one another.

Its pearly-white and silver scales glisten like starlight, *like the moonstone in my wedding ring,* while its massive wings cradle its body almost like a blanket. I cannot deny its beauty, but I also cannot deny the way my mouth has gone dry or the rapid rise and fall of my chest. Or, the strange longing I have to reach out and touch it but run away at the same time.

I hear footsteps nearby and barely turn in time to clasp my hand over Einar's mouth before he speaks and wakes our inevitable doom. His eyes are wide, and his body is tense as he follows my gaze to the firedrake behind me.

When he nods in understanding, I remove my hand from his mouth. Khijha glances back at us, and I silently urge her to come to me. She tilts her head in confusion, then looks back to the dragon like she doesn't want to leave, but she eventually follows me as Einar and I tiptoe away.

When we make it back to Gunnar, Einar's voice is far quieter than it had been before as he insists we be on our way.

I'm still in shock, speechless, and terrified, but I don't miss how he neglects to mention the dragon. The king has always been a man of few words, but I sense that it's more than that. The glance he shoots me confirms it.

He is protecting it. And he doesn't have to tell me why.

Whether Gunnar is trustworthy or not, there are always people out there who are willing to pay for information, who are willing to hurt the innocent for what they can get out of it, and I can only imagine what someone might pay for something so exotic. Or its parts.

Besides, it's only fitting. I think about what I have seen in Jokith thus far — the massive wolves and the giant horses and my rapidly growing kitten — and I can only imagine what manner of beasts lurking in the forest and the mountains, any one of which might have wandered into a cave to seek heat.

Yet, we were unbothered last night. Unintentionally or not, the dragon had protected us, too.

I understand better now why Gideon had thrown me, why he wouldn't come any closer. He had sensed the dragon. I certainly couldn't hold that against him. A shiver runs through me as I think of the massive dragon.

I press my face into his enormous neck, letting him nuzzle me in return before mounting him again. This time, when Einar lifts me up, it doesn't elicit the same feelings as before. His touch is gentler, more tenuous, as he helps me right myself on the saddle.

All the while, I can feel his eyes on me, but he hasn't said a word since we left. I grab one of the snacks I had packed from Gideon's saddlebags, and the king does the same. I am not hungry, not really, but I know that I need to eat even more after everything that happened last night.

And this morning.

When Gunnar rides ahead and Einar still says nothing, I finally break the silence for a change.

"You were right, before."

He looks sharply at me.

"About the language. I knew Jokithan before."

"Then why lie about it?" His face is closed off, but not as angry as I expected.

"When you refused to let anyone accompany me, I was...concerned. Curious, even." I meet his eyes to let him see the truth in mine. "I wasn't sure how much you would be willing to share, and I didn't want to be kept in the dark."

None of that is a lie. In fact, it's a perfectly accurate accounting of what did happen.

He nods, accepting what I tell him.

"You were right, also. I'm not used to sharing my load with another person. When I didn't want you to come --" he begins, but I cut him off.

"Please, don't explain. I see now that it was valid, you not wanting to be slowed down." I look at Gideon's saddle, at Khijhana, anywhere but the king, while the truth comes crashing in like the frigid waters of the lake last night.

Sigrid is sick, probably getting worse, and I have delayed her help by several precious hours. I have no doubt that Einar would have ridden through the night to get back to her, something I can still barely wrap my head around. A king who cares so deeply for a servant. But then, the mistress of my household never cared for anyone at all, so it's hardly as though the servants were unique.

"What happened last night was not your fault." His eyes are wide with disbelief, as though he can't believe I would think such a thing.

But he's wrong in so many ways.

"If I hadn't come, Gideon would not have been here. Let alone the obvious fact that I'm the one who fell in the lake. I'm the reason you lost time. You told me not to come." Even in spite of everything that's happened, I still have to grit that part out between my clenched teeth. "And I did anyway, and now Sigrid might pay the price."

Is this the cycle of my life? An innocent person paying for my disobedience in an endless continuum of death?

He studies me a moment before responding.

"My people have been ill for a long time, and it was only happenstance that you were here before Sigrid got as bad as she did. Besides," he tilts a corner of his mouth up with considerable effort, "you could hardly have known there would be a dragon interrupting our journey."

I take the out he has given me, because the other does not even bear thinking about right now. What's done is done, and I will pile it on the list of my substantial sins back in the darkest parts of my mind where it can keep the rest of my mistakes company.

"Why do you think it didn't attack us?" I remember what he said about the dragon sparing people who are pure of heart, but even if I did believe in fairytales, no description has ever been less apt for me.

He answers without missing a beat, as though we hadn't just been talking about someone dying who he clearly cares for. Perhaps I am not the only one in need of a distraction.

"I've been thinking about that," he says. "The dragon was sleeping, and in the old legends, the people would only seek it out under an old moon. Maybe there's some truth to that. Maybe that's the only time it's awake?"

I shrug, because that sounds implausible, but I don't have a better explanation. Before I can come up with another topic of conversation to fill the empty chasm that seems to be stretching between us, we round a corner and a sprawling mansion comes into view.

"So your ambassador has been, what, travelling the world to look for a cure?" I ask as we draw nearer.

Einar scrunches his face in confusion, then understanding dawns on his face.

"I suppose I didn't mention the important part. He is more than my ambassador. He's also an alchemist."

I mull that over for a second.

"Is he the one who chose me?" The words are barely audible.

"He is," Einar confirms.

"And you still trust him?" I try to say the words as a joke, but they come out as sharply as I had thought them.

Einar shoots me a cautious grin.

"He could have chosen worse."

I return his smile, but mine is weak in comparison. Because now I know, beyond a shadow of a doubt, that the man we're going to see is a traitor.

CHAPTER 44

Shimmering black stones makes up the base of the house, sparkling like tourmaline, stones that shouldn't even be used in this manner. There was no expense spared for the architecture of this place. The stones lead to wide windows that stretch around the expanse of the building.

The main door is a large, ornate thing with metal details that form arcs and whorls nailed into the spruce egress.

"A bit over the top," Einar tells me in an undertone.

"Says the king of a castle," I tease, and he smiles.

It takes a moment before I can tear my gaze from his lips, which only makes his grin widen.

I'm not really surprised at his excess, so like Madame's. For an ambassador, maybe, but alchemists can name their prices. That level of understanding of the properties of each everyday thing which surrounds us is rare and valuable, so, of course, he would live in a place like this.

"I can't say much for the man personally, but he has worked with my family for generations," he adds as we make our way toward the elaborate staircase.

It doesn't escape my notice that he's offering up information I didn't ask for, and I look at him askance.

"I suppose a king explaining himself on occasion isn't the worst thing in the world." His expression gives nothing away, even as he uses the words I hurled at him only yesterday.

"I suppose not." I give him the barest hint of a smile.

In spite of the snow falling around us, the flurries melt on each of the steps as soon as they land. Heat radiates from each one, preventing any ice from forming that could cause us to slip.

It's probably impressive for most people, to see things such as this. But considering my history with alchemists, the showy display only nauseates me.

Khijha takes tentative steps in front of us, her tail twitching and her ears perked on high alert.

Einar gestures with a hand for me to precede him to the front door, but he doesn't hold out his arm or his elbow, and I realize how he has hesitated to touch me since the cave aside from his cursory assistance in mounting and dismounting Gideon.

I witnessed plenty of displays of affection at the festival, so I doubt it has anything to do with Gunnar's presence. The king is an enigma, but not one I have time to contemplate right now.

He knocks on the frame, and a voice calls for us to enter. As soon as we open the door, I can see that the man is not Jokithan. His back is to us as he muddles something in a wooden bowl. His hair is a mousy shade of brown; it's sparse and balding atop his menial frame unlike any I have seen here.

The hands at work are several shades darker than Einar's, but not as dark as even mine, let alone the other Jokithans. It must be something in his alchemy that has kept him alive this long.

But where he comes from is the least of the surprises the alchemist has in store for me. When he turns around, I take a step back. Shock stills my movements and steals my breath.

Khijha steps between us, a low growl coming from her chest.

I always knew that there was a chance I would see him again, but

I assumed it would be on an errand for Madame. I wouldn't have even put it past her to invite him to the château.

I am utterly unprepared for the sight of him before me now.

A thousand images flash through my mind, each more haunting than the last. I have had nearly a decade to train my mind not to go back to that night, but his unexpected presence here threatens to slither through my defenses.

I force myself to look anywhere in the room besides his small round spectacles and my reflection in them, so different than it was then. But he hasn't changed at all.

I can practically feel his hot breath on my neck, and I want to vomit. My gaze lands on the king, who is already looking at me with some concern. Fighting for composure, I focus on him and think of our conversation on the way in.

I can't say much for the man personally, but he has served my family for generations.

The king trusts this man against his better judgment, and I know it is a mistake, just as I know I have no way of telling him that without damning us all. Khijha's body ripples, and I swear she grows another several inches as her lips curl back to display her metallic fangs.

I put a hand on her head, shushing her while my mind goes back in time.

Aika is maturing quickly. Each day she grows nearer to womanhood, my panic grows. I know that I cannot protect her any more than I could protect myself, any more than I protected Rose, but I have to try. I go to Madame's sitting room -- Mother, I correct myself. She refuses to be called anything else by us. Her 'daughters'.

"Zaina, this is Dvain, Jokith's most renowned alchemist." Einar gestures toward the man, but his words sound far away.

Her sitting room is set up more like a throne room from where she holds court for all those who dare to win her favor.

"Whatever price you will fetch for her, I will get it for you another way." I keep my tone neutral as I approach, though sheer panic bubbles at the surface of my façade.

"You had such potential. It's a shame you turned out to be such a stupid girl." Mother shakes her head. "And such a drama queen, at that. What I barter for your sister will be worth more than money. And honestly, it's one night. Why must you make such an issue out of every little thing?"

I am stunned into silence for a fraction of a second before fury rears its ugly head, edging out the fear I can never seem to move past with this woman.

"Little thing?" The words are barely a whisper.

Madame notices the tiniest shift in a person's emotions, and my anger is no small thing right now. She fixes me with a brutal stare that dares me to go on, and I belatedly tried to collect myself, but I can't seem to stop the words from pouring forth.

"My Lady." Dvain steps forward, a grin stretching over his vulgar mouth. "What a pleasure to meet you in person. I've read so much about you from your aunt's letters, it feels like I know you already."

"What did you get in exchange for me?" I had only ever dared ask that question one time, and she had been vague.

But this time, she smiles, like the memory makes her happy even now.

"For you, my dear, insolent, wretched girl, I received something no amount of money could buy. Loyalty."

I had never truly understood what Madame meant that day, and she had refused to explain any more. But I think of how it has taken one of the world's most renowned alchemists seventeen years to find a cure for a poison he has access to the source of.

And whatever Einar is paying him, I know that money is no object for this vile creature, nor much of a motivator. No, he takes his rewards in an entirely different fashion, one that the king I have come to know would die before offering him.

Dvain stretches out a hand for mine, and Khijha's jaw opens wider in a hiss. His beady eyes narrow ever so slightly, his mustache twitching under his sharp, long nose as he chuckles under his breath.

"Does it?" I force the words out, breathing as much calm into them as I can muster while placing a comforting hand on Khijhana instead. "Sorry for my cat. She's not too fond of strangers."

Einar shoots me a look, but I ignore it. I ignore everything and will myself to imagine scenes of the death I promised myself I would give this perverted monster. Instead of the way he'd robbed me of whatever innocence I'd had left. Instead of the way he cut into my flesh, one shallow, stinging slice after another.

He had taken everything from me that night, things I can never get back.

Dvain breaks his eye contact and turns back to Einar, patting him on the back in congratulations for the match.

I let out a shaky, silent breath when they are no longer looking at me.

What the hell do I do now?

CHAPTER 45

Einar leans over the small table with Dvain while Gunnar stands guard at the door. Every part of me wants to run or slit the man's throat, but that's not what I'm here for. Not yet.

I approach the men, standing at the opposite side of the table from them. They're examining several vials and notes and some of Dvain's personal journals.

"So, no more of the petals have fallen?" he asks, and Einar shakes his head.

I paste a look of polite confusion on my face to cover the torrent of emotions I am only barely controlling. Because seeing this man again, unexpectedly, is its own sort of hell. And then there are the petals.

"There are still two left. It should happen any day now, if the pattern holds." There is a sadness in his voice, and Dvain rests a placating hand on Einar's shoulder.

I force down my revulsion at the false kindness.

The king sighs.

"There are still the stem and thorn. It's not a method we've tried yet." But even he doesn't sound overly optimistic.

"We've been over this, Son." Dvain sighs. "The poison is far too potent there. You could die in the process. You could kill yourself and them if you're not careful. Alchemy is an exact science. Not magic. There are only facts in this case."

Einar nods, his eyes pinching tighter.

I feel my chalyx stiffen beneath my hand, her body rumbling from the perpetual low growling she's been doing since we got here.

It's more than her not liking him. It seems every time my feelings intensify, hers do as well, as if we're linked on a deeper level. If I'm not careful, she'll give away every single one of my thoughts, even if my carefully controlled expressions don't.

I focus back on the conversation at hand and desperately try not to allow myself to feel anything. Good or bad.

"Besides, as you said, there are two petals left. That means we have two more chances at this. I am working with my contact in Socair to see if we can get our hands on another rose. We have time yet."

Einar's fists slam down on the table, making everyone in the room jolt from the sheer force.

"That is the one thing we do not have." His voice is full of rage, sadness, and something else...defeat.

"I wish you would just allow me to test the flower myself. With the equipment I have --"

Einar cuts the man's words off with a shake of his head.

"I appreciate the offer, but the rose stays with me."

Dvain and Einar speak about several of the recent ingredients he has tried, and the one they settle on having the most promise is the 'hydrolysate extract'. The alchemist hands a large vial of the sparkling blue-green liquid over to the king before we turn to leave.

Which isn't soon enough for me. Every second we spend in the man's presence makes me feel like I have another layer of grime on my body that I'll never be able to wash off.

We take an alternate route home so as to not pass by the dragon's cave again. Einar says that it adds an hour onto our journey, but I am too distracted by my thoughts to notice. Besides, it is still so much shorter than the journey here was.

We ride the hestrinn as fast as we are safely able, which leaves little room for conversation.

It's just as well. I can hardly form coherent thoughts in the wake of everything I have discovered in the past two days. More than once, I shudder at the memory of the vile man's bespectacled face, prompting Einar to ask me again if I am cold.

I assure him I am fine, but I am certain he sees it for the lie that it is.

All the broken pieces of my life are converging in the worst possible ways, swirling around me like one of the deadly sandstorms I remember from my childhood, and I am standing in the middle, as I did then, powerless to stop it all.

I am anything but fine.

"I'm surprised your ambassador is not Jokithan," I finally manage when we stop to water the hestrinn.

"He practically is. My grandfather gave him citizenship for *services rendered*, and that was several hundred years ago."

My jaw drops. Several hundred years of terrorizing innocent victims. Einar notes my surprise.

"The average Jokithan doesn't live nearly that long, but I imagine he has concocted some sort of fountain of youth for himself."

I think of Madame, the way she hasn't aged even as much as Einar has when she has undoubtedly been alive longer, and I nod my agreement.

"But he's here," I muse aloud. "Not in whichever country he is an ambassador to."

"That was only luck on our part," the king responds. "He comes back every few months."

Luck. Madame's scheming, more likely. For someone so brilliant, Einar can be so incredibly naïve sometimes.

I want to tell him the truth, or at least that he can't trust the disgusting little man. But...the alchemist is in contact with Madame, and he will be on alert now for any sign that I have betrayed her.

If I tell Einar, and he acts on it — which he surely would — my sisters will be punished. Probably even killed.

If I don't tell him, Sigrid might die. And not only her, but his entire castle.

I think back to what my Madame had told me. The alchemist doesn't work for her as much as they make deals together. He could be genuinely working toward a cure in exchange for his opulent life here.

It's a slim chance, but more of one than my sisters will have if Madame takes out her wrath on them.

There are no good choices here.

Einar sets me back on my saddle, but his touch is markedly gentler this time, and it breaks something inside of me. I am silent again for the rest of the journey.

When we arrive back at the castle, we leave the hestrinn for the stable hands to care for and head straight inside. I do my best to acknowledge Sarah Agnes as she takes Gideon's reins, but I don't have the energy to pretend right now.

I hold my breath, scrambling to keep up with Einar's longer strides, though I understand his urgency. Guards push open the enormous doors, and a figure is hurrying down the stairs as fast as his uneven gait will allow.

It takes me a moment to place him as Leif, because he is not wearing his mask. He's nothing like I expected, though I should've known by now to expect nothing at all.

Leif's skin is green and yellow, like the deepest colors of a bruise. His eyes easily take up a third of his face, and large boils — no, warts — cover his cheeks and head.

When he opens his mouth to speak, it widens a hair too far, revealing a clear lack of teeth.

"Your Majesty," he croaks and begins to bow, but Einar waves it off as unnecessary.

"Please, how is she?" the king asks.

"She is stable, but she is not well." Grief emanates from him in a cloud that soon consumes me as well.

"The alchemist has given me another solution. I should be able to try it any day now," the king tells him.

I look sharply to Einar.

"Why would you wait?" I have to believe that there is some hope in the solution the alchemist gave us, as much as it is difficult to attribute anything good to that man.

But surely, he wouldn't go so far as to kill an entire castle full of people he's known for generations...

Leif's gaze travels between us, understanding and maybe even a trace of satisfaction in his features. Einar, for his part, studies me a moment before answering, and I wonder what it cost him to be open or honest about something he has fought so hard to conceal from me. From everyone.

"It's not that simple. We have to wait until the petal falls on its own," he explains. "Or we risk killing our only source for an antidote."

He says that like it should make sense to me, but it doesn't.

"And you risk killing Sigrid if you don't," I say quietly, in case there is a chance he has missed the obvious.

"Don't you think that I know that?" he growls.

"I hoped that you didn't know that rather than that you knew and just didn't care," I bite back.

There is no part of me that comprehends why he is willing to let her die when there's something he can do to save her.

"Of *course* I care, Zaina." He steps closer to me, staring down at me with a mixture of hurt and disbelief.

I almost feel guilty before I remember one of the few decent people I have ever met is upstairs painfully dying, and he is just going to sit by while it happens on the off chance that something bad will happen if he doesn't.

"You don't understand," he grits through his teeth. "I have a castle full of people depending on that, depending on me."

"You're right. I don't." Because I would burn the rest of the world down for the people I love.

I practically have. I probably will, by the time this is all over.

"And that is why I declined to make a stranger a queen. There is more to ruling than putting on a crown and ordering people around!" His jaw is clenched, and his pale blue eyes are burning like the hottest part of the fire.

A beat of silence passes before Leif cuts in smoothly.

"If I may, Your Majesty, she has been asking to see you."

"Of course." He takes off toward the stairs without so much as a backward glance

I briefly debate following him, but she hadn't asked for me. I'm just a girl she has known a handful of weeks who was fortunate enough to be the recipient of her kindness, and I won't intrude on this moment.

I can't quite bear the thought of heading back to my rooms alone, knowing she will not be there to welcome me as she has each time I have come back here, something I have taken for granted. So instead, Khijhana and I head up to the study.

I pass more servants than usual today, but I'm surprised by how many of them are still wearing veils or masks.

I am seated at my favorite sofa, the one closest to the fire but facing the window, away from the door, when Khijhana abruptly stands up from where she was already seated between me and the entryway. A split second later, I hear a set of footsteps gliding across the floor toward me.

I sigh. Odger is the last person I am in the mood for.

"To what do I owe the pleasure of your spontaneous visit?" I try to keep the sarcasm from my tone.

I am expecting Odger's oily tone, but the voice that answers freezes my bones to ice as surely as the lake had.

"Come now, Zaina. Is that any way to speak to your brother?"

CHAPTER 46

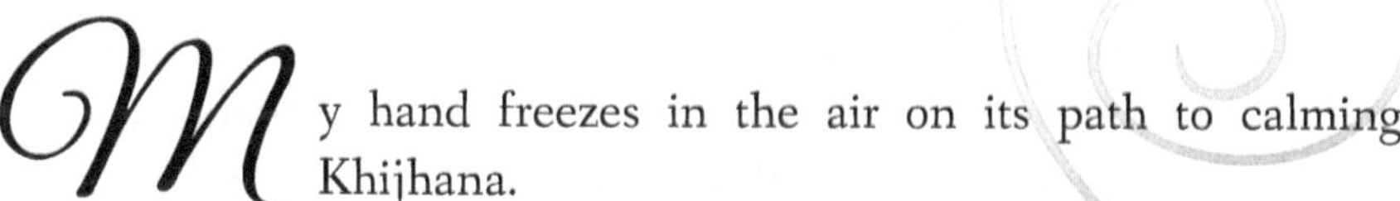

My hand freezes in the air on its path to calming Khijhana.

"What are you doing here, Damian?" How I manage the words when I am not even breathing is a mystery to me.

I knew that I was running out of time, but his presence here means it is already up. That's the only reason Madame would let him risk coming to me directly.

And he does nothing without her approval.

"I figured you would be expecting me after you saw me at the festival," he says.

I still haven't turned around to see his face, but his voice is all false pleasantries.

"If I didn't know any better, I would think you weren't happy to see your favorite brother." Bile rises in my throat as it does every time he bastardizes that term for his own use.

I may claim the other girls Madame owns as my sisters, but I do that by choice because they are as trapped as I am.

Damian, though, he lives for this.

He moves toward me, and Khijhana growls. "Control your beast, or I will do it for you."

In the decade I have known him, he has never sounded anything but collected. Whether he is taking someone's life while they beg for mercy or asking how you like your tea, his tone is the same. So, although his voice is calm, I know that he means it.

I take a deep breath, forcing a calm I don't feel while I reach out to comfort Khijhana.

"Good girl," he directs the words at me, not the actual animal in the room, but I am just as happy if he never acknowledges her presence again.

Growing up with Madame, there are few people in this world who scare me, but I would be a fool not to be cautious around the boy she collected only shortly after she found me.

Whether he was born this way or shaped by circumstance and molded by his dear adopted mommy, the fact remains that he is ruthless and deadly and entirely without remorse.

They are two sadistic peas in a pod, except that while Madame has a purpose for everything that she does, whether it is to further her own power or exact revenge, Damian inflicts pain for the fun of it.

He sidles up next to me on the couch, each point of contact a distinct pinpoint of revulsion. His cruel, flawless features are covered with a beaked mask identified by a small lightning bolt, one I have noticed in passing at dinners.

As much as I would like to believe he stole it or had it replicated, I am sure I can guess what he has done with its original owner.

"Dare I ask how many people you had to kill to get in here? Surely you know that will raise suspicions." A lifetime of practice ensures that I ask this question with little more than irritation in my tone.

He studies me, as though he can sense whatever shred of a conscience I have left, and his posture relaxes a bit.

"You know that I would never be that sloppy." He refuses to answer the part I care most about.

Instead, he takes one of my hands in his. I am absurdly grateful for the thin stretch of leather keeping his actual skin away from mine, but it's still an effort not to yank my hand back. I fight to keep my breathing even, to stay calm so that Khijhana will as well.

He brings his other hand around and places it on top of mine. To anyone else, it would look like an affectionate greeting, but I feel something jagged press against my palm.

It's a short-stemmed rose with a single thorn, to replace the one I am supposed to steal. It feels so much heavier than the sum of its parts, laden down with the weight of the betrayal it symbolizes.

I slip it into my cloak pocket before he speaks again.

"Switch them out and meet me outside with the original. I leave for the old man's house tonight." It isn't hard to guess who he's referring to, though Damian generally disdains anyone else Mother works with.

He means the alchemist.

My mind is racing for a way out of this, but every path seems to lead to the same inevitable destination.

"I haven't found it yet." I track each falling snowflake as they drift to the ground, or dissipate against the window, all the while lulling myself into a false sense of serenity. Whatever I do, I have to keep Khijhana focused on anything but the despair that sinks deep into my bones.

"I told Mother you weren't ready for this," he sneers. "Too busy letting the king warm your bed and the chambers of your fragile heart to do what needs to be done?" His words are barely above a whisper as his hand finds its way to my upper thigh.

"Don't be ridiculous," I snap back. "We both know I no longer have a heart, let alone a fragile one." Does he hear the lie for what it is?

I search the skies for answers, staring at the fading crescent moon before I speak again.

"It's a delicate project. I need another week, at least."

"I'm feeling generous, so I'll give you until tomorrow night." He reaches up, caressing my cheek. When I keep my gaze transfixed ahead, he jerks my chin toward him more forcefully.

"What do you say?" Condescension drips from his tone, and I want to slap him. Better yet, to push him backward into the fireplace and watch him burn. I wonder if his tone would be so calm then.

But there's no way Madame sent him here alone. She has a system, one man to keep an eye on another, and without knowing who the other person is, I can't risk upsetting her. Not unless I want my sisters to die, or worse.

So, I grit my teeth and say what he wants to hear.

"Thank you."

He doesn't move from his perfectly poised position with his hand on my face, doesn't huff, doesn't show any outward sign of impatience. He just sits next to me with an eerie stillness until I say the rest.

"Brother."

He looks me up and down with a gaze that is equal parts predatory and lustful, and I wonder if he fantasizes about the myriad of ways he might kill me as often as I dream of his untimely demise.

And maybe I'm as broken as Madame always wanted me to be, because a small, twisted part of me almost hopes that he does.

CHAPTER 47

I don't leave, even when Damian finally does. I remain seated on the elegant sofa, angling my body toward the dancing fire that has become so familiar to me.

I watch a thousand possibilities for my future play out in the flames and then dissipate into the smoke. In this rare, brief space, I acknowledge the life I might have had, something I have not done since my sister died and with her, whatever tiny part of me dared to dream of something different.

I let myself linger in this moment, in this fairytale world where I am just a girl who was reluctantly wed to a man who turned out to be so much more than she expected.

Then, taking a deep, fortifying breath, I bid farewell to all that might have been. I rise from the sofa, grim determination edging out every single unwanted, irrelevant emotion from a moment ago.

No matter how it sickens me, I have known what I had to do from the moment Damian appeared. Before that, if I'm being honest with myself.

The first step is finding Einar to give him the apology he needs to hear. I head to my rooms first, but they are empty. I almost smile, because I should have known Sigrid would insist on being moved again as soon as I wasn't here to stop her.

I remove my cloak and hang it on the stand but pull the false rose out of the pocket. It has a black stem at the base of four pointed red petals, and a single jagged thorn. Never having seen the original in person, I can only assume this one is a close enough match to pass for it. I don't think any servants will be coming in here, but I conceal it just in case.

I deliberate for a moment when I hear the footsteps of a familiar, confident stride. Not wanting to have this conversation in front of anyone else, even the guards, I take the passageway to his room instead of intercepting him in the hallway.

Khijhana follows, of course, as she always does.

The door opens to reveal the king looking twice as haggard as he had on the road. Surprise widens his eyes when he sees me, but not before I catch the grief in them.

He closes the door behind him, then walks over to a cupboard in the corner of his room without speaking. He doesn't question what I am doing here or order me out, which I take as a decent sign. Instead, he pulls down a decanter and two glasses, filling his own substantially higher than mine.

It shouldn't mean anything to me, that he has noticed what a moderately observant person would, but the way he has grown to know me tears at something inside of me that I am already barely managing to keep together.

I take the glass he offers, bringing it to my lips and taking a tiny burning sip before speaking at last.

"How is she?"

The king takes a much longer dreg before answering.

"She's stable, for now," he says simply, echoing Leif's assessment, but I can see what the words cost him, and it makes this next part easier for me.

"I'm sorry," I say, walking closer to him.

He nods, a mechanical response to a situation that has no words. I peer up into his endless blue eyes and make my meaning clearer.

"I'm sorry about Sigrid, and about what I said earlier. You were right."

He raises his eyebrows, likely because I've said something he never thought to hear from my lips twice in one day. I give him a half smile.

"Truly, though," I say, placing a hand on his arm. "You have to make the kind of choices no man ever should, and I... I have never had choices." I admit what I am sure he has already guessed.

But he surprises me with his answer.

"Everyone has choices, Zaina." He pierces me with his stare like he understands far more than I have ever intentionally let on. "There aren't always good choices, and sometimes all we can do is choose the lesser of two great and terrible evils." He takes another sip, backing away from our contact. "But still, there is a choice."

For a fraction of a second, I wonder if my cover is blown. If he knows, if he discovered Damian this very evening. I stand frozen, robbed of my breath, waiting for him to pass down the judgment I know how deeply I deserve.

But then, he lets out a slow sigh and abruptly changes the subject, setting his cup down.

"You didn't come to see her," he says, sinking down into his chair and reaching down to unlace his boots.

I am weirdly transfixed, watching him perform casual, everyday tasks in front of me like we are an ordinary husband and wife, so it takes me a moment to respond.

"She didn't ask for me." I tell him the truth, but as usual, not the entire truth.

And, as usual, he sees more than I mean him to. He looks up at me with more sympathy than I deserve.

"She would have been happy to see you."

"Tomorrow," I promise.

He picks his cup back up and drains his glass before setting it back down, but he doesn't refill it, something I appreciate about him. He traps me with a pondering gaze, one I return without quite understanding it.

"Stay," he says the word softly, somewhere between a plea and a command.

Either way, I am powerless to refuse him. I nod wordlessly, my gaze sliding unbidden to his massive bed.

"We are both exhausted. I only meant to sleep." His voice is cautious.

I haven't turned to face him, and I know that he has misread my anxieties entirely, but I don't correct them. Because as close as we came in the caves, I don't know if that's something I can give him, or something I can take from him when I know so much better than he does how our story will end.

There's no way I can sleep in my heavy furs, though. I debate for a moment going back to my room for my nightclothes, but he has shown me a rare moment of vulnerability. I am unwilling to burst this precarious bubble we've found ourselves in, to do anything that might change his mind.

Besides, he has seen me bare more than once already, lain next to my naked form, and has never made a comment about my scars.

All of those reasons make sense, but I am not a good enough liar to convince myself they are why I don't leave this room.

CHAPTER 48

My hands snake around to the buttons at the back of my shirt, and I hear a muttered curse. I turn to face him only to see that he is digging around in the drawer of an armoire. He holds a hand out behind him with some sort of garment in it.

"I said I was tired, Zaina, not a eunuch," he groans. "At least wear one of my shirts."

An unexpected laugh escapes my lips, because he has still not turned to face me. I have been forced to use my body as a distraction, a lure, a weapon. I never thought I would find myself feeling gratified by a man's reaction to it.

Still, I decide to show a little mercy on him and take the shirt he has offered. I finish disrobing and throw it over my head. It reaches to my knees, and the gap with the laces is nearly at my belly button. I am still drawing them in to tie them when he turns around.

His lips part, and he shakes his head.

"I'm not sure that's better." He rubs a hand over his face, letting out a low chuckle. "Just... Get under the covers."

It's freezing in here, so I am quick to oblige him. The furs on his bed aren't as heavy as those on mine, but they are still exponentially warmer than the air outside. Khijhana crawls up into his plush armchair as if she owns it, and he groans but doesn't tell her to move. It offers the tiniest fragment of relief, knowing that he will take care of her when I am gone.

I am providentially distracted from that line of thought when Einar reaches for the hem of his own shirt. He may have been a gentleman when the tables were turned, but I greedily soak in the sight of him, knowing what a limited time I have to admire the hard planes of his abdomen and the clearly defined V that leads into the soft trousers he decides against removing.

I force my eyes to travel upward, my gaze snagging on the small, unusual golden key that hangs from his silver chain, before finally lifting to meet his own amused eyes.

I smirk at him, and he sighs, looking skyward as though looking for assistance. Finally, he climbs into bed. He stays so close to the edge, I almost laugh again at the lengths to which he is going to behave. For my part, I'm somewhere between appreciating the gesture and being utterly baffled by it, but I also know that the last thing I need is something else coming in to complicate my feelings even more.

We stay like that for a moment, both lying on our backs and gazing up at the ceiling, neither of us anywhere near sleep from the sounds of his breathing, before he abruptly rolls over onto his side to face me.

He is still a solid couple of feet away, but I swear I can feel the heat emanating from him. He studies me, and I can see a question in his eyes.

I shuffle a bit closer, close enough to be within arm's reach, rolling over as well to face him.

"What are you thinking?" I whisper.

His behavior tonight has made me bolder than usual.

Instead of answering right away, he cautiously moves a hand toward my face. His fingers gently play along the chain that leads from my nose to my ear.

"I was wondering about this. It's unlike anything I've ever seen, even in pictures from the Eastern Lands." On the way to the alchemist's, he had been interrogating me, but I sense nothing but genuine interest from him this time.

"It's...a symbol of purity," I try to phrase it delicately. "Normally, it would be removed on the wedding night." I hedge, trying not to think of the way I stood naked before him and the way he'd refused me, trying not to think of every inch of his bare body pressed against mine in the caves. "But since ours didn't go exactly according to plan..." I can't help the small wry laugh that escapes my lips. "I suppose I have just gotten used to having it on. Besides, I assumed no one here would know the difference."

He matches my laugh with a chuckle of his own.

"Nothing about our wedding went exactly according to plan, though, did it?" He grins down at me. "It didn't help that you were late."

"I was not!" I say with some offense.

I am never late.

"You most definitely were." He raises his eyebrows. "Why did you think the thing was already in progress when you arrived?"

I think back to that day and how angry I had been that no one had given me even a moment to rest or freshen up.

"I just assumed you were a thoughtless ass." My tone is teasing, but we both know it's the truth.

I should have assumed Madame's hand in it, as it is in everything else, but I wasn't exactly in a mind frame to think critically that day.

"And I just assumed you were a selfish, spoiled heiress." He smiles to soften the blow, but I don't blame him, considering his side of the situation in hindsight.

He moves his hand from my face to my shoulder, running his fingers gently up and down my arm.

"Is that why you insisted I come alone?" It's something I've been wondering about. If he was willing to let one person into the castle, I wonder what harm a couple of servants or companions would have done.

But his hand stills.

“You’re freezing,” he comments, shifting to get out of bed.

I get the impression he’s buying himself time to respond, but I let it slide.

“A hazard of living here,” I comment wryly.

He pulls several thick furs from a chest at the foot of his bed, then walks around to spread them over me, tucking the ends around my feet.

My throat clogs at the unexpectedly tender gesture, something no one has done for me in at least fifteen years, but I manage to croak out a thank you.

He nods, then gets back into bed. Only when he is settled back in on his side of the bed does he finally answer my question.

"In hindsight, perhaps that was...overly rigid of me." He sounds uncomfortable again, and I realize he is on the verge of another apology. “There was so much going on here in the castle, so much at stake. My people were clamoring for me to find a wife, but it seemed imprudent to add anything else on top of that.”

His reactions at the wedding, his fierce anger, make more sense in the light of that revelation. The subject is clearly making him uncomfortable, though, so I settle on another one.

"You are one to talk about interesting jewelry. I haven't noticed any other men here wearing a chain." I reach my hand out toward his chest, grabbing hold of the small worn key on his chain.

With lightning-fast reflexes, his hand closes over mine. The motion is gentle, but the sentiment is clear. His grasp relaxes a bit around mine, an apology in his eyes.

"That is a longer story." He sighs, moving his hand away.

I let go of the chain and entwine my fingers with his.

"Then I suppose it's fortunate we have time."

Einar studies my face for something before his gaze travels to our linked hands and he takes a deep breath.

"You're not what I expected." His eyes flick back up to mine, a question lingering in them and something that looks like hope.

It's the second part that breaks me, but I can't let him see that.

"Oh? And what did you expect?"

"Nothing." He shakes his head. "It hardly matters now."

I nod back at the chain around his neck.

"Does it have to do with that?"

"It does."

I wait for him to continue, allowing the silence between us to grow until he's ready.

Visibly steeling himself, he removes his hand from mine and examines the key he always has on him.

"Seventeen years ago, I was engaged." He begins to weave a tale of intoxicating beauty and parties, exchanged letters, stolen kisses and laughter. And of how he truly believed himself to be in love, in spite of the fast and furious way he'd found it.

I listen intently. I know this story doesn't have a happy ending. Not only are they clearly not together now, but I recall the comments I overheard from the servants that day about "the other one."

"She came to Jokith to finalize our engagement, and it must've been the fact that she felt our alliance was so assured that she could allow herself to let her guard slip so much.

"Before, I had been so distracted by her beauty. By her wit and charm. But when she arrived, her disdain for my people was shocking. Her vanity and pride were overwhelming. And her cruelty..." He takes a steadying breath, his knuckles going white from his grip on the key.

My stomach churns. I'm getting a sick suspicion of who this woman was, *is,* and I hope against reason that it's one of the many things I've been wrong about lately.

"She slapped Sigrid." He pauses again. "She often abused or ridiculed the servants, forcing them to bend to whatever ridiculous whim she had. She had no respect for anyone she viewed to be beneath her."

My heart beats a furious rhythm, and heat rises to my cheeks. I don't have to feign anger on his behalf. I know there has to be more than one heartless woman in the world, but the coincidences are mounting. And if I'm right, I have had half a lifetime of watching Madame mistreat those she considers beneath her.

"She wanted to push the wedding up, but something was telling me not to. She was in such a hurry." A humorless laugh escapes his lips. "She wanted more than that."

Of course, she was. I do the math in my head. She was pregnant with Melodi, the only one of us who actually belongs to her. With that, I lose my last shred of doubt that the woman he was engaged to was Madame.

My anger mingles with an abrupt surge of jealousy. The man in front of me, the one who would never truly belong to me, had belonged to *her* for some period of time.

The realization shouldn't come as a surprise. Hadn't she always taken what she wanted? Hadn't she left nothing for my sisters or me that was untainted by her?

"She was desperate to climb into my bed. She threw herself at me at every turn. But something about it never felt right. It was never genuine or real with her."

My cheeks flush at the memory of our wedding night, but now for a wholly different set of reasons. No wonder he hated me. I hate myself for bearing any resemblance to Madame that night. Or ever.

"Anyway... one night, I went to confront her about it all, went to tell her we were through, but she must have already known. When I arrived at her chambers, she wasn't alone. Odger was with her."

"No." My eyes widen, and my mouth pops open in surprise.

Not because I would put it past her, but because it's so unlike Madame to be careless with her plans. *Unless it was part of her plan?* My head hurts from analyzing this.

"Yes. And I'm sure I don't need to explain the compromising position he had her in up against the wall."

I actually cringe. His disdain for the weasel makes so much more sense now.

"Were you terribly upset?" I ask, unreasonably afraid of his answer, and he shakes his head.

"Not in the way you would think. It stung, but I had already planned to break off our understanding. That she slept with Odger was just a slap in the face after the fact. But I never imagined that she would be so cruel..." He closes his eyes as he fidgets with the smooth key.

I try to put myself in his shoes, to somehow believe that the woman who now goes by Madame had a shred of kindness in her. That he could believe himself *in love* with her.

Was she softer then? Her very essence unmarred by every black and twisted thing that she would do in the years to come?

It's no use. It's impossible for me to imagine a version of that woman who is anything but a liar and a monster.

CHAPTER 49

I hate the turn this conversation has taken. I hate everything about Madame and the way she manages to slip her way into every last nook and cranny of my life, spreading her particular brand of devastation like wildfire.

But for all that I hate her, in this moment, I think I hate myself just a little bit more for asking him for this story.

"She poisoned them?" I phrase it like a question, although I already know the answer.

How better to punish the man who refused her advances, who refused to acknowledge her unearthly beauty, than to surround him with ugliness. There's only one thing I still don't understand.

"But she didn't poison you?"

He looks up at me with such fathomless remorse in his eyes that I am hit with a fresh wave of self-loathing for forcing him to relive the moment of his castle's downfall.

"Not for lack of trying," he mutters. "It was the day of the midwinter feast that I caught them. She told me she would leave quietly while everyone was preparing for that night. I thought she was protecting him. What Odger had done was punishable by death, but not without dragging her into it as well. I should have known she would never give up that easily."

He shakes his head, and I can tell he hasn't forgiven himself, even after all these years. Another thing we have in common, I suppose.

"For that matter, I should have seen how little she cared for anyone but herself. But I was so anxious to be finished with the whole affair, so I let her go.

"In the weeks she had spent here, we had dined every night in the hall together with my courtiers and staff, as was my father's custom, eating and drinking from the same table. She despised it, of course."

I can only imagine.

"She put it in the wine?" I guess.

"And the water," he adds. "But midwinter feast is the one time a year where I don't eat at the same time as my people, or before them. I wait until they are finished eating to get my own plate and drink. It's symbolic, putting their needs before mine."

He pauses, lost in the memory.

"To this day, I don't know if she knew that. If she was trying to punish me by inflicting something on my people that I was unable to protect them from, knowing how I feel about them.

"Or if it was an oversight, if it was only timing or a flair for the dramatic that made her choose that night and she was unaware that I would not be partaking." He lets out a huff of frustration.

I wish I could help, but truthfully, I'm not sure, either. Even if I was, I could hardly tell him without explaining my connection to her.

Madame had gleefully passed along stories of what a beast the king was, but she never offered any insights of her own, never indicating for a moment that she knew him personally. It's not surprising, since she hoards each of her precious secrets like a single drop of water in the center of an endless desert.

"In hindsight," he interrupts my thoughts. "I see that she must have been plotting it all along, at least as a back-up plan. She never could have gotten it together so quickly, otherwise. Part of me even wonders if she wanted me to find her with Odger, to blame myself for putting it in motion."

Another question I can't answer, though I wouldn't put it past her. The woman deceives as easily as she breathes. There is nothing solid I can tell him.

What's worse, though, is realizing how many more unanswered questions I will leave him with when I go.

He seems to have lost himself in his thoughts again. I speak to pull him out of his reverie.

"And this?" I ease my hand out of his and move it back toward his chest. This time, he allows it, though his gaze carefully follows the movement of my fingers.

"This," he says, entwining our fingers together around the key. "Is all the hope we have left."

I hadn't fallen asleep until well after the king, but I still wake before he does.

My subconscious has clearly indulged in every craving my conscious mind denies, fusing my body so closely against his that I can hardly tell where one of us begins and the other ends. I am warmer than I have been since I arrived in this place, maybe warmer than I have been since I was taken from home all those years ago.

I gently disentangle myself, yawning and stretching my limbs. I open my eyes to find Einar's appreciative gaze on me. I'm sure I don't mistake the hungry look I find there, but before either of us can act on it, my stomach growls with an entirely different sort of hunger.

I let out a small laugh, but he looks at me with concern.

"When was the last time you ate anything?"

I am so used to going without meals that I haven't honestly thought about it, but I'm not about to explain to him, so I just shrug.

"On the ride back yesterday?" I guess.

He frowns, and I try not to be disappointed when he rolls out of bed. He strides to the door, opening it a couple of inches to speak to whoever is on the other side. I catch the word breakfast before Khijhana interrupts him, putting her nose in the space and shoving the door open wide enough to allow for her frame.

I appreciate Einar's attempts at discretion, but they will certainly know I slept in here now. Though, why I should care when we are husband and wife is beyond me.

"She needs to go outside," I call quietly to the slightly bewildered-looking king. "Usually one of my guards does it," I offer.

He blinks a couple of times, and then nods and finishes his brief conversation before closing the door and coming back to me.

"I suppose I never thought about how she was taking care of her business," he says.

"Speaking of..." I trail off, padding toward the door to his privy.

He looks at me strangely, and for a moment, I wonder if he objects to my using his facility. Then I realize, I shouldn't know where it is. It is in the most obvious place, though, so I pretend not to notice his scrutiny and head in, shutting the door behind me.

I had only popped my head in for a moment when I was snooping through his rooms before, but now I can truly appreciate the opulence. Although there is a large bronze bathing tub, similar to the one in my chambers, there is also a curious section in the corner.

Stone covers the walls in a large rectangular area a few feet high, and a bronze faucet of some sort hangs from the ceiling.

"What is that in the corner of your bathing chamber?" I ask him when I come out.

"I'm not sure there is really a name for it. My father liked to design things, so he had the faucet installed for when he came in from a day of outside work. The water drips down from the top and gathers into a drain so that the dirt and grime don't sit in the tub."

That was all well and good, but there was something far more enticing to me about the structure than the cleanliness of it.

"And no water pools in it?" I reiterate hopefully.

"Right, it all goes right down the drain." He takes in my expression, and his lips draw into a slow smile. "Would you like to try it?"

My mouth goes dry, because I'm not sure if he is offering for me to use it or asking if I would like to try it with him, and I'm not at all sure that I trust myself to choose the right option if I am presented with both. He solves that problem for me, though.

"I'll get you some clothes from your room and wait for breakfast," he says, leaving and pulling the door mostly closed.

That's the right answer. I'm sure it is. Then why is there a tiny, ugly thing inside of me rearing its head...something that feels a lot like rejection?

CHAPTER 50

This is glorious. Einar explained it to me while he was turning it on, something about how the water travels through the same kind of rocks that were at the festival in layers so that it's warm coming out, but I was only half listening, because he still hadn't put a shirt on.

Steaming water cascades from the faucet, falling like one of the warm rain showers on the island. Einar has an array of soaps on a raised tray, so varied that I am almost amused. There is a bar that smells like citrus and has a grainy feel, and a lavender one so soft it is already losing its shape.

I wonder if someone else stocks these for him or if he specifically requests soaps in seven different scents at all times, but I take a moment to sniff each one before I decide on sandalwood. The one that reminds me of him.

I staunchly refuse to think about how today will end, about the fact that I have less than twelve hours left with the only person who has made me feel safe in sixteen years.

Instead, I focus on collecting little pieces of this place to take with me, to wherever I will go next. Einar's voice surprises me out of the line of thought.

"Shall I plan to serve your breakfast in here, or do you think you might be finished anytime soon?" There is laughter in his voice, despite the high-handed words.

"The former, thank you," I shoot back.

He chuckles, a deep, growling sound that I react to low in my abdomen.

"I'm not sure how to turn this off," I offer more seriously, though that is hardly the reason I'm still in here.

"That's all right. I was going to rinse off once you are finished."

I frown, although he can't see me. Last night, he was right. We were both tired. But I am beginning to wonder if he regrets what happened in the caves.

I know that I should, but I can't quite bring myself to.

With all the boldness of the ticking clock my life has become, I call out before he shuts the door.

"You could just rinse off now."

I can't see him, but the door freezes in its path. One beat of silence, and then another, an interminable stretch that makes me wish I could pluck the words back from the air and swallow them before they reach his ears.

The door eases shut, and I am certain my humiliation is complete. But then, I hear solid footsteps, the whisper of cloth sliding against skin, and then he is standing before me.

His gaze is fixed firmly on my face, and what was respectful before is beginning to feel insulting in the wake of the past couple of days.

I don't know how to put into words what I want to ask him, though, so I say nothing, only move aside to make space for him under the wide stream of water.

He steps under the cleansing rain, but carefully keeps a solid couple of inches of space between us. And I know I'm not imagining it, the way he is trying so hard not to touch me. I just can't figure out why.

I stare, transfixed by the rivulets of water rolling down his body, by the way he moves the cedar soap he chose in a circular motion across his chest. His eyes burn into mine, and I am so caught up in this moment that I find myself asking what I want to know in the bluntest way possible.

"Why won't you look at me?"

His eyes widen, and the soap falls to the floor.

"I am looking at you," he replies with a strained sort of calm.

Slowly, pointedly, I let my eyes roam from his tousled white-blonde locks down the muscled planes of his chest, all the way down his body before dragging them back up again. I raise my eyebrows.

His lips are parted, questions and lust vying for attention on his features. Then, his face hardens in resolve.

In a challenge.

It's the face he gets when we are playing chess, and every part of my body tightens, even before he lets his gaze drop. And though I am the one who initiated this, I suddenly feel very unsure, because I have spent the better part of a decade keeping a tight rein on my emotions. I am not used to feeling so out of control.

A frenzy of feelings runs wild through every inch of me. Desire and revulsion war with one another while I drink in all of him, soaking this image into my memory to save and hold on to, but nevertheless being terrified of wanting him. Of wanting *this*.

But that's what Einar does; he makes me want things I never thought I would.

His eyes linger on each inch of my skin like a caress. They travel down, and he doesn't stop or pay any extra attention to the stark white scars decorating my abdomen.

Which is just as well, because I don't want to pay any attention to them right now, either. By the time his eyes meet mine again, they are filled with a heat so intense, it is more like lightning. He leans down, his mouth hovering just above mine when he whispers.

"Because when I look at you like this, it's all I can do to keep my hands off of you."

I hold his stare, my chest going tight and every fragment of me burning with desire.

Then don't. For as bold as I thought I was feeling, I can't seem to voice the words aloud.

Slowly, he reaches toward me, and I have a moment of panic before I realize he's reaching around me to turn off the stream of water.

Einar steps out of the space and grabs a towel to wrap around my shoulders, pressing a kiss to my forehead as he does so. Somehow, the gesture makes me want him even more, even as I wish I could crawl into a hole and die.

After wringing out his hair, he grabs one for himself as well, quickly wiping down his muscled body before wrapping it around his waist. He gestures to where he has left my clothes on a vast counter before turning to leave.

I am unreasonably irritated by his thoughtfulness, by the way he seems to know my mind better than I do. Heart still racing, I take my time getting dressed.

By the time I emerge, I tell myself there will be no more encounters like this. I tell myself I don't care, that I never did.

I lie harder than I've ever lied before, and still, I don't believe it.

I study Einar over breakfast, and I sense his scrutiny in return, but neither of us speaks until we are both finished eating. We had gotten dressed in a charged silence, one with more questions than answers, questions neither of us had voiced aloud.

Khijhana is back, but she is curled up in his chair again, napping. There are no sounds aside from the scraping of his spoon against the bowl and the sharp crack of me breaking off another piece of my flat bread.

"I don't regret the caves," Einar says out of nowhere.

Sometimes, I feel like he really is reading my mind.

"You just aren't anxious to repeat them?" I don't look at him when I say that, because I don't want him to see whatever emotions are swirling in my eyes.

Besides, you don't care, I remind myself again. *And it soon won't matter, even if you do.*

But he reaches over and tilts my chin up until I am looking into his eyes.

"I am not anxious to do anything you are not entirely ready to do."

My lips part in surprise, both at his words and the sentiment that no man has ever expressed to me before.

"Perhaps I have misled you." I point to the chain on my face. "I know I said this was to symbolize purity, but I'm not -- I haven't been considered pure in some time." Nine years, to be exact.

"You don't have to explain yourself to me. I'm not concerned about your past."

I look at him for a long, drawn-out moment, long enough to think that life is even crueler than Madame for showing me a man like this and making sure he can never truly be mine.

"You never asked about the scars," I say quietly.

His expression doesn't change, not a single trace of consternation at my abrupt change of subject.

"And I never will. As I said, your past is your own, Zaina. You don't have to tell me anything you don't want to tell me." He says the words with such sincerity.

I want to tell him everything, give him every truth that's in me, but I know that isn't possible. So, I settle for this one.

"Someone gave them to me... on the same night he took something else from me."

I thought I had seen the king angry, but the rage that enters his gaze now is on another level entirely. I'm grateful. If it was sympathy, I'm not sure I could go on.

"I was thirteen." I don't know why I said that except that I know how he feels about choices, and I want him to understand how very few I had.

"I see," he bites out in an ominous tone. The words sound more like a death sentence than anything, and I wish I could tell him who was responsible to watch him carry it out.

When was the last time someone was furious for me rather than at me?

My sisters and I empathize with one another, but we hardly have the energy for the kind of righteous indignation the king shows now.

Khijhana growls, and I wonder if she is picking up on his emotions instead of mine for a change before I catch the telltale trembling of my fingers. Not with fear, but a singular, all-encompassing rage that always seems to thrum just below the surface.

"So, you see," I finish up, fiddling with the chain at my nose to hide my reaction. "I never should have worn this to begin with."

He blinks several times, the fury in his eyes warring with another emotion I can't quite put my finger on, and all at once, it is too much. I shake my head, sliding my hand across the table and reaching up to touch the chain around his neck.

"More importantly," I force my tone to be breezy. "You never did tell me what this was."

He stares at me for another moment, and I wonder if he will give me the out I am practically begging for. Finally, he nods.

"It would be easier to show you."

CHAPTER 51

Einar pulls back the tapestry on his wall, and I pretend to be surprised, as if I haven't already explored the room beyond it.

What piques my curiosity, however, is how once we are in the large study at the top of the stairs, he heads straight to the bookshelves lining the back wall. With his left hand, he runs his fingers over seven of the spines in a seemingly random order, quickly pulling on them but not removing them from the shelf. Then, with his right hand, he pulls an older copy of a book on the history and properties of Pennyroyal all the way out before replacing it again.

My brows furrow as I try to remember the books he touched and in which order when, suddenly, the entire wall vibrates. A doorway appears in the middle of the shelf next to him, completely disguised to the untrained eye.

Khijha's eyes widen, and she scrambles back a little. I can't help but be a little shocked as well. I am genuinely amazed as I follow him through the corridor into a hallway.

"Where are we going?" I ask as he removes a torch from the wall to light our way.

"The West Wing."

The way he says it sounds so final, and I'm taken aback a little.

The West Wing.

The one place I was refused entry and have been trying to get to since I arrived.

A million thoughts flit through my mind, and my heart races as it always does when I think of what awaits us there.

Instead of saying any of those things, though, I simply nod as he leads the way.

We're fairly silent as we walk the length of the hall, twisting and turning down each passage. It's nerve-wracking to have only my anxious thoughts to keep me company, but I'm not sure what to say. Everything that comes to mind, every question I want to ask, feels wrong.

So, I keep them to myself until we eventually come to a stop at a dead end.

Einar rests his torch on the hook next to us and runs a hand along the right side of the wall until his finger finds purchase in a nearly invisible crevasse. He pulls out another key and uses it to grapple with a small lock.

A red light filters in, revealing a rectangular frame.

Fascinating.

He pushes it open wider, and, suddenly, I know exactly where we are.

A rose-shaped mosaic lights the floor and walls around us, casting a haunting reminder of every reason I was sent here.

There are even more alchemist's tools in this room than in his private study. Beakers and metal frames, small candles, and mortar and pestles line the long table in the center of the room. Along with shelves holding hundreds of jars of ominous-looking substances.

Einar looks back at me with a sad smile.

"This is where I spend most of my free time," he says, finally breaking the tense silence between us. "This is where I've spent nearly two decades searching for a cure."

I marvel at that, at him, at how dedicated he is to his people, and at his endless amount of hope.

"Once I realized what had happened, I went to search her rooms." He doesn't need to clarify the *her*; I know too well who she is. "On her bed was this single, blood-red rose, along with a note telling me it was my only hope for a cure. After that, she disappeared. Even the substantial resources of a king couldn't find so much as a trace of her."

Madame can change her features on a whim. The resources of all the kings in the world couldn't find her if she didn't want to be found, but there's no point in telling him that now.

So I say nothing, because there are no words to express my fury or the overwhelming sadness that has crept its way into my bones at her callous calculations. Even sending me here, knowing he possessed a flower with a rare poison she required for reasons only she knew.

She knew he had it because she gave it to him. And now, she wanted to take it away. To ensure he didn't find a cure? To keep punishing him?

Or was this her plan all along. If she truly had meant to poison him the first time, perhaps she needed more of this to finish the job in a way no one would be suspicious of.

Your first task is simple. Marry the king and produce an heir.

I swallow back a fresh wave of revulsion. But really, what had I expected? How would she possibly control a kingdom still in the possession of a strong-minded king?

The second one might be trickier. I need you to steal something valuable. My sources say it is well hidden. You'll need to gain his trust, first.

I had been relieved when she had sketched it out. A flower. It seemed simple enough. But now...

The sound of Einar's footsteps forces me back to the present. He walks directly toward the stained-glass window I noticed when we first arrived and removes the chain around his neck. He inserts it in an ordinary looking pane in the window frame. I understand the basic mechanics of lock picking, a skill I picked up courtesy of Aika, but I don't think even she would be able to tackle this one.

The pane swings open to reveal a single, black-stemmed flower in a small vase. *Or what is left of one.* The mosaic above the rose, of sorts, is an exact replica, far more accurate than the loose sketch I was shown before leaving. Except the glass version still has a full array of petals, whereas the flower before me is down to two.

It is identical to the one Madame sent with Damian. That must have been quite a challenge, even for her, but then, her mind was never the broken part. It's her soul that's been rent in pieces.

Of course. I sigh, cursing him internally for showing me this place, even as I know that I set this all in motion.

This is why I'm here, is it not? The whole cursed thing that started this mess, the reason for every damned thing I've done and am about to do.

"Why would you trust me with this?" I can hardly hide the note of accusation in my voice, even though I know, rationally, he isn't the one to blame.

Even if he has sealed both of our fates.

"After what happened with Ulla, if that was even her name, I've learned to trust my gut. I'll admit that when you arrived, I allowed my suspicious nature and the weight of all that was happening here to cloud my judgment...but for better or worse, I trust you now."

Worse. It's for worse, I want to tell him.

Instead, I offer him a wan smile that barely reaches my eyes, tainted as it is by the sick feeling in my own gut.

He studies the rose for a moment before placing it back in the vault.

"No fallen petals today," he says, resigned.

I walk toward him slowly, wrapping my arms around myself. My heart is breaking for him. For his people. I hate the despair that is permanently etched into his ruggedly handsome face.

Einar takes in my expression and moves his hand toward my face.

"I still have the flower, and it still has petals." He gently caresses my cheek, his own features turning sympathetic, as if, against all reason, he wants to comfort me in this moment. "There is still hope to be found."

And that's what undoes me completely. I squeeze my eyes shut, closing the gap between us and hiding my face in his chest. She has made a game of torturing him, with me as her most recent pawn, and still, he tries to offer comfort rather than receive it.

"I'm so, so sorry that she did this to you," I say, my voice breaking.

I'm sorry for all of it. The poison, the rose, and so many other things that I will never be able to explain to him.

He stills in surprise for a fraction of a moment before wrapping both of his arms around me, holding me tightly to him while I steal the comfort I don't deserve.

CHAPTER 52

He holds my hand, his fingers interlocked with mine the entire way back to his rooms. I can't find the strength to let go of him, to allow anything to separate the connection I have with him in this moment.

My time here is running out. Damian will be waiting for me tonight, and this bubble I've allowed myself to linger in will burst, raining down around me like a thousand jagged shards of glass.

When we get back to his room, there is a note from Leif that Sigrid is asking for Einar. I make the excuse that Khijha needs to be taken outside again and that I will meet up with him after. His brows raise, but he nods wordlessly as I take the passageway back to my rooms.

Throwing a cloak around my shoulders, I grab the small coin purse that I have been saving and stuff all of the jewels I brought with me inside it before making my way toward the stables.

I close my eyes against the cold, taking deep gulps of the crisp, fresh air. When I open them again, I spend a while just soaking in each and every snowflake, admiring the way they shimmer under the sunlight.

While the icy landscape doesn't have the bright, flashy colors of the island, it's hard to believe I missed the way it sparkles with a kaleidoscope of subtler shades.

Images of a vast desert crawl back out from the recesses of my mind. The light would glint and glimmer on the dunes the same way it does on the vast snow-covered hills, shining like gemstones all around me.

While the Mirrored Desert had sandstorms that you could see from miles away, Jokith has something majestic in its own right, like the way the storms roll off of the mountains, billowing clouds of fog, and snow streaming down to the ground in a wave of icy air.

Khijha makes a show of rolling around in a pile of snow, and I can't help but smile at her as she shakes it off and does it again. She was made for this. A small part of me wonders if, after all of my protesting, I could have been, too.

It hardly matters now.

When I reach the stables, Sarah Agnes is overjoyed to see me. She prattles on about how hard she's been working with Gideon and the new tricks they've been mastering.

Her sincerity is overwhelming, and it's all I can do to hold up a hand to stop her.

"Sarah, thank you for taking such good care of him. But I need you to do me one final favor, and please, I'm begging you, do not ask why."

When I've finished giving her instructions, she pinches her eyes shut, but nods stoically.

If any of this is going to work, I need to be able to trust her. It doesn't escape my attention that the last time my plan hinged on trusting someone else, my sister died.

But I am not that girl anymore, and when Sarah promises me she will do this, I allow myself to trust my gut and believe her. I pull her into a hug, surprising both of us, before I force myself to leave.

The next stop won't be nearly as easy.

I take a deep breath as I approach the staircase that leads to the West Wing. The guards, who I am used to seeing in masks, stand there far less imposing now than they were before.

Now, instead of fearing the men who tower over me, I pity them. Their faces are misshapen. One has scales and bony plates covering his skin, his mouth and teeth jutting out at an elongated angle, the skin around his lips reddening with the effort. The other is covered in a thick pelt of coal-colored skin with sparse, matching hair, and his eyes are small round orbs that match, while his nose turns up into a snout with two large tusks on either side.

Under the guise of their masks, they are intimidating, terrifying even. But without the covering, it is easier to see their isolation. Their pain and their fear.

I take a tentative step past them, and they do not stop me. Instead, they shrug their shoulders and nod.

When I reach the top of the stairs, I'm not quite sure what to do with myself. I follow the halls to the left, and several doors are shut to me, while a few are cracked open, revealing more pain and unnatural changes happening to the people inside.

A richly dressed woman with fawn-colored fur, freckled with white spots stares at me from the end of the hall. Round eyes that are too large for her head blink slowly; her pointed ears flit forward and to the side. I gesture for her attention.

"Excuse me," I speak in a hushed tone, not willing to intrude on their obvious grief unnecessarily.

"Yes?" She takes a couple of small, hesitant steps toward me.

I recognize her light voice as the veiled noblewoman who spoke kindly to me at the dinner table, and I curse Madame all over again for inflicting her twisted brand of vengeance on these innocent people.

"Do you know where I can find Sigrid and the king?" I ask her.

"Yes, Lady. I lead you there." She gestures for me to follow her down the bleak hallway.

One door reveals a man with wilted wings like a butterfly's and a woman with a round, furry face and small slits for her nose. They cry at the foot of a bed while its occupant takes stilted, wheezing breaths.

I squeeze my eyes shut against the desperate words and the soft cries, imagining myself back in the dungeons of Villa Paradís all over again.

We reach the end of the hall, and she points me to a smaller set of stairs leading upward again. I'm barely on the first step when I hear Einar's deep voice resonating and filling the floor above.

I follow the sound up to the servants' quarters, nearly slipping on the last stair. A girl slowly moves ahead of me, her tall, filmy antennae wobbling from side to side with each step she takes. I don't miss the way that her feet drag slowly along, leaving a trail of green slime on the floor in her wake.

I take in each of her movements, and the sound of her labored breaths. Then it clicks for me -- that day with Einar on the tour. Him telling the servant to keep her mask on. What I thought was rudeness on his part was kindness instead. He didn't want to add to her pain with my reaction.

I watch the snail-like girl head toward her room before I continue to follow the sound of Einar's voice down the hall.

The servants' quarters are far grander than the ones Madame has given hers in either of her houses. The rooms are fairly spacious, from what I can see, and along the far wall is a small lift that looks newly installed. A scale-covered servant is cranking a lever that lowers it downward.

I'm certain that the contraption has a practical use, but I know the castle's owner too well now to imagine that it wasn't a sentimental reason that motivated him to install it.

Einar's voice floats from further down the hall, and I follow it, passing more of what I had seen on the other level. Pain. Mutations. Suffering.

When I arrive at the room I've been looking for, the door is open, revealing Sigrid sitting up on her large four-poster bed.

Her feathered fingers are cupping Einar's cheek, and he leans into her touch. The gesture is so matronly and so foreign to me. I debate whether or not to interrupt their moment when she catches sight of me and waves a weakened hand. The king turns and smiles when he sees me, and it is all I can do to not to break down and tell him everything.

"Come, dúllan mín." Her voice is scratchy, but she's smiling. Or trying her best to.

Einar chuckles and, in Jokithan, asks her why she calls me this.

"Because, inside, she is sweet little girl, still. Underneath her defenses, she is good," she answers back, and the words she thinks I cannot understand cut deeply.

If only she knew there was no part of me that was good or sweet left. There isn't room for those things in the world I grew up in.

I force a smile and walk toward them, keeping my darker thoughts to myself.

Einar nods and continues to speak in their language, but his eyes never leave mine.

"Yes. I believe she is," he says in the common tongue, offering me a smile that I do my best to return.

"You're looking better than the last time I saw you," I say when she turns to face me.

I don't want to confuse her or invite too many questions by speaking Jokithan, not when this is the last time I'll see her.

"Am I?" Sigrid follows suit, speaking the common tongue as well.

She chokes on a laugh, examining the feathers that now cover all of the skin on her arms and hands.

"Yes. You're talking and even laughing." I push away images of her collapsing on my floor and gasping for air.

Einar's smile fades, and Sigrid wraps a loving hand around his.

"That is the gift and curse of this poison. Some days, we are have pain and others we are better." She coughs, and the sound is raspy.

I grab the glass of water on her bedside and offer it gently to her dry, cracked lips.

She takes small sips and thanks me before continuing.

"But I have know it will be over soon." She looks at the king, and they have a brief, unspoken conversation between the two of them.

Whether she is assuming he will find a cure soon or that she will be gone, hardly makes a difference. Either way, the look on Einar's face tells me he is still desperately clinging to hope.

CHAPTER 53

"I should get you two some lunch." Einar stands up.

His excuse is feeble. There are plenty of people who could help with that, but I don't fault him for needing a moment to collect himself. When he's gone, Sigrid stares at the doorway and sighs.

"He is have too much pain for someone so young." She squeezes my hand that still rests within hers. "When his family passed, he was still just a boy. I sit with him every night while he grieved them, while he wish he passed, too. I sing his *móðir's* lullabies to him, so he could find sleep."

I hate the part of me that asks her for the rest of the story. I don't deserve to know something so personal about him, but I can't help myself when the question bubbles from my lips.

"What happened to them?"

"Einar was very sick. He had the rashes and fevers and he need isolation. His family went for ride to visit mountain villages. There was avalanche." She pauses to cough. "They never come home. The dogs find them buried in snow weeks later."

Again, my heart fractures and breaks apart in this very room. The fear he had when he found me alive after falling down the mountain. The way he is so reverent of the peaks, his caution. It isn't just respect for nature that made him that way. It is also that he has seen firsthand what the mountains can claim for themselves at any moment.

And I had selfishly followed him, triggering one of his worst fears.

"What are you think, child?" Sigrid pulls me from my thoughts, her face carefully examining everything she sees on mine.

I'm too tired to hide my feelings at the moment, too tired of death and loss and pain. So, I give her a truth.

"I was thinking about how sad I am for him. For all of you. I know what it is like to lose family..." I hesitate about how much I want to give away before settling on the loss I feel most keenly. "My sister died very young." It is a struggle to keep the emotion from my voice. "I used to sing to her, too."

Sigrid's head tilts to the side, her eyes softening. But when she opens her mouth, what she asks isn't at all what I was expecting.

"Would you give this song to me?"

I startle and feel the heat rise to my cheeks.

"I haven't sung in ages." I attempt to dodge her request, not sure if I am capable of singing Rose's lullaby after so long.

"Please?" she asks again, and I freeze.

I deserve to relive the pain of losing my sister. I deserve to now associate it with the pain I have suffered and inflicted here.

So, I take a steadying breath and close my eyes and listen to the melody in my head from so long ago. My father holds a sitar, his fingers strumming and plucking my mother's, my *true* mother's, favorite song. And it's her voice I hear when I open my mouth to echo the words.

The lyrics speak of the love of a man and how it makes this woman whole. They run away in the night and are married by dawn. She needs him like the ocean needs the moon, and he needs her like the desert needs rain. Their love is limitless, all-powerful, and complete.

As the lullaby continues, their love creates a child. This child fills them with so much joy they nearly burst. In spite of the storms around them and the terrible creatures that want to steal the child away, the parents' love protects it and keeps it safe from all harm.

Each note and every word remind me of how much I wish love was capable of such a thing.

I see Rose's limp body. I remember being terrified when strange hands pulled me from my parents' sides in the marketplace. I think of Aika and Melodi and every reason that I have to do my part to protect them, because no one did that for me.

By the time I sing the final note, I open my eyes, but my vision is blurry. I reach a hand up to rub them, and my fingers come away wet. I'm not sure how long I've been crying, but the tears I've shed are reflected on Sigrid's face as well.

She says nothing as she gently pulls me closer to her, wrapping her arms around me, and it's all I can do to pull myself away.

When I sit up, I see Sigrid's sad eyes fixed on something behind me.

Einar has returned. He's holding a tray of food, but his gaze is utterly transfixed on me. I don't ask how long he's been standing there. I don't need to. It was long enough, regardless.

I finish wiping my face, and he silently approaches, resting the food on the middle of the bed. I feel far more vulnerable now than I ever have before. I would rather be naked in a room full of strangers than face the way my soul feels so exposed in this moment.

Einar helps Sigrid with the bowl of stew he's brought up for her while I silently pick at the bread and cheese.

"Thank you, Ùlfur," she says after a few bites, her eyes flitting back and forth between the two of us. "But I am so tired now. Please, let me rest. You two finish your meal together."

Her hand grasps mine, tugging it gently, and I follow her lead by leaning in to hug her again.

"Thank you," she whispers in the common tongue.

I smile, but the gesture feels empty. Just like everything else about me.

CHAPTER 54

Einar and I walk silently down the halls of the West Wing. Halls I now realize he kept me from for very particular reasons.

These people deserve their privacy. They deserve to have a place of their own to rest and grieve and cope.

No wonder they despise me.

I'm the monster who tried to force my way in, who took so many things for granted while they suffered and fought just to trudge on with their lives.

And it is here that he keeps their hope for a cure, protected by and for them.

We eventually find ourselves back in his rooms, and I've been so distracted that I'm not even sure how we got here.

"Are you all right?" Einar's deep voice rumbles through me, cutting through the silence.

The timbre of his voice coupled with the sincerity in his stare threatens to unearth the catacomb of emotions I've worked so hard to bury.

"What helped me get through the years after I lost my family was talking about it," he steps closer. "Sharing the pain and finding a way to let it go."

I'm not breathing. My mind does not begin to fathom what that is like, because I came from a house of suppression and avoidance. I can't speak or find the words to express what this offer means to a person who has never been allowed space for their own emotions.

I want to say no, to shut down and close myself off, but as his eyes search mine, my lips begin moving of their own accord, and nothing I do can make them stop.

I'm so tired of the pretense, and of keeping everything in and pretending the pain away.

"My childhood has been very different from yours." I begin with the obvious. Einar doesn't move, doesn't speak.

"Where I am from...family doesn't mean the same thing as it does here. Family is ownership, not love." I try to break down my sordid tale, in the pieces that are safe to give.

"You are more valuable to the family if you have something to offer." I swallow hard, thinking of the pieces I've already given him and how to present the rest. "My value was my age, my virginity." I pause, not looking at him when I add the last part, because it's not something he has ever specifically commented on. "My beauty."

Einar clenches his fists and his jaw, his entire body going taut with fury, but he stays silent.

"These are things that are highly sought-after. After mine was sold, I knew they were going to do the same to my sister."

"Who did this?" His voice is strained. "Where was your aunt?"

I close my eyes for the briefest of moments, willing away the images of them before I answer his second question. I can't give him an answer to the first, even though a selfish part of me wants to.

"She was the one who brokered the deal," I say flatly. "I tried to run away, and I took my sister with me. I had planned it out, down to every last detail, but nothing went exactly right. We were found right before we would have boarded a ship to freedom."

Einar's face is pained. He moves forward like he wants to touch me, but then pulls his hands away as if he is afraid to.

"She was furious." I carefully choose my words while the reality of the situation plays on a loop in my head.

"Rose --" I nearly choke on her name. "Rose wouldn't stop crying."

She was afraid and wailed, as a child should be able to do.

"The family guards," *Madame's soldiers,* "were too rough with her... They beat her. At Mother's orders."

Madame knew they were going to kill her. She played God as if she had the right to, then forced me to watch as the sentence was carried out.

Einar's eyes are wide as he soaks in every word, and I wonder if he can read between the lines to everything I still can't say. Some small part of me wants him to.

"It's my fault that she died." I speak the words aloud, giving life to the guilt I have carried with me for so long.

She was calculating. She chose which of us was most valuable to her and decided how she could prevent something like this from ever happening again. And she was successful.

Einar walks toward me, his voice calm, his eyebrows gathering inward as he speaks.

"No. You were a child. Your family was supposed to protect you. This is not your fault, Zaina."

"This is the price of your disobedience, child." Madame's voice was cool, no hint of anger as she sat back to watch her orders being honored.

"I haven't been a child in a very long time." My chest aches, and I rub absently at the pain that I know will never fade.

She forced me to watch as the soldiers tortured my helpless sister, my only friend. She forced me to listen to Rose's cries while her men held me back, preventing me from helping.

"Do not fail me again." Madame said coldly when it was all over.

She handed me a picture of Melodi in an unspoken promise of the fate she would share if I did.

And then she found Aika, and no amount of sense or reason kept me from growing attached to her as well. My sister.

That was my punishment. Reliving Rose's death, knowing I was powerless to stop it.

"I try to remember our happiest moments," I add after a while, doing anything to quell the misery that accompanies the memories of that sands-forsaken night. "I try to remember the sound of her laugh, the music she played on the piano, the way she begged for one more lullaby." A bitter smile tugs at my mouth.

"The song you sang for Sigrid," Einar says, and I nod. "I can see why she loved it."

This time, my smile is a little more genuine. "She did. She was learning to play it on the piano."

"I would have loved to meet her. I am certain that her life was better for having you in it."

This time, I look up at him, truly seeing him. Realizing that there isn't a single thing he has judged me for, things other men would have. But it's more than that.

For so long, I have thought only about the death Rose suffered because of my incompetence. Because of my bad decisions. It never occurred to me what kind of life she would have had before that if I hadn't been around to protect her. For the first time in nearly a decade, the squeezing pressure around my heart eases just enough for me to breathe.

"How?" I ask, baffled by everything that he is. "How are you like this? Full of hope and life after what happened to your own family? After what happened to your people?"

Einar takes hesitant steps toward me, slowly moving his hand to my cheek, giving me plenty of opportunity to stop him if I wanted.

"Because there is more to life than pain, Zaina. We just have to find those moments." He tucks a strand of hair behind my ear. "And hold fast to them."

I close my eyes and try to think of the moments he's referring to. The music and the laughter, and, most of all, the love. All of the little bits of her that I can keep for myself, even though she's gone.

"Thank you," I say when I open my eyes.

He nods, and his body is still so close to mine.

I don't deserve his kindness, but I am a sea sponge, and I take this, too. I close the space between us, wrapping my arms around his waist, pressing myself against him as though I can force an ounce of his goodness and hope to seep into my tainted soul.

CHAPTER 55

I don't know how long I stand wrapped in his embrace, but he doesn't make me feel rushed or awkward. He doesn't falter at all.

He never seems to.

He was right, though, about the relief in saying the words aloud. The grief I have held on to for so long has edged out just enough to make room for another emotion.

Enough for me to realize his shirt laces have loosened, revealing the dark-blonde hairs on his solidly muscled chest. Before I can stop myself, my hand has traveled upward, my fingers drawn like a magnet to that space of skin.

I tilt my head up, meeting his eyes, letting him see everything that is burning in mine for a rare change.

"Zaina." His voice is hoarse when he says my name.

"Yes?"

But he appears to be at a rare loss for words, staring down at me with a thousand emotions swirling in his eyes.

I war with myself, because I will be gone tomorrow and he will be here, left with only the memory of this and a thousand questions he will never have answers for.

Does this make me as cruel as Madame?

There is one thing I can clearly discern from his expression. I see my own desire mirrored in his features, and it is larger-than-life, like everything about him. Imposing and overwhelming and, just for the tiniest fraction of a lifetime, mine.

I close the gap between us, standing on my toes and wrapping my arms around him. I pull his head down until my lips reach his. My fingers go to the laces on his shirt, untying them in record time. I tug on his hem, and he stills.

Opening his eyes and placing his hands over mine, he fixes me with a steady gaze.

"Are you sure you want this?"

For everything I am uncertain about, never once have I doubted the depth of my wanting for him.

"Yes." One word, breathy and barely audible.

His expression morphs into something far less controlled, white-hot desire edging out every other emotion on his face. But he reaches up with gentle hands, placing two fingers on my chain.

"How do I take this off?"

My eyes widen in surprise.

"I told you, it doesn't matter. I'm not --"

"Don't you dare finish that sentence with the word 'pure'. He does not get to take what you did not offer and change the way you see yourself." He says the words with such conviction.

Tears stab at the back of my eyes, threatening to spill down my face with the overwhelming weight of all the emotions I can't quite identify. I put my hand over his, guiding him through the motions of unhooking the chain. He places it on the small table next to the bed, then returns his attention to me.

My fingers have traveled back to the hem of his shirt, but there is no need. He pulls it off with one swift motion, then sets to work on mine. His hands are surprisingly deft for their size, and he has undone each of my tiny, complex buttons in a matter of moments. Our pants follow, and we are soon standing bare before one another.

I try not to think of all the time we have wasted, time we could have been together that we will never have now. Instead, I stay in this moment of perfect intimacy.

He backs against the bed, pulling me toward him. Gently, he lifts my knees up to either side of his torso, and my lips meet his with urgency. I tilt his head to the side and kiss his neck, then push him back against the bed. I take my time exploring his shoulders, his chest, making sure to memorize every line and scar on his perfectly shaped body. He finally groans and flips us so that he is on top to do some exploring of his own.

He starts with my mouth, then moves downward, leaving a scorching trail of kisses all the way down my body. When he makes his way back up to my lips, he pulls back and asks me again.

"Are you sure you want this?"

Last time, the words were quiet, but this time I say them earnestly.

"Yes, Einar."

The sound of his name on my lips must be his undoing. But for all I have robbed him of his self-control, every point of contact is a gentle reverence. He moves with a deliberate slowness, broadcasting every movement and giving me every opportunity to stop him, opportunities I would die before taking at this point.

I didn't know it was possible to feel this way, like another person is an extension of your very being. I didn't think I was capable of loving a man in this capacity.

But in this moment, belonging to each other wholly, I realize just how much I have been fooling myself, because I could spend the rest of my life tucked inside Einar's protective arms.

In a way, that's what I am doing.

I lie awake for an hour after Einar falls asleep, memorizing the steady sounds of his breathing. Sixty minutes of silent tears that won't stop falling, of soaking in his endless supply of warmth and using it to bolster myself for what's ahead.

My eyes are finally drying by the time the clock chimes midnight. I give him another few minutes to make sure the sound didn't wake him, but he doesn't stir, his breathing deep and even. Content.

I snake my hand between us to the key around his neck, and deftly maneuver it over his head, going slowly to avoid the chain clinking. His breathing stills, and for a tense, awful moment, I wonder if all of my plans have been for nothing.

I place my free hand against his chest where the pendant would usually be, and his breathing evens out again. But it's too soon to sigh with relief, because that was only the first step.

Besides, there is no relief to be found in any of this, only a sick revulsion that creeps all the way through my being to my very core.

I wait another moment before easing my way off the bed and crossing the room to where Khijhana sleeps in the chair near the door to the privy. I stand there for a solid moment where I would have a convenient excuse to be, but he doesn't stir, so I slip my clothes on as quietly as I can, keeping my gaze fixed firmly on his face the whole time.

I tell myself it's so I will know if he has been alerted, but the truth is that I want to linger in every last second I have with him.

Slipping my unmarked hand into a glove, I feel an unreasonable wave of sadness over that, too. The wedding markings are gone. It will be like I was never here at all.

When there is nothing else that could possibly give me an excuse to stay here, and I know time is running short, I tap Khijhana on her nose to wake her.

She is silent as a wraith and intuitive as ever as she slides off the chair and stands at my side. It is fortunate that I have already eked every last bit of moisture from my body, because her loyalty would finish me.

I pick up my boots and cross the room on soundless footfalls, opening the panel just as quietly. With a final glance over my shoulder to see that Einar sleeps soundly, I ease the door to the passageway shut.

Speed becomes as important as stealth as I make my way to my rooms. Hastily, I throw on my boots and grab the artificial rose from its hiding spot. I pull off three of the petals, and they fall to the ground like droplets of blood from the shattered pieces of my soul.

I have to backtrack to Einar's room. I give him a quick look to ensure I haven't disturbed him, but I don't allow my gaze to linger beyond that. If I focus on him for too long, my resolve will crumble and this will all be for nothing.

Quickly, I slip across his room, all the way to the passageway on the other side. It's a matter of moments before I am back in the room I had assumed to be his study before. Hurriedly, I pull the books in the exact same order he had, and the bookcase slides open. I hate myself for how easy it is to betray a man who deserves it less than anyone I know.

I am back to my room with the real rose in a matter of minutes. I slide my boots on, then scrawl a quick note at the small writing desk. I put the flower and the note in a small black satchel, then slip it into the pocket of my heaviest cloak.

Finally, I turn to Khijhana on knees that will barely support me, wrapping my arms around her neck.

"You can't come with me where I am going," I whisper as if she understands.

And maybe she does, or maybe she merely senses my anguish, because she lets out a tiny, keening mew. Damian thinks I am handing off the rose to him, but I have an entirely different sort of plan in mind.

"I would take you if I could, but he will kill you, and I couldn't bear that on top of everything else. You'll be safe here." I thought my tears had dried away, but I have to fight back a sob as I kiss the top of her furry head.

"Besides, Einar is going to need someone when I am gone." I stand up, brushing the fresh wave of tears off my face, because I know Damian, and I know that none of this will work if he senses the slightest hesitation from me.

"Take care of each other," I say in a calmer tone.

Khijhana follows me to the passageway door, but I slip through and close it behind me, ignoring her forlorn meow. I know how soundproof these walls are, how I can only barely hear acoustic sounds like footsteps through them, but I hear Khijhana's cries echoing in my head all the way until I reach the outer door.

When the icy blast of air hits me from outside, it seems to freeze everything inside of me as well. Because this is it, the only way I could see through the thousands of possibilities I walked down. Even if walking out this door means I can never return, never see my sisters or Einar again.

This is the only way to save them.

End of Book One.

Pronunciation Guide

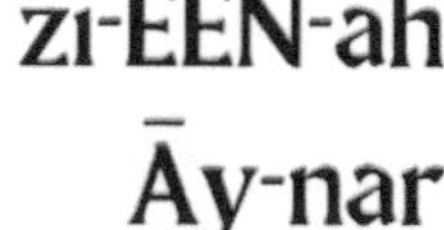

Zaina	zī-EEN-ah
Einar	Āy-nar
Jokith	JŌ-keeth
Khijhana	kee-JAUN-ah
Chalyx	CHAL-ix
Corentin	COR-en-tin
Aika	Ī-eek-ah
Madame	Mah-DAUM
Ulla	OO-lah
Bondé	BON-day
Leif	LĀYF
Sigrid	SEE-grid
Odger	OD-ger
Dvain	DVĀYN

A MESSAGE FROM US

We need your help!

Did you know that authors, in particular indie authors like us, make their living on reviews? If you liked this book, or even if you didn't, please take a moment to let people know on Amazon, Goodreads, and/or Bookbub!

Remember, reviews don't have to be long. It can be as simple as a star rating and an: 'I loved it!' or: 'Not my cup of tea...'

So please, take a moment to let us know what you think. We depend on your feedback!

Now that that's out of the way, if you want to come shenanigate with us, rant and rave about these books and others, get access to awesome giveaways, exclusive content and some pretty ridiculous live videos, come join us on Facebook here: https://www.facebook.com/groups/driftersandwanderers

For even more freebies and some behind-the-scenes content, you can also sign up for Robin's newsletter here: https://www.subscribepage.com/robindmahlenewsletter_tse

ELLE'S ACKNOWLEDGMENTS

Where do I even begin? I feel like this part is always difficult because there are so many unsung heroes that go into making a book what it is.

Robin, this is our sixth co-write! Can you believe we've made it this far? Six books down and a million more to go. I'm so grateful that we're in this together. Even when writing is hard, and we're arguing about non-essential plot points, I can't imagine it any other way. Thank you for being my forever octopus, my Stardew Valley co-farmer, my best friend and co- author!

To my husband, my main squeeze, the love of my life and father of my children... There are never enough words to explain how grateful I am that I have you in my life. You are my rock, my warm blanket and my shoulder to cry on when I am overwhelmed. Thank you for always being there for me, for helping me sort through frustratingly difficult plot-holes with ease. Thank you for always boosting my confidence and listening to me go on and on and on and on and on about bookish things. But mostly thank you for loving our children and taking care of our family while I'm crumbling under the pressure of deadlines and edits. I love you more than waffles.

Jamie and Brianna. You two... I seriously don't know where we would be without you.

Jamie, your constant reassurances and insight mean the world and I am so grateful that I know you. Thank you for putting up with us, forgiving us, and fixing us when we need it most. I miss you and love you more than you used to love peanut butter whiskey. ;)

Brianna, this book would never have made it to the release date if it hadn't been for you. Thank you for helping us with plot issues and errors and being so very methodical and careful with our book baby. You saved it from the mess it was and I will always love you for that.

To Jill, my bestie and second biggest supporter. Thank you for always having Marco-polo dates with me when I'm up working at 4 am. For listening to me complain when the characters wouldn't do what they were supposed to do. And for re- reading so many times and even when this story wasn't very good. You have been here since the very start of this whole author journey of mine and your insight, support and swooning over our stories is invaluable. Thank you, from the bottom of my heart for being you.

Ivy, you are a rockstar and a wonderful human. Having your friendship has meant the world to me, and having you on our team has been so so so helpful! You keep us organized and in check and are constantly slapping us around (verbally, of course) when we are too hard on ourselves. Thank you for jumping into the middle of our chaos and helping us to make sense of it all. Also... you deserve a medal for all of times you re-read the beginning of this book. I love you to the moon and back! <3

Lissa, you are irreplaceable! You have been a loyal reader from book one when our writing was new and rougher around the edges. Thank you for the fan art, the gifts, the messages of encouragement and support and reminding us that we can do this, even when we don't believe it ourselves. <3

Joy, Charlee, Amanda, Michelle, Allyssa, LeAnn - you ladies are the best bookish friends a girl could ask for. Thank you for listening to us complain, check for errors, support us and believe in us. You each played a different, but very vital role in helping us get this far, even if you didn't realize you were doing it at the time. So thank you.

Kate, thank you for being so kind and supportive and for actually wanting to help us with this story! You are an amazing human. Blessed be the fruit...

Sarah, thank you for pushing so hard to win a spot in this book. But really, *we* were the real winners here... This story would not have been the same without Gideon! We needed him, Zaina needed him and our readers need him too. I'm so happy that we were able to include him in this story, quirks and all. <3

And finally, our ARC team and Drifters and Wanderers...

Where would we be without you?? Thank you for offering hours of entertainment and laughs when we were losing our sanity. Thank you for gushing over Zaina and Einar and even for your anger when we left you with another ridiculous cliffhanger... That just means you're invested, right?

We love you all and are grateful for the loving support you've given us. You make us feel like real authors!

ROBIN'S ACKNOWLEDGMENTS

It's always hard to remember who to thank at the end of a book when it's such a huge team of amazing people making it all possible, but I'm going to give it a shot.

First and foremost, my husband is amazing for being so patient when this book took longer than expected, for keeping my babies occupied with board games and anime while I spent yet another day in my writing/editing cave. Thank you for listening to me rant about plot-holes in my permanently exhausted, nonsensical haze. You are the most supportive husband anyone could ask for and, without a doubt, the best daddy ever!

To my co-author, the icing to my cupcake, the jelly to my peanut butter, you also deserve a thank you for patience. This book was rough around the edges, and we had to work long, frustrating hours to make it come together. Thank you for not giving up on this project or me, even when neither of us (me or the book) was at our best.

To my big sister and Auntie-bear to my children, you also have had the fun of hearing me talk endlessly about this book in the months it took to finish. If that wasn't fun enough, you even read the bad iterations and watched my wayward monsters while you were at it. You are the best. <3

Jamie, I will thank you in every book from here to eternity because without your unending well of optimism and fantastic eye for errors, nothing I write would be what it is. Did I mention I love you for putting up with me even when I can't stick to a deadline or remember to book you in advance?

Brianna, you have once again saved my butt with your uncanny ability to root out plot-holes and inconsistency errors. I think sometimes your sheer determination on my behalf is the only reason I don't throw in the towel. You'll never know what your straightforward nature does for my motivation. Thank you!

Ivy, I honestly don't know how you forced yourself to read at least four iterations of the beginning of this book, but it was impressive, especially when I happen to know one of them was very, very bad. You are seriously awesome for all the hard work you put into helping us shape this story and everything else you do. I'm so glad you're on our team!

Lissa, Jill, and Joy, you guys are the best betas anyone could ask for! Laughing and crying and swooning with your comments was hands down, the best part of writing this book.

Kate, you came in late and threw on a cape and helped us perfect this story! Thank you for still loving us even after we kept you awake at PennedCon.

Sarah, thank you for lending us Gideon and helping us to do him justice! He became such an unexpectedly spectacular part of this story, all from your invaluable input.

Michelle, you're still my favorite mentor, even if I thrust you into that title without your desire or permission. :P Thank you for always being a listening ear when writing gets rough!

We had so many amazing readers and author friends who got us through this story, it's impossible to name them all, but I love our Drifters and Wanderers! You guys encourage me even when you don't know it, you vote on things we can't decide on, and you are generally entertaining when I need a boost. Here's to hoping the road to the next book is a lot less bumpy!

ABOUT THE AUTHORS

Elle and Robin can usually be found on road trips around the US haunting taco-festivals and taking selfies with unsuspecting Spice Girls impersonators.

They have a combined PH.D in Faery Folklore and keep a romance advice column under a British pen-name for raccoons. They have a rare blood type made up solely of red wine and can only write books while under the influence of the full moon.

Between the two of them they've created a small army of insatiable humans and when not wrangling them into their cages, they can be seen dancing jigs and sacrificing brownie batter the pits of their stomachs.

And somewhere between their busy schedules, they still find time to create words and put them into books.

Join them on Facebook: facebook.com/groups/DriftersAndWanderers

ALSO BY ELLE AND ROBIN

Coming Soon:

Of Beasts and Vengeance - Twisted Pages Book Two Shadow Kingdom - Assassin of the Isles Book One

Ready to read now:

Our first co-written series is complete! Check out the box set here:

The Lochlann Treaty

We had so much fun participating with several brilliant authors for this anthology. And don't tell anyone... but we plan to turn Rapunzel's story into a series next year too!

Aurelian Skies - Princess Bachelorette Anthology

And finally, the reason this whole journey started... Robin D. Mahle began as a husband and wife team to create Clark and Addie and their amazing story. Check out the first book in their fantasy romance series here:

The Fractured Empire

www.ingramcontent.com/pod-product-compliance
Lightning Source LLC
Chambersburg PA
CBHW020457310726
48979CB00016B/2693/J

* 9 7 8 1 7 3 2 5 5 9 2 4 0 *